RATS
IN A
CAGE

The Black Box of Misery

CHRISTOPHER CLARK

Rats in a Cage

The Black Box of Misery, Surviving Addiction and Trauma in a Brutal Social Experiment

CLARK, CHRISTOPHER, Author
RATS IN A CAGE
CHRISTOPHER CLARK

Published by:
ELITE ONLINE PUBLISHING
63 East 11400 South
Suite #230
Sandy, UT 84070
EliteOnlinePublishing.com

ISBN: 978-1-961801-88-2 (Paperback)
ISBN: 978-1-961801-89-9 (eBook)

FIC030000
FIC025000

QUANTITY PURCHASES:
Schools, companies, professional groups, clubs,
and other organizations may qualify for special terms
when ordering quantities of this title.
For information email ripfityoga@gmail.com

Dad, this book is for you!

Thank you for never giving up on me!

You'll always be my hero.

Love you always.

Guy Robert Clark

1940- 2019

INSPIRED
BY TRUE EVENTS

PRAISES

"***Rats in a Cage*** by Christopher Clark plunges deep into the underbelly of urban decay, following the spiraling lives of individuals caught in the throes of addiction and poverty. The novel opens with a gritty portrayal of Mike, a man who once had everything: success, a family, stability, only to lose it all to alcohol and drug abuse. His story is a stark reminder of how quickly life can turn when addiction takes hold."

–Johnny M.

"The book's setting in Houston, Texas, is vividly depicted, with Clark painting a realistic picture of the struggles faced by those living on the margins of society. The streets become a battleground for survival, where drugs, alcohol, and violence are ever-present. Characters like Pookie add depth to this landscape, illustrating various facets of street life and the complex relationships formed amidst chaos."

–Bret J.

"The narrative is straightforward yet powerful, with a rawness that feels authentic and unfiltered. Clark does not shy away from the harsh realities of his characters' lives, making "Rats in a Cage" a compelling, if at times uncomfortable, read. The dialogue rings true, capturing the desperation, humor, and resilience of those who have nothing left to lose."

–Natalie K.

"Structurally, the novel employs multiple perspectives, which adds depth but sometimes disrupts the narrative flow. Each character's journey is a reflection on societal issues such as systemic racism, economic disparity, and addiction as a disease, a progressive trap that ensnares even those who might seem least vulnerable."

–Marie C.

"Emotionally **Rats in a Cage** is heavy. The author's ability to evoke empathy for characters like Mike and Blake, whose descent into further despair is chronicled with a blend of inevitability and sadness, is noteworthy. Scenes in later chapters, including poignant moments of realization and rawness of human connection and disconnection, are particularly striking."

–Denise P.

"**Rats in a Cage** is a harsh and unflinching look at addiction and its impact on individual lives and the community fabric. Christopher Clark offers no easy answers but compels readers to confront uncomfortable truths with his stark prose and memorable characters. For those interested in gritty urban dramas that tackle serious social issues, this book is the one to read."

–Jeff W.

CHAPTER 1

Mike stumbled out to the median on Antoine and 34th. Drunk again and needing a hit of crack. This area was a hot spot in Houston Texas for panhandling, prostitution, and everything else you can imagine. This was his daily ritual. He was among the many poor souls, directionless and lost to their own devices. Some say it's corporate greed that creates more poor people. Others say systemic racism is to blame, creating a subculture of society that are destined for prison and defenseless against alcoholism and drug addiction. But, at one time, Mike was an extraordinarily successful college graduate with his own car dealership. He had a beautiful wife, three healthy children and a big house. He had it all. So, what happened? He drank excessively. He used drugs recreationally. One too many trips to the strip club and his wife caught him cheating. She divorced him, then alienation of the children caused him to find the solution to his problems deeper in the bottle. Drugs became a necessity to mask the pain. Medical journals state that alcohol and drug addiction are a progressive disease. This was evident in Mike's current standing in the community. Living under the bridge and panhandling for his daily supply of chemical relief from a life he so desperately tried to escape. In his mind, the only escape was being wasted.

"Hey Mike, what's up?" Pookie asked.

"Shit, another day, just another day fool."

Pookie was an interesting guy. Only his momma knew his real name, so he was called by his street name. Homeless and hustling in this area for twenty plus years, he thrived in the "street life." His vices were hoes and "drank" as he liked to say. The crack and heroin bug never bit him. He was the guy that could get you what you wanted, for a price of course.

"I hear ya, man." Pookie lit up a cigarette, and Mike holding out his hand said,

"Let me get one of those, brother."

"For a dollar."

"What? A dollar, Pookie?"

"Yea man, inflation!" At that Pookie laughed and his laugh was infectious. And Mike, through his laughter said,

"Okay, gimme one, I'll pay you later."

Since most people like Mike smoked and/or drank up their money through the night, Pookie could make a profit by charging a tax on everything from cigarettes to that morning 40oz. beer to stop the shakes. He would loan these items to people knowing they would earn throughout the day. This helped him to afford plenty of drinks and an occasional motel room for a "lady." He seemed content with this lifestyle and always had a smile on his face. Even the police liked him because he never started any shit.

As Mike lit up his cigarette and walked off Pookie yelled,

"Don't forget my dollar fool!"

Mike waved him off and went to his hard-earned corner.

Some people might think homeless people just randomly choose which street corner to panhandle at. In reality, it was a territorial claim like gang turf and people will fight and even kill for that corner. Mike would switch off periodically with a friend of his named Bam. But lately, the corner was all Mike's because Bam went missing. While standing on the corner thinking about his buddy Bam, a guy in a brand-new Corvette pulls up to the light. Mike held out his change cup and tried to look sad to elicit a compassionate reaction from this obviously rich guy. At first, Mr. Corvette avoided eye contact, then he looked directly at Mike and shoved his hands in his pocket and pulled out a knot of 100's so big it made Mike shudder.

"Here you go, bro." He handed Mike a $100 bill. "Oh my God," Mike exclaimed. "God Bless you sir!"

"Fuck that, dude! Smoke one for me!"

And with that, Mr. Corvette peeled out and stopped a block away to score from Pookie. Mike ran over as the corvette was peeling out again.

"Hey Pookie, who the hell was that?"

"Some rich dude wanting to get high. Never mind that, I saw him hook you up so pay me mine before you smoke it all." Mike paid Pookie, scored some dope, and took the rest of the day off.

CHAPTER 2

Blake bought a new house, an SUV for his wife and a Corvette for himself. He had just settled a lawsuit from a major car accident where he sustained serious injuries. He was prescribed pain killers which he took according to the doctor's instructions when needed, then they became a necessity. But like most alcoholics and addicts, early in their use, he remained functional. Not having to work and plenty of idle time on his hands, he was introduced to cocaine. Since he was athletic most his life, he would work out a few times a week and was still somewhat healthy. He had a beautiful wife that was one of those women that didn't act like they knew they were pretty. Humble and loyal to a fault. She was the exact opposite of Blake. She was Blake's voice of reason when he would listen. She had a distinguished career in Finance with a six figure income and was not a snob. She cautioned him when his spending was out of control, and he would shrug her off. After one weekend of major spending his wife confronted him.

"Honey, you spent $3,000 this weekend?" shock in her voice.

"Leave me alone! We have enough money to not have to worry about money, so get off my back!"

"Please be careful sweetheart. I worry about you."

One morning while snorting all night, his wife walked into the living room to Blake hovering over a pile of cocaine on the coffee table. He looked up when she came in and she noticed a patch of white powder covering his nose.

"Did you get high all night again?" more accusatory than a question.

"So, what!" he shouted.

"How much did you spend this time?"

"Leave me alone woman! It doesn't matter!"

"It does matter if you spend it all or worse than that, die!"

Blake never physically hurt his wife but the mental torture from an addict had her seeking legal counsel recently.

"I'm leaving, honey." Sadness in her voice.

Blake snapped his head up mid snort and asked,

"Where to?"

"I don't know where, but I'm leaving. I'm leaving you, Blake."

"What the hell are you talking about?" He dropped his head down for another line. He lifted his head back up and looked her in the eyes and in his best manipulative tone said,

"I'll get help sweetheart, don't worry."

"You have said that before! I've made up my mind." Blakes face went whiter than the coke on the table, then beet red.

"Fuck you then!"

"Baby, get some help and I'll come back." She was crying as she opened the front door. As she closed it, he screamed after her,

"Fuck you bitch! At last! No more nagging! All alone! Party time!"

CHAPTER 3

Back in the hood, Mike was shopping from the assortment of narcotics in Pookie's stash. He bought crack, pills to come down, and some cigarettes. Next step, some company for an hour or so. Prostitutes were readily available, and Mike was looking for his favorite, Big Booty Betty.

"Yo, Pookie, where is Betty?"

"Gone fool. No idea"

"What do you mean gone?"

"Told you, I don't know. It's like Bam and Milo and whoever else, just up and disappeared."

When people in the hood went missing no one cared, but Pookie paid attention. Since Betty was unavailable Mike chose Janine. She was a little older than Betty but definitely poke-able. Once sex was out of the way, Mike smoked up all his money and started the cycle all over again. Bum, score, smoke.

Next day Mike walked out to see Corvette Blake pulling up to the light. Hot damn, Mike thought, and ran up to greet him.

"How's it going, bro?"

"Great" He gave Mike another $100 bill and said,

"Old lady left me, time to party full time!"

The corvette peeled out as usual and Blake hooked up with Pookie, then took off. This time Pookie came up to Mike and said,

"I don't know what's up with that dude but anyone "chunkin' Benjis" like him is crazy or got nothing to lose."

"I don't know either, " said Mike, "but I'm glad for it!"

Back at home, Blake broke out another eight ball (three and a half grams) and snorted a huge line as a rapid knock made his heart skip a beat. Cops? He sneaked up to the door to take a peek and saw it wasn't the cops. He opened the door to a fat guy with a big legal envelope in his hands and says,

"Yea, wassup?"

"You Blake?"

"Yes, what can I do for you?"

"You've been served."

The process server handed Blake the envelope and walked off abruptly to Blake yelling after him,

"Fuck you punk!"

Once inside, Blake sat back down and set the envelope on top of the eight ball. As he opened the envelope, the realization that his wife was really gone hit him with the fact that she was filing for divorce. But before any sadness could take over his mind, he snorted another line and shouted,

"Fuck, Fuck, Fuck I don't care!"

But he did. He tried calling her and of course, she changed her number. As usual, he buried his sorrows in the white powder of oblivion.

Court was awful. His wife got more than half the money and the house. Blake got the money left over and his car. Blake was so high it didn't matter much. He moved into the same crack motel Pookie and Mike hung around. He became everyone's best friend and was the life of the party. As long as his money paid for it of course. Every hooker kept throwing themselves at him, but he refused. The rumor circulating was that he was gay. But Blake insisted he still loved his wife and was hoping for a reconciliation one day when he "got sober."

The fact was he never cheated on his wife much less with prostitutes. Plus, when he was high, all he cared about was the next line.

"Hey Blake," Mike yelled across the motel room.

"What?"

"Dope is getting low, want me to go score some more?"

"Here." Blake tossed several hundred dollars to Mike. Mike jumped up and flew out the door. "Be right back!"

CHAPTER 4

Betty woke up in what appeared to be an all-white hospital room. It had soft white light with white bed sheets and blankets. She, in contrast, was in blue hospital scrubs. A little disoriented, she exclaimed,

"Where in the hell am I?"

The last thing she remembered, she was on the stroll, looking for a trick, when a van pulled up. There was a nice enough looking guy, then the side door slid open, and something went over her head. A little sting in her neck. Was this a kidnapping? Why would they take me to a hospital? She continued this thought process as she cautiously got out of bed and investigated. Her eyes took a minute to adjust to the soft lighting then there was flashing. She was alarmed at the sudden brightness coming from each wall. She walked closer to the nearest one and read the letters as they lit up. An eerie feeling came over her as she read aloud the first strange message.

Choose life not death. "What the fuck?" She was scared and with reason. What kind of people would kidnap her, place her in an extremely comfortable hospital room, then have the walls talking crazy shit?

"Who are you crazy people?"

"What do you want from me?"

More messages.

Give up the drugs, not your life.

You are worth it.

Love yourself.

Then she saw something that registered from somewhere deep in her memories. Once, when she was on probation, she had to go to these corny meetings with a bunch of old people. She started to read.

"God grant me the Serenity…"

When she was done, she was choked up and felt a lone tear on her cheek.

What was that all about? These people are nuts! There was no one here. No windows. No doors. She didn't even see any surveillance cameras.

"Hey! Someone let me know what is going on!" She stopped walking around as she stepped to a white refrigerator that was approximately four feet tall. When she opened the door, she was stunned by the amount of food and by the variety. Tuna salad. Fruit. Grapes. Oranges. Pears. Eggs. Sandwiches of all kinds and Yogurt! She tore open a container of yogurt and squeezed the whole thing down her throat. She realized she hadn't eaten a decent meal in years and nothing probably for a few days. She gorged on everything she could. On her third sandwich she noticed a note inside the fridge. Was that there before? She opened and it read,

"Eat. Get well. Change your life. Get prepared for a new beginning or die in your addiction. It's your choice. Choose wisely!"

Now, she was scared.

"This is crazy! Someone tell me what the hell is going on! Please!"

She finished her sandwich while she relieved herself on a toilet in the corner of the room next to a decent sized walk-in shower. She needed one of those badly. She showered then felt extremely exhausted. She started looking for an exit or something else that would explain all of this when the exhaustion took complete control. Mainly because the food was laced with anti-withdrawal medications. She was out like a light as soon as her head hit the pillow.

Betty had grown up like some street girls. Parents divorced, then an abusive stepdaddy comes along. Sexual abuse started at a young age. Her compliance was awarded with praise and gifts. In her late teens, when she was smart and strong enough to speak up, she told her mother and confronted the abuser. But her mother chose the side of this man that had set her on a path that would almost destroy her. She left home and used what she had learned. Sex as a transaction for what she needed. Money. With that lifestyle came alcohol and plenty of drugs. She was in the middle of a dream where she had a family of her own and a loving husband. Then, the dream turned dark and she was a little girl again and "Hank" was sneaking in late at night to touch this innocent girl in the most inappropriate ways. She screamed "NO!" and was sitting up in bed. She jumped up and ran to the nearest wall. She shouted,

"Who are you people? Answer me God damn it!" She banged and beat the wall until her hands were red and her knuckles were starting to bleed. She fell on the floor sobbing.

CHAPTER 5

At the motel Blake noticed his funds were getting low. "Say, Mike, maybe we should pace ourselves."

"Why?" Mike asked. "We're just getting started."

"I know, but my wife's voice about watching my spending keeps echoing in my head." Blake managed a laugh.

"Say, Blake. I've got some hoes coming over later."

"Mike, I told you, I don't mess around with prostitutes."

"Dude! Your wife left you! She took almost everything you owned! Fuck her!"

"It's not that, Mike." "I've never been like that. All I care about is getting high, not getting laid. I still love my wife and in reality, she did the right thing, man. She escaped my madness. She was a good woman. Always was. She didn't deserve the hell I subjected her to. She saved herself because I was beyond saving. She still held out hope in the end. She told me if and when I get sober, she would come back in a heartbeat, yet here I am. That's why I don't mess with hoes."

"Well, I do brother!" Mike laughed all the way out the door.

CHAPTER 6

Milo had been in the hospital for seven days. As far as he knew he was alone until he heard a woman's voice screaming for the same answers he did when he arrived.

"Hello?" He banged on the walls.

"Hello?" Betty managed to squeak out. "Who is that? This is Betty. Hello?

"Betty? Holy shit, Betty! It's Milo!" Milo was another local junkie that had gone missing before her.

"I thought you were in jail or dead Milo. How did you get here and where the hell are we."

"I don't know, Betty, but this place is Awesome! Everything you could ever want! I mean everything!"

"Well, it is nice but there is no way out!" She was puzzled as to why Milo was so excited by being imprisoned after being kidnapped.

"No way out? Why would anyone want out, Betty? This is paradise! Everything we could ever want is right here!"

"What do you mean, Milo? We are trapped!"

"Oh wait, you haven't seen the black refrigerator yet."

"What's that?"

"Oh, you just wait," Milo continued in a conspiratorial tone. "After a few days it appears, it just magically shows up in your room while you are asleep."

"What the hell does it do, Milo?"

"Anything you crave is in there, Betty! Anything! At least anything I crave. It's like these people, whoever they are, know exactly what drugs and liquor I like!"

"Drugs? Liquor?" Now Betty was extremely confused.

"Yes, Betty! Coke, Meth, Heroin, Pills, and plenty of whiskey! It's amazing! I never want to leave, Betty! Never!"

Betty was incredulous.

"Drugs? Drugs? Why would a hospital give you drugs and alcohol?"

"I don't know girl, but I think it's some kind of facility for testing or some shit"

"You mean we are part of an experiment?"

"Yes, Betty! Look at the messages on the wall. Make good choices. Choose life not death. God grant me the serenity and the rest of that bullshit!"

"But why? I don't understand, Milo." The fear in her voice was evident.

"Why would they kidnap us off the street, provide a beautiful and comfortable room and feed us? Then give us a refrigerator full of drugs and alcohol. It Makes no sense, Milo! It's insane!"

"Don't forget all the messages, Betty."

"How can I? They won't stop flashing! Do you think that maybe the experiment is for us to not use drugs Milo?"

"That never crossed my mind."

"Because the last thing on my mind is to get high. I mean, I am craving a little bit, but I am still trying to figure all this out and I need a clear head. Now Milo seemed puzzled.

"But why give me access to all these drugs, high quality I might add. And somehow, the black fridge stays full!"

"But Milo, the walls say 'Life is about choices' 'Make good choices' 'choose life not death. It's like a rescue with a catch."

"Say, woman, you're too smart and you think too much. I'm going to enjoy this free ride and stay high as a kite! I would like to find a way out of this room though. Even though it has all this great stuff, I am starting to feel trapped!"

CHAPTER 7

Back in the motel room Blake lined up a huge rail. His nose was trickling blood down his face. As he dabbed the blood with a piece of toilet paper, the TV was on in the background. A new virus called Monkey Pox and the newly elected Donald Trump is talking. He says he is the best person to combat the Pox.

"There is no one better, just ask!"

"Oh God, I can't believe they elected this guy again! Maybe it is the end of the world as we know it."

"What's that?" asked Mike.

"Oh nothing. Turn off that bullshit and put on the music channel, will you?"

"Sure thing."

Mike changed the TV and Blake went over his finances on his phone. Credit cards almost maxed out. Only several thousand dollars left to his name. And a Corvette. Soon, he thought he would be homeless. No way! Not him! How did he end up here? He remembered his wife's final words before she left.

"Baby, come back to me, get clean and sober. I'll always love you."

"I can't," he replied, "I'm an addict. I have a disease."

"I know Blake. But life is still about choices. Choose me not the drugs! You could die!"

The memory fades as the music is turned up to a Pink Floyd song.

The lunatic is on the grass.
The lunatic is on the grass.
Remembering games and daisy chains and laughs.
Got to keep the loonies on the path.

And the cocaine, once again, overrides all sense of belonging. Pain and feelings of sorrow are gone. The coke is the feeling. The coke becomes the soul. The coke is his spirit. The coke is his God. All problems for the moment cease to exist. Everything ceases to exist. There is just the high. Cocaine becomes all that matters in life. All that he knows. All that he can see. Pink Floyd continues to play as his face goes numb like an arctic explorer lost in the snow.

And if the damn breaks open many years too soon.
If there is no room upon the hill.
And if your head explodes with dark foreboding too.
I'll see you on the dark side of the moon.

CHAPTER 8

Bam had been in the facility for what, a week now? It was so hard to remember. The same van pulled up and asked where to find some good dope. While he was answering, a couple of people jumped out. The problem was these "jump out boys" did not have the complete 4-1-1 on Bam. Yes, Bam was a homeless addict. He was even a mental health patient, but at one time he was a professional MMA fighter with a 2-0 record. He was far from fighting shape, but when those goons attempted to apprehend him, his fast twitch muscle fibers and his muscle memory kicked in. He beat one of the abductors senseless, but he was eventually subdued.

Bam had not always been this way. He came from a wealthy, two parent family. He started drinking in high school as a weekend hobby. Peer pressure convinced him to try meth. After school, he became a fighter, and only experienced the occasional party. He would swear off drugs, when training, then beat someone half to death and celebrate! But, the partying got worse and more frequent. As with most addicts, he neglected his responsibilities and even failed to show up for a few fights. Promoters stopped calling him.

His manager dropped him. Eventually, he became a full-time meth user and chased it all down with plenty of beer.

His family committed him to a psych hospital a few times and he was diagnosed Bipolar. And like so many Bipolar patients, drugs and alcohol, they thought, were the best medicine. Now, in society's eyes, he was another worthless, homeless person no one cared about. Except for someone in this facility. Bam had woken up like the others, puzzled, scared, mad and starving. But he ate and ate. Then came the black fridge. Like Milo, he drank and drugged. He was so out of control that the "Watchers" took special notice and thought to intervene but the doctor in control of the facility said it wasn't time and to let the patients make their own choices.

This morning for Bam was the same as usual. He was so drunk and high he could touch the ceiling. All of a sudden, was that his mother? He saw his dead mother standing before him. 'They' were watching from the control room as he shouted, "Mom!" "Mom!"

The apparition spoke to him, "Son, look around you."

"This is your choice. This is what I have always tried to tell you."

"Mom!" I miss you, mom!" I'm sorry I..."

"Son, listen, stop killing yourself!" "Pay attention to all the signs around you." Bam jumped up from his bed and fell on his face from the blood rushing to his brain. He stood back up to the image of his mom still talking.

"You were a wonderful child growing up with amazing talents. It was the alcohol and drugs that set you on this current path. Then, I got sick. I am sorry that I had to leave you. That pain made everything worse. You have to let go of all the hurt inside you before it destroys you. Only you can make it right. You must find hope once again and save yourself.

And with that, she was gone.

"No! Mom!"

The watchers in the control room knew he must be hallucinating. Bam fell to the floor sobbing and was still calling out to his mother. When he stopped crying, he looked up at the flashing messages. Everything his mother had ever tried to tell him was swimming through his mind. He didn't know exactly what came over him, but he closed the black refrigerator.

A comfort he hadn't known since he was a child in his mother's arms embraced him. He knew he was done. Something deep in his psyche or his spirit changed. Did he believe in that shit? His mother sure had. He felt something click like a light turned on. That's it, he thought, that sounds right.

The light switched on and he knew. He really knew in his alcohol and drug riddled brain that he was done. And what a phenomenal moment it was. Clarity washed over him. When the black fridge first arrived, he stayed wasted and ignored all signs designed to help him. He had also ignored people banging on the walls from the adjacent hospital rooms around him. He never spoke up or even cared. He wanted to shout to the entire world he was done. He wanted to scream so loud that his mom could hear him in Heaven. Now, he found his voice.

"Mom! I'm ready!" Then he crawled to the nearest wall and shouted,

"Hey! I'm here! Who else is here?"

Betty was the first to speak up. "Who is that?

"It's Bam!"

"Bam? Oh my God, Bam!"

"Betty, is that you? How in the hell? Why are you here?"

"I don't know, Bam. Same as you I guess?"

"How long you been here, Bam?"

"A week, I guess."

"I've been here a couple of days. Wait, why didn't you speak up this whole time?"

"I'm sorry, Betty. I've been wasted for days! Wait! Before I forget. Do not open the black refrigerator. Don't even go near it!"

"It hasn't got here yet, Bam."

"Ok good. It will suck you in and it's hard to escape. I opened it and was consumed by it. But somehow, for some reason, I don't want to be wasted anymore! I want to feel alive again! I even want to feel the shitty parts."

"What do you mean?"

"Well, it's like I don't need drugs or alcohol anymore to live. The desire is gone! Do you know what I mean?"

Just then Milo chimed in,

"I do! It means you're a fucking quitter!" And Milo followed that joke with a drug-fueled, maniacal laugh that echoed throughout the entire facility. Betty, ignoring Milo said,

"I guess I get it, Bam." The doubt was obvious in her voice. She continued,

"I am craving right now but the black fridge isn't here yet. I know I don't want to live like I've been living but I don't think I am strong enough to stop. I feel like this whole crazy thing is a test!"

Milo screamed,

"Y'all are both quitters! Everything you will ever need is right here, except, damn I could sure use a woman! Hey Betty, find a way to my room so we can get busy!"

"Fuck you, Milo!"

"That's the idea bitch!" Milo's maniacal laugh sounded so evil it gave Betty chills.

CHAPTER 9

On the monitors in the control room, they watched the patients twenty four hours a day. It was sometimes exhausting, but in their minds it was worth it. This experiment would save lives. On one hand, if they chose life and gave up the alcohol and drugs they would be transformed for the better. But, if they continued on the same path before they got here, then the inevitability of death would be brought to them much sooner. After all, isn't that what every alcoholic and addict wanted? To numb themselves into oblivion? This is the kind of philosophy that the doctor running this facility would "educate" all his employees into believing as he did.

This facility, in his eyes, was performing groundbreaking work, albeit illegal. The doctor reasoned that he could give these hopeless people a new lease on life without alcohol or drugs or put them out of their misery.

Walter Van Hook bankrolled this place after he lost his son to an "accidental overdose." He hated that phrase with passion. He would share a news story of an accidental overdose then scoff that it was a farce and that there was no such thing. When met with opposition he would say,

"Isn't death what every person toying with drugs wants? Oh, they might not feel like dying that day but surely they know that any time could be the day their heart stops or their brains cease functioning.

His son was the exact image of his mother that left when he was eleven. She had caught the doctor and his nurse together and never came back. His son, of course, blamed his father. At thirteen he started smoking pot. By eighteen it was ecstasy, and by twenty, cocaine. His heart couldn't take the constant abuse. Doctor Van Hook could do nothing to curtail his son's drug use and felt helpless.

Racked with guilt after the death of his son, the doctor poured himself into every study on how to cure the addict. Most were 12 step programs or Psychiatry with various drug cocktails and were mostly experimental. It seemed the people that were cured or stopped, was due to this Psychic change concept. But the main thing from his studies showed him each and every person had a choice. A choice to change. A choice to do something different and a willingness to live. They no longer chose the route that was killing them. They had somehow found hope. These success stories chose life over death.

Hope was a recurring theme throughout everything he read. Somehow these miracles, and doc was not a traditionally religious man, but he saw these triumphant stories as nothing less than a miracle. Hopeless individuals, from all levels of society, found hope and chose life. So now he was offering the lowest parts of society, the shunned, the forgotten and the ignored, a second chance. In reality, they probably had dozens of chances in life but were too wasted to see it.

The other person in the monitor room with the doc was his newly acquired assistant. She found this place through a friend of a friend and wholeheartedly stepped into the position. Her family was also affected by the pain of addiction. The passion she had for helping these patients was second only to Doctor Van Hook's. Her hope was to perhaps one day rebuild her family. At first, she had some trepidation about the whole kidnapping and secret facility aspect, but she believed in the doctor. And she had asked herself, "Wouldn't anyone given this opportunity do anything to save their family?" Determined, she devoted every day to these patients and rooted for every one of them. But she knew, statistically, some of these patients would fail. Especially, when offered the never-ending supply of paradise in a box, to use one of Milo's favorite sayings. The party that never sleeps. Until the final sleep that never wakes comes to claim the hopeless addict.

She had heard from the doctor numerous times that is what addicts most want. To never feel pain again. To numb their body permanently and maybe not wake up from their miserable existence. She often pondered; how did someone get to that point in life? What horrible trauma created a sense of hopelessness? What person would traverse this road until insanity and/or death came to claim the willing participant? She could not fathom giving up like that. That is why she would not give up on her family.

She had her own trauma. Her stepfather. Why did it always have to be a stepfather? He would visit her room and she remembered closing her eyes tightly, and wishing herself away to a dream safe from the monster. Although she dived into drugs early on like so many others, she eventually found a good man and settled down. She found hope. She thrived in the devoted wife role. Like the doctor said, she woke up with hope and made the choice to change. Now, she was watching the monitors taking notes. Guiding each one with flashing signs on the walls and helping them realize there is a better way. A way to find hope. A way to find life once again. The black refrigerator no longer bothered her. What bothered her was when they succumbed to the cravings and was one step closer to death."

The drawback of this experiment was that someone could die. She was told some already had. But the doctor believed that some people became so hopeless they chose death over life whenever they use. So, she vowed to do everything in her power to bring hope to these patients so they would choose. Choose life.

CHAPTER 10

"**D**amn it!" Blake slammed down the motel phone.

"What's wrong?" asked Mike.

"Well, the rent is due for this damn crack motel!"

"What's wrong with that, big money sonny?"

"Big money sonny is almost broke that is what's wrong!"

"Broke?" Mike laughed so hard he almost swallowed the crack rocks he kept in his mouth like a squirrel hiding its nuts. "You can't be broke, no way dude!"

"Yes way, Mike. I mean, I can pay rent, but my money is almost gone."

"How the fuck did you…"

"Not me Mike, Us. We have snorted and smoked and drank and partied for several weeks now. I knew it would run out one day but not this soon." Blake choked back tears at the realization that his life was a complete disaster, and his only escape would be out of reach.

"Well, what are you going to do?" asked Mike.

"The only thing I can do right now. Pay rent and get fucked up! I'll cross the being completely broke bridge when I come to it." He slammed his fist on the nightstand for effect.

"Sorry to be a Debbie downer, here." He handed Mike a few hundred dollars. As Mike was leaving, Blake felt like that money was his blood and that his addiction was literally bleeding him dry. Every $100 bill had been oozing from his veins one drop at a time. He remembered a church song from way back in his childhood,

"There's power in the blood, Power in the blood."

Well, his power was almost gone. There were only a couple of thousand left in the bank and that would only last a few days at the most. He had a bunch of decent jewelry. Daydreaming, he saw himself pawning his last few possessions, then living in his car. How could a person sleep in a Corvette? Maybe he should buy a tent now. He couldn't sell his Corvette because he still owed $30,000 on it! My God, he thought. How do people wrestle with these types of decisions? Pay the rent or get high? To eat or get another hit? Or worse yet, feed their children? He was horrified at these thoughts. He shook them away and buried his nose in the remaining small pile of snow before him, and waited for the fresh avalanche to arrive.

Most people he met on the street seemed content with this lifestyle. He didn't think he could survive like they did. "I would rather die than be on the streets." He said out loud and his skin crawled. Mike arrived and his heart skipped a beat and the morbid thoughts escaped for the time being, but he knew they would be back.

Mike and Blake snorted and smoked their way to heaven once again, and all reality was banished into a different dimension. Blake stood in front of the mirror and was petrified. He was once an avid bodybuilder that garnered looks from the ladies. He had lost thirty pounds. That would place him at 145 pounds in a six foot frame. From the epitome of health to a,

"Fucking crackhead, loser junkie and soon to be homeless." He had not noticed he had said this out loud to which Mike asked,

"What?" dude?"

"Nothing bro, just thinking out loud."

"Yea, you have been doing that a lot lately Blake. You okay?"

"I'm good, for now. I was just thinking about what I would do when the money runs out."

"Well, that would mean the party is over!" Mike's sense of humor was lost on Blake.

Mike's signature, obnoxious laugh hurt Blakes brain.

"No, seriously, Mike. Soon the money will be gone and then what? Will I live under the bridge with you?" The desperation in Blake's voice tinged with fear troubled Mike.

To lighten the mood Mike replied,

"Not with me bro! There is only room for one in my sleeping bag!" It worked and Blake managed a slight laugh but did not completely shake the feeling of impending doom.

Mike stood up and was still laughing which triggered a coughing spasm. He stumbled his way to the sink and spat up a blood filled "loogie" and possibly part of his lung by the sound of it. Once he finished hacking up several more bloody, God awful concoctions, mostly missing the sink completely, Blake yelled,

"Make sure you wash all that nasty shit down the drain this time dude! Last time it hardened up like glue and I had to scrape it off with a knife!"

"Ok Blake, sorry about that."

"I think I got cancer." Mike said with no real concern in his voice.

"I mean we all have to die sooner or later right, Blake"

"I guess. The goal is to be later though."

"Well, we might as well die partying our asses off!"

Just then, during another session of Mike's laughter, Blake imagined himself dead. Would his wife come to the funeral? Would his children? He had not talked to his kids in months. They were distant since his drug use and divorce. He didn't notice Mike turn ghostly white, then stumble out the motel room door. He heard a loud "Ugh" then a loud thud. He shook himself out of his "day-mare" and looked around.

"Mike?" Mike?" He walked toward the open door and saw Mike collapsed in a heap on the concrete walkway outside the room.

"Mike!" screamed Blake.

Frantic, he knelt by Mike and shook the lifeless body of his only friend and party buddy.

"Mike!" No reaction. "Someone call 9-1-1," Blake yelled to no one in particular. The other dope fiends peaked out their windows, but no one dared call 9-1-1 or offer any help. Paranoid and "stuck" in their rooms, they ignored the drama as it unfolded. One snake cracked opened the door to get a better look, then slithered back in his hole. Blake jumped up, found his cell phone and called an ambulance.

"Come quick, please! I don't know. My friend collapsed! Hurry! Um, I'm at the Motel on 34th street. Um, it's called Paradise, I think? Room 224! Upstairs! Quit asking so many fucking questions lady and send a fucking ambulance. Jesus!"

With that, Blake hung up and searched for a pulse. When he found none, he started C.P.R. by pushing on Mike's chest with both hands. When he heard the sirens, he relaxed and heard Mike start to breathe, although still unconscious. He suddenly realized there was dope in the room. He jumped up and cleaned as fast he could before the police arrived.

CHAPTER 11

octor Van Hook's assistant was named Marie. So dedicated, that she took barely any breaks and sometimes slept there until her next shift. There was a tiny restroom located in a closet within the monitor room. She was looking at herself in the mirror after relieving herself and saw the disheveled person staring back at her. At forty, she was still an attractive and youthful woman. Because she was used to being in charge at her previous job, as well as her household, she thrived in this position. She was the doctor's "right hand woman." Because of the trauma she experienced in losing her family to addiction, these patients became her number one priority. And she never gave up hope her family could be restored one day. She wondered if her husband would make the right choices if he was here? Would he choose life instead of death? All she could do was hope. Hope is what kept her going most days. She often said hope is what everyone needs.

CHAPTER 12

Bam had settled down in his room after reuniting with his friends. He was going over the last few years of his life. The details were extremely hazy in his drug and alcohol flooded brain, but the parts he did remember gave him anxieties. A few months ago, he had been robbed and even stabbed. The evidence of this attack was the grotesque scar from chest to waistline. He remembered holding in his intestines as he ran for his life. He came to a convenience store on Montrose Blvd and the glass door was locked. He banged his bloody hands on the glass until his view was partially obstructed. What Bam could not see was a clerk frozen with terror and would not press the security release button under the counter for him to enter, despite the gut wrenching screams for help.

Bam had turned around, slid down the bloody glass and sat on the concrete in front of the door resigned to die. He was tired. Tired of his life. Tired of the nightmare. He felt ready to let go. His next thought was feeling like he was floating above his body watching himself die. He felt at peace. The misery and horror were finally coming to an end. Then flashing lights and the ambulance. The paramedics worked quickly to stop the bleeding and loaded him up in the meat wagon. That was the street's affectionate term in the hood for an ambulance because most people that entered, while in the most violent parts of the city, often died en route. Sometimes from gunshots or just beaten senseless by rival gang members. But this particular day as Bam recalled, he was saved by the E.M.T. 's and the doctors at the hospital. He was in a coma for a week. When he was let out, the first thing he did was grab a 40oz. of beer and start his journey of destruction all over again.

Now, lying in this pristine white hospital room, he methodically started to plan his future. Did he have a future? What would he do with this newly found hope? Was this what hope felt like? When had he last been hopeful? Maybe as a child, hoping Santa would bring him a new bike. He remembered hoping his mom would be saved by God because she developed cancer. His mom helped him to hope. She was ever the optimist. She had been sober for years and was always preaching about making the right choices in life. But she died. A horrible pain filled, cancer riddled death. He had held her pale, frail, and lifeless body so many days and cried out to God. But to no avail. No one answered his prayers. He came to the epiphany that it was then that he had lost all hope. It died with his mother. Now he remembered his mother before she died. Beautiful, with long black silky hair. Big, perfect smile. Ever affectionate and attentive to him. Was that joy he was now feeling? How…. Stop questioning it fool, he told himself. He felt hope and joy and noticed his mouth was turning slowly upwards into a smile. Not as nice as his mother's because he had lost most of his teeth, but a smile nonetheless. Then he choked back tears that were threatening to flow but thought twice about it and he let those tears come until he was blinded like he was in the middle of a rainstorm. He had not cried since his mother's funeral. But this sobbing was distinctly different than anything he had experienced. For these were tears of joy. His mouth still showed a jagged toothed smile. When the rain of tears stopped, he offered up thanks to his mom and whatever God was listening.

As Marie watched this miracle of choice transpire before her eyes, she silently cried. Cried for life. Cried for her husband. Cried for all the people still suffering from addiction that may never experience this renewed hope. This joy that Bam was overwhelmed by. This made what she was doing worth it. This really works! People can heal. People can make the right choices when spending most of their life trying to die. Bam had chosen life over death.

CHAPTER 13

The ambulance took Mike to the hospital, but the police stayed behind to grill Blake. Pookie, and a few others, watched from a safe distance never wanting interaction with the police.

The Sgt. on duty was a typical overweight, crew cut, hard ass and pulled no punches.

"So, what kind of drugs were y'all doing?" asked the Sgt.

"Um, er, uh we, I don't really know but.."

"Hey!" the Sgt. interrupted. "I've been at this job for 20 years, so don't bullshit me or I'll lock your ass up so fast you'll be picking out a new set of China for you and your new husband in the county jail!"

"Ok" Blake sounded defeated. Head bowed he said, "We were doing cocaine officer. "

"Uh huh, I figured that."

The Sgt. was poking around the motel room looking for a reason to haul this crackhead to jail. The Sgt. Looked back at Blake standing in the doorway trying to not look worried and said,

"You know what? I don't really give a shit! You want to kill yourself too? Go right ahead."

As he stomped out of the room, he shoulder checked Blake. Blake stumbled but caught himself from falling and heard the Sgt. Mumble, "crackhead" under his breath. He shut the motel room door and peaked out the window until he saw the last police car drive away. Pookie tapped on the door a few minutes later.

"Woo wee! That was close man! Is Mike going to be ok?"

"I don't know. I'm tired, Pookie. Tired of all of this." Blake waved his hands around for emphasis.

"When does it end, Pookie?"

"End?" Pookie scratched his head and said, "I guess when you decide to stop? Or die? It's your choice, I guess."

Blake thought, there is that damn word again. Choice.

"That word is burned into my brain from my wife and keeps coming up periodically. Is there really something to that? Can I really choose?"

"My grandma used to always say life is what I make of it so, maybe so. What the fuck do I know? I'm a mutha fuckin' hustla'!" Pookie chuckled a little.

"You know I had a sponsor once that told me I had to work these bullshit steps and go to meetings and blah, blah, blah. Choice? Fuck that! Oh shit! Where did I hide all my dope?"

Blake searched frantically for his stash.

"With that, I am outta here Blake. Holla at me when you need something."

Blake didn't acknowledge Pookie. The obsession to get high prevented him from hearing anything but his heart pounding in his chest.

Blake was in mid snort when there was a soft knock at the door. This time it was Janine. He let her in and went back to his pile. Janine placed her hand on his shoulder.

"Are you ok, Blake?" The genuine concern in her voice was lost on Blake.

"I will be, as soon as I get my buzz back." The closeness of a female other than his wife made him uncomfortable, so he delicately eased out of her soft grasp.

"All this drama stole my buzz!"

"I bet."

Janine wasn't as pretty as Betty, but she was cute and petite. Slightly sun weathered and pushing 40. She had long brown hair and freckles, which helped her look younger than she was. She also had all her teeth intact, which was uncommon in this area, so her smile was exceptional. He could tell she took care of her hygiene and that was more than he could say for himself. Blake hadn't taken a shower in three days. It must have been a week since he brushed his teeth. He did that now, talking through a mouth full of toothpaste.

"You want to hang out and get high?" Blake asked shyly.

"Oh?" Janine's eyes opened wide, and her ears perked up like a cute Siberian Husky he once had. Then she looked at him in a somewhat curious and sexy way.

"No, nothing like that I mean," he was stammering now embarrassed. "I uh, um, I just don't like being alone.

"Ok." The look of disappointment quickly changed to that of disinterest.

"I'll pay you for your time, but I just want to hang out and get high, if you're cool with that."

"Sure." It sounded robotic.

"Can I ask you a question Blake?" He lined up 2 huge rails of the "booger sugar", another street name for the coke.

"Go ahead."

"How come you never asked to be with any of the girls around here? He did not look up from his stash as he continued to snort.

"I heard your wife left you a while back and put you through the ringer.

"People talk too much." She could tell he was irritated. She followed up with,

"I'm sorry, Blake I didn't mean to.."

"No big deal." He waved her off and lined up two more lines. There must have been a quarter gram in each one. He inhaled one and offered the other to Janine.

After she did the line, she said.

"Again, I'm sorry if I sound like a busy body, but you're obviously hetero and I have never seen a man roll through here and not hook up with one of us. You must be really in love with your wife."

Blake wiped away a tear before she saw it and replied,

"Yes I do, wholeheartedly and the only pain reliever I need is…" He held up his bag of escape and shook it for effect.

"No offense to you Janine, but I have no interest in prostitutes or any other type of woman for that matter."

"No offense taken."

"I just want to block out everything and feel nothing." Blake bowed his head for a second and looked to be in prayer. Truth be told he was fighting back tears. When he looked up, she couldn't help but feel empathy for this man. That was something she was not used to working on these streets. She couldn't afford to get close emotionally to a man. That was rule number two. Rule number one was no kissing.

"I wish someone loved me that much. She is or, forgive me, was a

lucky woman."

"I guess."

She continued,

"I have never heard of anything like that except in a couple of romance books I read a long time ago." She giggled.

Blake looked up at her and spoke as he handed her the coke lined mirror.

"She was, is, a good woman that stood by me much longer than she should have. I put her through hell. I don't blame her." Janine listened intently, now feeling regret by starting this subject of conversation.

"She only wanted me to get clean and come back to her emotionally. But I checked out so to speak. I wish I could get clean."

"Me too," said Janine. "Me too."

CHAPTER 14

Mike woke up in the hospital to a beautiful nurse attending to him. Hazily he asked,

"Am I dead? Is this heaven? Are you an angel?" The nurse laughed.

"No sir. You are in a hospital, and you are going to be fine." His vision was slightly blurry from the meds they gave him but from what he could tell, this nurse was gorgeous! Better than what he was used to.

"I'm nurse Pierce. You had a mild heart attack. Should be a wakeup call for you."

He looked at her with a sheepish grin,

"If this is a dream, I don't want to wake up, beautiful!"

She managed a smile, but remaining professional said,

"You tested positive for all sorts of narcotics. Your liver has taken a beating from alcohol as well. You are also malnourished so eat this tray of food." She rolled a portable table to him, and he realized he was hungry, so he began eating.

"We'll do our best to clean you up and feed you, but in the meantime, would you like to talk to someone?"

"Talk to who?" He said through a mouth full of food. "I'm talking to you."

"No I mean a pastor, or a therapist or.."

"Hell no! I mean no thank you ma'am." He quickly nipped that bullshit in the bud he thought.

He didn't want any preacher or psych doctor picking at his brain.

"Keep them away please!"

"Ok. But it's pointless for us to make you all better then, you get out just to do it all over again. Next time you might not be so lucky."

"Maybe not." Mike replied.

"But I will go out on my terms. It will be my choice."

As Nurse Pierce walked away, she stopped in the doorway and turned slightly to face Mike and said,

"You're right, everything in our lives is about the choices we make. Good luck sir."

And with that, his angel was gone. Mike thought to himself, everyone is a fucking philosopher.

He shouted,

"I don't need anyone's fucking help!" But deep down he knew he did.

He tried to remember a time when he was not drunk or high. 11 or 12? Damn. He started drinking and smoking weed at 13. Holy shit. He was 58 now. 45 years of non-stop getting wasted. How had he made it this long? How was he still alive? His mother used to say "everything happens for a reason." So, what was the reason he was a worthless, homeless, drunk crackhead? When does it end? He dismissed the pointless questions he had no answers to, and fell asleep once more. He dreamed of his angel and him having a grand old time. If anyone had walked in while he was asleep, they would have seen the big grin on his face.

CHAPTER 15

etty woke up. This was the 5th day, and her cravings were not that bad. The withdrawal drugs in the food were doing their job. She blinked away the haze of sleep and sat up. She looked around her room and terror froze her gaze. The hair on the back of her neck stood up. Her breath was stuck in her throat and her heart seemed to stop beating. She wanted to scream but could not find her voice. There it was. Ominous in the pure white room. The Black refrigerator. No, no, no, no, no, she thought. At last, her voice came although soft and squeaky,

"Please God, no." She finally yelled,

"NO!"

She jumped up out of bed and banged on the wall.

"Bam! Bam! Are you awake? Please help me!"

The walls around her were blinking their messages. She read them to herself. Choose Life! Life is about choices. Make the right choices. Choose life not death! Bam must be asleep.

"Jesus! Please help me!" She shouted. She was a foxhole Christian, only asking for help when in trouble.

"I don't want to get high anymore!" She was crying hysterically now calling upon the God of her understanding to rescue her from the black fridge.

"Please God! Give me the strength!"

She went to the white fridge and stuffed all the food she could down her throat hoping that would help. She looked like a ravenous animal that was eating for its life. Eating was an instinctive reaction to help stop cravings and kill the butterflies in her stomach begging for dope. But deep down she knew only drugs and alcohol could fix those rumblings within her.

After she was full and satiated, she collapsed in front of the white fridge. No blanket. No pillow. She cried while thanking the God she barely knew until the tears ran out and sleep took over.

CHAPTER 16

Blake ran out of dope. He was terrified. Mike was gone. Janine had left to turn a trick even though Blake had given her $200 to hang out. He was all alone for the first time in who knows how long. He jumped up off the bed a little too fast. He passed out from the dizziness. Also, he hadn't eaten or drank any water for that matter, for a few days. When he came to a few seconds later, he rushed to the sink and turned on the faucet. He bent over and inhaled water until his belly hurt. Standing up and gasping for air, he looked at the man in the mirror. Hardly a man looking back at him. Hair crazy, spotted and a patchy white beard. Sunken eyes, haggard and wrinkled face that seemed to look like one of those horror movies where a skeleton comes to life. He turned his face side to side to see the hollowed cheeks that once had cute dimples according to his wife. X wife. His once disarming smile was empty. The crazy smile staring back at him had reminded him of another flick he saw where a mad scientist, that was drunk on his own genius, resuscitated dead flesh back to life. A maniacal, evil, skeleton man. He felt like a zombie. Although his Heart was still beating, he was dead to the world around him. Whatever he looked like it wasn't him staring back. He was an empty shell of a man with no soul, no life, and no hope. Nothing.

"I am nothing." He said out loud.

He was jolted out of his "day-mare" by a knock at the door. His heart seemed to jump out of his chest. Police?

"Who is it?"

"It's Pookie, fool! Open up!"

Relieved, he stumbled to the door still feeling extremely weak and needing a fix. He opened the door to Pookie standing there with a smile and a sack in his hands from the convenience store around the corner.

"You need to eat brother." He stepped in the room gently pushing past Blake. Pookie set various chips, a sandwich and two cokes on the table. Could he eat? He had been up for five days now. He felt a twinge of hunger at the sight of the food, so he tore open a bag of chips and chugged half a coke in one breath. The sandwich was gone in three bites.

"Slow down bro!" Pookie tilted back the forty ounce bottle of Ol' E and wiped his mouth when done and said,

"You should really take a rest."

"I'll rest when I die," mumbled Blake.

"What's that?"

"My father used to always say that. Rest when you die."

"I ain't never heard that shit before."

Blake now snapped back to his only life goal, more dope.

"I need more dope, Pookie." He said this as chips flew out his mouth.

"Yea, no problem but first pay me ten dollars for this food."

Blake paid him a few hundred and gave him a list of his necessities.

Pookie left. Rest when you die was echoing in his mind while he waited.

CHAPTER 17

Marie watched intently as Betty cried out to God. She hoped her God would answer her and give her the strength to continually abstain from opening the black fridge. She watched her as she was devouring the food. A desperate image because she was using both hands to shovel it in. Betty finally went to sleep. She looked so peaceful. Curled up in a little ball in front of a white fridge and eating yourself into a coma was not enough to keep someone sober, Marie thought. Had she achieved that psychic change like Bam? She was astonished but pleased that Bam was the first one to "come to" so to speak. And all this after he had partaken of the black refrigerator. It was also incredible that immediately after getting sober he attempted to work with Betty to make a change. Bam evolved into a hero in this facility to save people from themselves.

As she typed her notes, she periodically looked up and watched the other patients. Milo was nodding out with a needle in his arm, high on heroin. There was a shattered crack pipe on the floor. A meth pipe on the side table. The black fridge was ajar with baggies of narcotics strewn on the floor in front of it. She choked back tears. Her hope was dwindling. She feared that Milo would be another victim of his own bad choices. He seemed to have chosen his path. The path of destruction. The journey to oblivion. Choosing death instead of life. She wanted to talk to him and to encourage him, but it wasn't time. She knew there was no interaction until Doctor Van Hook said so. So, she resigned to observe and take notes. She felt helpless.

"It is up to them." She said out loud.

"It is their choice. May their God give them the strength to do so." She bowed her head and whispered a silent prayer.

"God grant me the serenity
To accept the things I cannot change
Courage to change the things I can
And wisdom to know the difference."

She recited this powerful prayer to herself several times every day. It always brought her peace and offset her anxieties that affected her work.

She wished everyone knew this prayer. She daydreamed of a time when she and her husband were happy. Way back when. Dancing all night. He was such a great dancer. Country, Hip hop and even salsa. When they met, she had no rhythm. Two left feet. But he would pull her so close and move her hips with his to the beat and allow her for the first time in her life to feel the music through him. Hips swaying side to side. They were so sexy together. Then the money and the drugs took over the images in her brain. She shook herself out of the daze before it ruined her mood. She noticed Betty had sat up. What would she do now? Would she succumb to the calling of the Black fridge? Once again Marie bowed her head.

"God grant me the serenity..."

CHAPTER 18

Milo's life was more screwed up than most. Father went to prison when he was eight for killing his mother. He had caught her cheating. So, he was raised by his grandparents. They did the best that they could for this child, but it was apparent early on that Milo was extremely troubled. He exhibited anger issues. He never shied away from a fight but wasn't a bully. Other kids tried to bully him because he was little, but they would find out the hard way that he was not the one to pick on.

By the time he hit high school he was six foot and two hundred pounds. He was suspended several times in eleventh grade and despite having average grades, he chose to drop out and take a job in construction. At seventeen, he moved out of his grandparents and lived with other construction workers. He made good money and led a simple life. This is where he discovered alcohol. One day after work, when it was ninety degrees plus outside, a friend handed him a beer. When that cold brew hit the back of his throat it was like magic. A switch turned on and all the fear and hurt disappeared for the moment. He and his friends would party all weekend after working hard all week. It was a tradition among these guys, and he loved it. The alcohol made him feel invincible and liked by everyone. Except for the occasional fight by someone drunker than he was, his life was normal to him.

Then he met a beautiful girl at a bar. They moved in together and soon she was pregnant. They had a small trailer park wedding and all his friends attended. He got so drunk that he passed out during the consummation. She didn't care because she was drunk as well. The baby was born healthy even with her drinking while pregnant. His drinking became more frequent and was compounded by the fact that she stopped partying, "For the baby," she said. She also wanted him to do the same, but it was too late. The bug had bitten him and poisoned his mind. He would come home drunk to her nagging,

"You drove home like that?"

"What if you were pulled over?"

"What if you got into a wreck?"

"You could have hurt someone or hurt yourself?"

All he heard was- *"Blah, blah, blah, blah"*

So, he started coming home with a case of beer and drinking there.

After 10 years of this drunken neglect to his wife and child, plus the occasional bout of physical abuse, she left.

One day while he was at work, she just packed up and left. No note. Nothing. He shrugged it off and got wasted. His daily ritual of beer graduated to cocaine and heroin use at the introduction of another girl he met. He started missing work so much that he got fired. He went on unemployment and blew through his savings. Not to mention that twenty percent of his money went to child support. He was living off credit cards and they were about maxed out. Once unemployment stopped, he lost his place and of course, in true fashion, the new girl left.

All alone, homeless and wasted, he devolved into a wandering, hopeless man. Panhandling, petty theft and a couple of robberies were his ticket to the next drink or high. He met Pookie and learned other ways to hustle. He was on a path of destruction with no foreseeable way out, until he woke up in this bizarre hospital.

At first, he was comfortable, but experiencing withdrawals. He ate and slept his days away. Then the black fridge appeared. His heart literally skipped a beat and he threw up the instant he looked inside.

"Jackpot!" He screamed.

He devoured the contents of that black fridge like he was a third world child introduced to an American buffett. And what a buffet it was! Everything he had ever used in the largest amounts he could ever dream about. He thought he was in heaven. The first time he saw the signs on the wall he shrugged his shoulders and ate until he had his fill. He ignored the signs once more and got high, because he had chosen the path of death.

And every day since the black fridge appeared, it was a drug induced maniacal journey for Milo. At times he would hallucinate and see his x wife and his child in the room. They would be there staring, judging him. He would scream, "Get out of here! Leave me alone!" He switched to heroin and the hallucinations stopped.

Heroin was so much better than meth he thought. He felt so peaceful when he cooked dope with a spoon. This place was the best thing that had ever happened to him. Silently, he thanked God as he injected another syrup like concoction into his veins and nodded off into extinction. He didn't care if he woke up or not. If this wasn't heaven, this was as close as he would ever get. Marie watched from her place in the monitor room. She was saddened by what she saw. But this was his choice, she reminded herself.

CHAPTER 19

Mike was in the hospital for a few days when the nurse gave him the news.

"You're going to be discharged today, Mike."

"Already?" asked Mike

"Yes sir. We have done all we can for you, and you are good to go."

"I don't feel good to go." Mike was feeling the effect of withdrawals.

The nurses smile waned, and she looked directly in Mikes eyes and said,

"It's more than likely you're going through withdrawals. But the other tests indicate you're cleared for discharge."

"Okay." Mike couldn't hide his disappointment. This place was so nice and comfortable.

"That offer to talk to someone still stands."

"Oh no! Don't need anyone to talk to. Thanks, but no thanks. It's almost lunch time, can I eat before y'all kick me out?"

"Certainly, of course." Said Nurse Pierce.

An hour after lunch, Nurse Pierce and an orderly came into his room. She gave him some meds to go and placed him in a wheelchair. He was wheeled through the lobby onto the sidewalk in front of the hospital and they said their goodbyes. He had a knot in his stomach. He needed a drink. Bad. He walked towards the bus stop. He had just enough change to drop in the receptacle and found a seat next to a priest. The priest noticed the medical armband he still wore, and Mike noticed his gaze.

"Oh, this? No big deal. Just a little heart scare. This old ticker is indestructible." The priest looked intently at Mike like he was seeing into his soul.

"You know, sometimes God gives us signs that he is there waiting for us to come back to him." Mike thought, Jesus! Another person trying to meddle in his life.

"Well, Father, I think to come back to someone you would have had to be with them in the first place. And I ain't never been with God." The priest gave this statement some deep thought before he spoke. Mike could tell he was struggling with some wise words to impart to him, so Mike spoke up,

"My life ain't about shit, excuse the language father. It never has been. I'm too far gone for God to even care." As if a light went off in the priest's mind, his eyes lit up and he spoke,

"Son, don't you know? God will never leave you nor forsake you. He is always there for you. You still have a choice. He longs to hear you call out his name for help. Will you call to Him now? Can I pray for you?"

The sincerity in the priest's voice moved Mike so much he teared up but choked back and swallowed any crying that tried to escape his proud lips. Mike bowed his head and squeaked out,

"Okay, father." The priest reached for Mike's hands, which at first startled him and he pulled away slightly. But then he relented and allowed the father to take him through a prayer. The prayer was beautiful and was about love and forgiveness. He also asked God to help Mike make the right choices. The priest continued,

"God, lead this man to the path of righteousness." Righteousness Mike thought? How could he ever be righteous? He was about to go find his buddy Blake and get wasted. The same old choice he always made. As the priest finished and said Amen, Mike said Amen as well then looked up and saw he had missed his stop.

"Shit!" He shouted. "Sorry father. I missed my stop! Hey!"

He jumped up and pressed the stop alert button on the wall of the bus. The bus driver stopped at the next available intersection. As Mike started to exit the bus, he looked back at the Priest and managed,

"It's too late for me father but thanks anyways!" He heard,

"It's never too late!" the father shouted as he stepped off the bus. Where was he? Damn! At least a couple of miles away! Starting to run he said to himself,

"I hope I don't have another heart attack on the way back to the motel!"

CHAPTER 20

Blake cracked open the door to his room and stuck his head out. Where the hell is Pookie?

"God, I hate being alone in this place," he said softly. He could see Janine walking back and forth in front of the motel looking for a trick. A car stopped and spoke to Janine, she got in. How unsafe that is Blake thought.

Janine had told him her story. It didn't make sense to him. She came from a loving home with both parents. She was in college studying to be a nurse. Even though she was date raped, twice, she stayed in college and made decent grades. She never told the police or her parents. She felt ashamed because her parents were devout Christians and knew they would blame her. That was why her parents sent her to a Christian University in Texas. Christian University, what a joke. She was confused by all the hypocrisy with the wild parties and drinking and drugging she saw. Someone introduced her to Xanax. She often wondered why it was always her so-called friends that introduced her to all these chemical escapes from life?

Being on pills caused a lackadaisical attitude, to say the least, about going to class. She failed out of college and her parents gave her the choice of being sent away to a faraway college in what, Montana? "Fuck that," she remembered telling them. They literally disowned her. They cut off all her funds and refused her request to come home.

That is how she ended up here. She controlled her own life because she had no pimp. So, she could turn tricks whenever and with whoever she liked. The only problem she had was being lost in the never-ending cycle of getting drunk. She would make money, buy some alcohol and the occasional cocaine or pills, then have enough for her motel room. She saw no way out of this life. She was usually too drunk to care. A couple of times she borrowed money from Blake to pay for her room. He didn't sweat the fact that she didn't pay it back. She even offered a few times to work it off with sex and of course he declined.

So, after a few bad experiences with her tricks and cocaine, she tried to switch to an alcohol and marijuana maintenance program. The effect on her life was less drama, but still destructive. A while back Blake heard she was doing badly and paid for her room a couple of weeks in advance anonymously, but deep down she knew it was him. That is why she made it a point to check on him every day.

Suddenly, Blake saw Pookie walking through the parking lot. Pookie looked up to the second floor and saw him peeping from the window. Blake looked like a scared turtle poking his head out of his shell. Pookie was savvy enough to know what Blake wanted. More dope. Pookie tilted back his head and finished his forty and slowly walked up the stairs. He got to the door and Blake opened it to let him in. Pookie asked,

"You ate? Slept?"

"Nope"

"Damn, Blake. At least drink some water, fool!" Pookie went to the sink and filled up a plastic cup with dirty tap water and gave it to Blake. Blake drank it obediently. Pookie saw a few hundred dollars in his other hand. He waited for him to finish the glass and noticed the desperation in his eyes. He had seen that look for decades. The never ceasing craving for drugs. The craving for that first hit experience that is always chased but never found. The chase was a lifelong marathon where the finish line is never reached, until death that is. Out loud Pookie said,

"That demon is never satisfied."

"What demon, Pookie?"

"The dope demon, Blake. You'll never be satisfied, my homey. Maybe when you die."

"Um, ok. Please don't preach to me right now. I mean, I appreciate your concern and everything," he held up the money in front of his face.

"Can you get me some?"

"You know I can, Blake." As he took the money,

"I just don't want to see you end up like Mike, brother."

"Thanks, Pookie but I'm good." Pookie walked to the door then stopped and faced Blake.

"You know, I never see you leave this room, how do you always have money?"

Blake shrugged. Pookie left with the unanswered question. Blake recounted in his mind his nightly ritual.

He would wait until around four in the morning. The magical time.

Most hustlers, hoes and tricks took a short break, to sleep or whatever. It was deathly quiet outside and that's when Blake would step out and walk down the street to an ATM. He would see people asleep at the bus stop and no one walking around but him. He would pull out his daily max of $500. As he did so this time, he saw his balance and it terrified him. That's it. The party is almost over. What in the hell was he going to do?

How much money had he given away because of the kindness of his heart? Money he would never see returned. He knew no one would help him out. Not that he expected it. He shook off the fear and the questions and just focused on getting more dope. He sat in the dark waiting for Pookie to get back. What a pitiful life. Out loud, he said,

"I had it all and blew it, I had it all. Look at me now. A fucking loser. I'm nothing. Nothing."

CHAPTER 21

Mike walked while cursing himself for missing his stop. He could feel the protest of his lungs for the extra walk it would take to get back to the motel. Damn, he felt old and beat up. He needed rest but all he could think about was getting back to his best friend and getting high. He turned down the wrong street. He was daydreaming of the next hit of crack or the next line of coke before he realized it.

"Damn it!" he shouted. He turned around to go the other way when a van pulled up and a big burly guy rolled down the window to ask,

"Hey, I'm looking for that good shit, what's up?"

Mike was street smart enough to know random people pulling up and asking where to score dope were probably the undercover police. Before he got a chance to answer, the side door slid open and three men with masks got out and grabbed him, while simultaneously placing a hood over his head blocking out the sun. Shocked and Blinded, he was thrown in the back of the van and felt a prick in his neck. He was warm and fuzzy. He knew this feeling. It was morphine. He thought this wasn't so bad as he fell asleep. His fear was gone and so was he.

CHAPTER 22

Betty was fiending out bad. The withdrawal meds lost their effectiveness. That often happens with heavy users. She was shaking but the cravings from deep within her gut were the worst. She was sweating as well but she knew what was behind the door of that black fridge would take away all her pain and make her feel better. Better? What a crazy thought to think that drinking and using drugs would make everything better!

This place was insane! All the signs on the wall made sense but were heavily challenged by the black fridge. Her head hurt trying to figure just what the fuck was going on. She thought about all the stuff Bam had said. Bam! How profound he sounded. He was never known for that!

She sat in front of the black fridge terrified. Frozen. Debating both sides of her mind. The problem was that both sides were each devils! With each side having an even more devious plot for her life!

Devil #1, "What is the worst that could happen?"

Devil #2, "Who cares, let's get fucked up until we end this miserable existence!"

Devil #1, "I'm just talking about getting high and making the pain go away. No big deal."

Devil #2, "What do you care about your life for anymore anyways? Just open the fridge and do all the drugs you have ever wanted to with no thought or worry about money!"

This insanity went on for several minutes and her head was spinning.

She came to and jumped up and ran to the wall separating her and Bam's room.

Banging on the wall she screamed,

"Bam! Bam! Help me!" The fear and desperation were apparent in her pleas for help.

Bam was dreaming of his mother as the screams entered his peaceful slumber and his mother transformed into a rotted corpse. Skin flaking off, showing dirty white bones and eyes protruding from the skinless skull. Her mouth was open, saying something.

What was his mother saying? "Please! Please! Bam!"

Bam shot upright and said,

"Betty?" He jumped out of the bed with a sense of urgency and went to the wall.

"Betty! I'm here! What's wrong?"

"Bam! I don't think I can resist these urges!" Tears were clouding her vision.

Her crying made her sound like a scared child with the boogey man in her room. The sounds tore at Bam's heart.

"Yes you can, Betty! Look at all the signs around you! Pay attention! Read them all!"

"I have, Bam! It isn't working!"

"These signs have been trying to speak to your heart this whole time. Listen with your heart! Betty, look around right now, what do you see?"

"Um," as she turned from facing the wall, she took in the scene.

"Um." She mumbled again.

"Read them. Read them out loud to me!"

"Which ones?" She asked.

"Any of them! All of them!" Bam shouted with frustration. "Just read them God damn it!"

"Life," she started. Paused, choked back tears.

"Don't stop! Just keep reading!" Bam shouted again.

"Life is about choices," she spoke too softly.

"Louder, Betty!"

"Life is about choice." She found her voice now.

"Choose life not death. Make the right choice! Easy does it! Forgive others! Forgive yourself! Forgive all!"

She felt more confident now. There were signs flashing all around her. The room looked like a giant Christmas display at Macy's.

"Your life has meaning. Alcohol and drugs are not the answer." Wait, back-up, what? she thought. Forgive? Forgive my stepfather? How can I? Again, she spoke out loud.

"Forgive all, forgive yourself?" She said this in a questioning tone and Bam interjected.

"Yes! Yes! Yes!" He sounded animated now. "Yes, Betty, That's it! That was the hardest one for me to understand!"

Bam was feeling the power of hope and willingness in every fiber of his being, and it was exhilarating!

"Forgive all the feeling of worthlessness inside you! Those feelings fuel my need to be wasted. My feelings of not deserving to be happy! That's why I needed to drown all my pain and resentment against myself and others with drugs and alcohol! It's all bullshit! It's all lies! Let it go, Betty!"

"I don't know if I can, Bam!"

"You have to, Betty! All the horrible memories of people that hurt us, or a God that we once believed in that ignored our pleas for help! All that anger and misery was the cause of our addiction! We must forgive. Keep reading, Betty!"

"Love yourself again." As she said these cheesy sayings, she felt her body and her mind slowly calm. The knots disappeared from her stomach. The more she spoke her shakes subsided. There was no miraculous light from heaven, but she felt different. Better. Even with access to all these drugs and all the alcohol she could possibly drink, she felt great. The urge to use drifted away! She was now feeling excited! She continued to recite the messages on the wall.

"Let go and let God." She really didn't understand that one, but it didn't matter. It was working. She hadn't believed in God for a while. But if believing in a God would heal her broken heart and mind, then that wouldn't be so bad. She turned toward another wall and noticed something that she hadn't seen before. A message above her bed. This message had stopped blinking and constantly shone. The letters were bolder.

"Betty! Betty! Don't stop now! Keep reading!"

"God, grant me the serenity

To accept the things I cannot change

Courage to change the things I can

And wisdom to know the difference."

"Say it again, Betty!" So, she read it again.

Marie was on her feet. Knuckles turned white from squeezing the desk with her hands. Doctor Van Hook was in the room as well. The hairs on the back of his neck tingled. Betty started to understand the prayer as she recited, slowly and methodically. Over and over.

She closed her eyes and peace and understanding filled her mind and comforted her heart. Courage to change the things I can. What can I change? Me! All I can change is me! I cannot change my past. I cannot change the horrible things that happened to me! Most of all, I cannot change people! So, serenity is for those things that are out of my control! And now I know the difference!

"Holy shit Bam! I get it now! Holy shit!"

She jumped up and down shouting to Bam like a child on Christmas morning realizing the box they were unwrapping was a PlayStation five!

"I really get it, Bam! All I can change in this fucked up world full of fucked up people is Me."

"Yes, Betty!" The feeling of triumph filled Bam's heart.

"I don't have to live that way anymore! Thank you, Bam! Thank you, Bam!"

'Don't thank me," Bam shouted back.

"I didn't do it, you did! You cried out for this girl! You found it! You realized it. You chose life!"

She was weeping now with such relief and joy. She had not felt this way since, well she couldn't remember in how long. All she knew was the horrible things she experienced as a child no longer haunted her. She felt a love for herself and others she had never dreamed of. She kept saying,

"Thank you, thank you, thank you." She lay down in the bed and dreamed of a beautiful life. One free from alcohol, drugs and free from misery. She was, at last, at peace.

Doctor van Hook looked at Marie. Always the professional, he broke form for a moment and grabbed her and squeezed her in an awkward hug. She was startled but welcomed the embrace. She too was overjoyed.

"Another patient breakthrough!" The doctor shouted.

"Yes, doctor." The doctor snapped out of his unprofessionalism and released Marie with an apology.

"Um, I, Uh, I'm sorry Marie. I didn't mean to…" she interrupted him and placed her hand on his shoulder.

"No, doctor. It's ok. It is something to be proud of." This breakthrough now meant two patients were seemingly cured. This filled her with such hope. She looked at Betty on the screen. Asleep. So peaceful. She chose life. Incredible.

"Doctor? When do we begin the next phase? I mean do we wait until all the patients on the list are acquired?"

The doctor turned toward Marie and she continued.

"Can't we start phase two with these two patients?"

"Patience, Marie. You know as well as I do what's at stake here. I know what you hope for too. Just a little while longer. A few more patients and we will be ready."

"Yes, doctor." She knew all of this, but she felt a sense of urgency.

"Milo is not doing well. We may have to intervene, but in the meantime, we have these two miracles to celebrate!" The doctor did not smile that often and seeing it now was refreshing to Marie.

"You're right, doctor. And with Milo we shouldn't give up hope. As long as he breathes, he has a chance to choose. If I have learned anything from all of this, it is that everyone has a choice."

"Yes, Marie, that is correct. They can choose life over death. My work is proving it."

CHAPTER 23

All alone. All the dope is gone again. It was four o'clock in the morning and Blake hated this feeling. He needed to get more money. He cracked open the door and peaked out of the motel room. All his friends were gone. All is clear.

He stepped out and casually made a beeline to the ATM down the street. Once in front of the ATM, he pulled out his debit card and took a deep breath. He knew this was probably the last of his money. His wife, x wife, was always the one managing the money and paying the bills, but he was smart enough to know the approximate amount that was left. He was partying too much to care about money anyway.

"This is it." He said out loud. Pin code. Balance $324.35. "Shit!"

He withdrew $320.00. The sight of $4.35 on his receipt made his knees weak. He steadied himself on the ATM before he started the quick trek back to the room. He did not ask himself how he got to this point. He knew damn well the reason. His horrible choices. He didn't listen to his wife. "Choose me or the drugs," she had said. He could see and hear her voice now drifting through his mind like it was yesterday, but the call of the high was more appealing.

He had taken her for granted. Hell, he took his whole life for granted, then she left. He had put her through so much torment with his nonstop drug use. She had a nervous breakdown at work because he would call dozens of times a day. All she did was worry that she would come home and find him dead. She couldn't even get a decent night's sleep because Blake would creep around the house all night searching the drawers. He said he was looking for signs of her infidelity. It was pure, drug induced delusion. By the morning, the house would look like it was hit by an F.B.I. raid.

She left and took a little bit of his soul with her. The rest was being erased a little more every day like a winter storm blanketing the landscape until Spring. Frozen and lifeless. Soon, he would waste away and be forgotten.

The familiar knot of lovesick pain hit his gut like a punch from a boxer. He felt nauseous. He shook his head clear from this frequent pity party he would have and focused on the matter at hand. Get more drugs.

Pookie came by with a delivery and Blake was ecstatic. Pookie thought to himself that this is the most miserable guy in the world. Pookie knew from his stories that one time he had a million dollars but smoked, snorted and drank most of it. The rest, he gave away to everyone that asked for it. Maybe he was so messed up after the loss of his wife that he had a death wish.

Pookie knew no one took advantage of him, but Blake was trying to help everyone he could. After Pookie left, Blake popped open a beer and smashed up the powder with a spoon. The line was so fat it would make Scarface cringe. The back drain from this line made him choke and it was hard for him to swallow so he downed another beer.

Oh yes! He was back. Back to the land of emptiness. All feelings were gone. Except for the feeling of nothingness. Some describe it as numbing in your body and a mind devoid of thought. Like floating in a space of darkness with no stars. No cold. No heat. Nothing. You're just there staring at the drugs waiting for the demon to summon you to take another hit. He got "stuck" and couldn't move. Almost like he was immobile, in a sitting and conscious coma.

When he came to and looked at the clock, it had been over an hour he was staring at the pile in front of him. Some inner thought returned to his mind. He wondered if he was insane.

Someone once told him the definition of insanity was doing the same thing over and over again but expecting different results. He googled it. That wasn't the real definition. That definition was credited to Einstein? WTF? But he also heard insane people never questioned their insanity. He wasn't crazy! He was just fucked up beyond any repair.

Pookie was walking down the street after leaving Blakes room. He was planning on how to spend the profit he had just made. He was also contemplating love, loss and Blake's problems and didn't notice the white van pull up behind him. He heard what sounded like an engine and a door sliding open. As he turned around, it was too late. Everything went black. He felt multiple hands on him. He struggled but it was no use. Pin prick. Cold. Then, warm. So this is what happened to Milo, Betty and Mike and everyone else, they were abducted… …..That was Pookie's last thoughts.

CHAPTER 24

Blake was sitting in his room. He was hoping Pookie would come by because his stash was getting low. But His cash was about gone. He had some jewelry. No, not yet. He peeked out the window. Damn it! Where is Pookie? Blake looked around the unkempt motel room. The trash strewn everywhere was a pitiful sight.

Blake would clean the room occasionally. Not for cleaning's sake mind you, but to look for misplaced dope. They called this "Carpet Farming." Now he was on his hands and knees searching every square inch of the floor. He came across a few baggies of powder. They each held at least a gram.

"Jackpot!" He exclaimed. He poured all of them out on his mirror and licked the baggies clean. He lined up his discovered treasure and threw the baggies on the floor. Once temporarily satiated, he peeked out the window once more. What happened to Pookie? He opened the door and saw Janine going to her room. Sensing eyes on her back, she stopped and turned suddenly. She faced Blake and locked eyes with him. Her heart poured out for this man. She could tell he was once handsome. Now he was an empty shell of a man. He always looked so sad and broken. She had seen pictures of his family. He would show everyone he talked to. That was strange because the majority of people out here did not have pictures in their pockets, much less any family to speak of. Most had no one to care about or anyone to care about them. They were the forgotten. No one gave them a second thought. Most people had nothing to lose. But Blake had so much at one time and was throwing it all away. To her, he was a decent man. Never came on to her or acted inappropriately.

Every man that she encountered wanted sex from her and for a price she obliged. But not him. When Blake would talk about his wife she could feel the love he had for her. To be loved like that! But no one could ever love a whore. That used to fill her with such deep sadness. Now, resigned to live this life of sorrow, she didn't fool herself into ever thinking she could be loved. She slowly walked to Blake.

She imagined she was Blake's wife coming home from work. Watching the nightly news and discussing current events. Kissing him on the lips after cooking dinner. Making love to him all night long. Normal things that normal people did. Something she would never know. A home. A good man. Love. Children. Never. She sighed and stepped up to Blake and gave him a big hug. Not for him but for her. For her because she would never have a man like this. A man lost to drugs but with a big heart that was broken by his addiction and the loss of a woman. A good man that had seemed to give up on life. She wished she could take away his grief. But in that embrace she knew he yearned for another. At first Blake stiffened, but then relented. He welcomed the momentary closeness of another human being. He imagined his wife's hugs. She used to hold him and kiss him all the time. As his addiction grew, that all disappeared. Then reality hit him once again and he felt wrong for this hug and gently pushed her away. Janine sensing the awkwardness,

"I'm sorry Blake, you looked like you needed that and to tell the truth so did I." They walked into the room and shut the door.

"It's ok, no biggie."

She took in the scene. How disgusting. She didn't come from much and lived in a motel too, but her room was immaculate. This once "well to do" guy lived like a bum.

"Oh, here." Blake cleared a spot for her to sit down. Hesitantly, she looked at the chair before she sat down.

"Can you help me?" The desperation in his voice was obvious. The voice of someone craving. She had heard and seen it a million times. She drank and did drugs but didn't think it controlled her life as badly as Blake. Or maybe she just managed it better than him.

"What do you need, Blake?"

"Well, I can't find Pookie and he usually scores for me."

"I ain't seen him for a few hours, but I guess I can help you."

He handed her what little cash he had left.

"Whatever that will get me, I guess, and keep some for yourself if you want."

She looked at the few crumpled up twenty's he gave her and said, "Don't worry about it Blake. I did rather well tonight. No charge." Blake breathed a sigh of relief.

"Seriously Blake, you have done so much for me in the past so it's cool. She smiled and left.

A long agonizing sixty minutes later, Blake fell asleep. She had to knock on the door several times for him to answer. It was at least six days without sleep, and he felt the effects. He jumped up to answer, and the room spun around. He fell on the floor and hit his head on the door. He opened the door rubbing the fresh knot and she asked,

"You alright? Did you fall or something?"

"I'm ok, I'm ok. Did you find anything?" His eyes were bugged out and he was licking his lips, like a dog that had not eaten in several days waiting for scraps, and watching his master walk in with a hamburger. His savior had arrived. His "white knight." His only soul mate.

"Yes." She handed him the package and he opened it feverishly. She had also brought him some beer and while he crushed up the cocaine, he downed the sixteen ounce Budweiser in one breath. Gasping he said,

"Thank you, Janine."

It was snowing in Texas as he skied down the slopes once again. Blake handed her the mirror.

"No, I'm good." Her heart ached for this man. She didn't feel like getting high. She felt a little guilty for even scoring for him. But she didn't want to leave him alone. He was a good guy, and she could feel his pain. But Blake was a grown man and responsible for his own choices.

"I'm pretty much broke now, but would you want to hang out for a while? I'll understand if you don't." He sounded like a little kid wanting someone to play catch.

"Blake, it's not always about the money. You have done so much for me, shit, you've done so much for everybody!" She saw that sadness in his eyes.

"I like hanging out with you, Blake, so relax."

He held up the mirror once more to Janine with a sheepish grin. "Ok, twist my arm." She smiled and giggled a little and it caused him to chuckle as well.

She took a nice sized line as Blake's thoughts raced through his mind like a high-speed internet connection. He was out of money. He had some jewelry he could pawn. His wedding ring cost two thousand dollars. He had a Movado watch that cost well over a thousand. A couple of necklaces somewhere. What else? His father's Rolex was left to him when he died. Stop! How could he ever envision pawning that? That is so twisted he believed. But that was him in a nutshell. Twisted and destructive like a West Texas Tornado.

He remembered in the corner of his mind at some long-ago Narcotics Anonymous meeting about hitting bottom. He didn't think he was there yet. He knew he had not reached his bottom because he couldn't stop digging himself deeper into a hole. At this rate, he thought, he would wind up in China by the end of the year. His thoughts entered the silent room. After a few dead zone moments.

"When does all of this end, Janine?" The words confused her.

"All of what, Blake?"

"You know," he looked around the room, "living like this."

She didn't know how to answer that question. He continued.

"You don't want to live like this for the rest of your life, do you, Janine?" She looked up from the shiny white flakiness on the mirror, some caked on the end of her nose. She looked like a lifeguard with fresh sunscreen watching the beach for people drowning. A small trickle of blood left her nose and touched her lips.

"Oh shit!" Blake jumped up to get her some toilet paper.

"Here." He started to hand it to her but decided to wipe away the blood himself. She let him do so. Drugs and alcohol aside, she knew he was a caring man.

"Thank you." She said shyly.

"No problem." She remembered the question he had asked a few moments earlier.

"End huh? Well, I guess when I get tired of this shit. I mean, of course I don't want to live like this but what choice do I have?" Blake started to counter but she kept going.

"Who is going to help me get off the streets? Who is going to give me a job? No one would hire a druggy prostitute.

"I don't really see you like that, Janine." She started to shake her head.

"No, I'm serious! I don't."

I know Blake, I believe you say what you mean because you never try to get into my pants." For a moment they both sat there staring, then they burst into laughter easing the mood.

"Although you believe that, Blake, that is what I am. Could I be something else?"

"Maybe you could. You used to be someone else before all of this right?" She lifted up her arms and looked around the room as she said,

"This is all I've ever been. She looked down after saying that and a lone tear ran down her cheek. Blake gently lifted her chin.

"Hey, I'm sorry, I didn't mean to…

"No." she stopped him. Stood up abruptly and walked to the door and turned to face him.

"Don't feel sorry for me, Blake. I stopped feeling sorry for myself long ago." Blake was silent and didn't know what else to say.

"I figured out a long time ago that this was my life, and this is all it will ever be. I can't be something else. People can't change. You had a wonderful life, Blake. A house, a wife. I had nothing. I never had a chance.

"Janine, um, I'm sorry. I didn't mean to get you upset."

"I said don't feel sorry for me, Blake!" She grabbed the doorknob. Blake jumped off the bed and grabbed her hand.

"Please! Please don't leave. If you don't have to go to work right now? Please, stay if you can." His eyes were pleading with her as well. Damn! She wished she had a man like this in the past. Maybe her life could have turned out differently. She shook away the fantasy.

"Ok." She walked back to the chair by the bed.

"I promise no more talk of anything."

"It's not your fault I got upset, Blake. My past and present are what it is. I often fantasize about living a different life, but I honestly feel this is it for me. So back to your original question. When does it end? It ends if I ever choose it to end. Or when I die. Either way I don't have much of a choice."

Blake thought about his wife and all her talk about choices. He could recall her begging him to choose her or the drugs. But the "calling" was stronger than his love for her.

"Janine, I wonder if we really ever have a choice or is that something people just say to make themselves feel better."

"I don't know, Blake. I don't know." What was left of her heart was becoming like the dust on the mirror, only to be wiped away and forgotten.

CHAPTER 25

"Marie. Look at this." Marie looked at one of the monitors that Dr. Van Hook was pointing at. It was Milo. He had been increasing his daily dose of narcotics switching between meth and heroin. It was such a dangerous combination and the Doctor had great concern.

They watched him smoke meth, drink whiskey, then pop pills and shoot heroin to come down. He kept repeating this maddening routine every day since the black refrigerator appeared.

"What do you think, Marie?" It took her a moment to answer.

"I think everyone deserves a chance to change. I also know that some will get it and some won't." She believed this and thought Milo was in the group that might not make it, but she still hoped. Milo was a difficult case.

He was educated and from what she knew, those kinds of addicts were usually too smart to get this simple philosophy. Because "they knew it all" and wouldn't listen to the truth. Or they were too stubborn or self- righteous. Or did Milo give up and decide to party until the party was over? She thought he enjoyed it all. The way he would dance around, sing, shout and pass out. Then wake up and start where he left off. It would be amazing if not so insane! All of these patients knew death was around the corner, didn't they?

From their investigation, Milo married once but divorced. His wife left him because of his addiction. Usual story. Eventually he was fired from his job and then got two D.W.I.'s. His money was eaten up by legal fees and child support. He managed to fool his probation officers and stayed drunk and high. He ran out of money and charged up all his credit cards. Lost his place to live, then overdosed in an alleyway. He woke up in a hospital and when they released him, he panhandled, hustled, stole, and robbed people at random. He was picked up twice for suspected robbery, but no case would ever stick. He was "Chasing the demon." Now in his new Heaven, he was satiated beyond his wildest dreams. Marie thought it was a nightmare. How much longer could he last?

His room had become so filthy that Marie sent orderlies through the secret entrances to clean up. Milo probably didn't even notice. What he did notice was his refrigerators were replenished when he woke up. That's all that mattered to him. Although most of the food was spoiled, he used most of the alcohol and drugs as fast as he could. She felt a twinge of guilt that Milo could die at any moment in his present state. She expressed her concern to the doctor.

"Doctor, is there anything else we could do for him?"

"Marie I already…" Marie turned to face him and interrupted his reminder.

"Maybe we could take away his black refrigerator for a few days?"

The doctor thought for a moment. Milo was by far the worst case, other than the ones that died. He didn't want to lose another patient.

"Ok, Marie. That idea might just work."

Milo was nodding off. He was still conscious. Eyes mere slits but still able to see through bloodshot eyes. His scattered thoughts were all over the place like deadly smoke from an active volcano. Where were the shadow people? These shadow people would come into his room and clean up and refill his fridge. He didn't know if he was hallucinating or if it was real. He was at the point that reality was out of reach. How did they get in here? Maybe he could find a way out? When Milo woke the next time from his heroin fueled semi-coma, He decided to take a shower for the first time in a week.

"Damn! I stink!" He showered, stepped out and pissed in the sink. Why not? This was his castle, and he could do whatever the hell he wanted and it would all be cleaned up! He subtly looked around the room for a hidden door. A gap in the wall or something. Hadn't he looked many times before? He couldn't remember.

"What's he doing?" asked Marie. She and the doctor were watching Milo on the monitor intently.

"I think.." The doctor started but Marie jumped in.

"Is he looking for a way out?"

"Holy shit! Where is my black fridge?" Milo turned around in frantic circles until he was dizzy.

"Fuck! Fuck! Fuck!" The black fridge was most certainly gone. All evidence of his drug usage was too. Baggies, syringes, pipes, the burned-up spoon and even lighters.

"Wait," He started. "No alcohol?" He looked up at the ceiling at what he knew must be hidden cameras somewhere.

"What the fuck guys! Not fucking cool!" Horror struck him like lightning and the knot in his stomach felt like he swallowed a bowling ball that was rolling down a lane towards a cliff. He projectile vomited all over his room. He screamed once again to his captors.

"Why in the fuck would you take away my shit?" All the messages on the wall ceased to flash. His hands were shaking, and he needed a drink. He hurt deep down in his bones. He needed a hit or a shot or a line. Anything. Something. The wall over the bed lit up.

"Now is the Time." These words did not flash. They were frozen.

"Time for what assholes!" Marie continued to type the messages.

"Choose Life." Then. "Find Hope Again." "You are worth it." "Believe in Yourself."

"You can change!" "Choose Life not death!" He started shouting.

"Fuck you! Bring back my fridge!"

"How long should I keep putting out this new sequence of messages doctor?"

"For at least a few days, Marie. His withdrawals are going to be bad."

"Give him an extra dose of phenobarbital and Ativan in his food to help. But do not hide them this time. Place them in a baggie in the white fridge and he will think they are a little gift. Hopefully, his detox won't be that unpleasant."

"I hope so, doctor."

She found herself once again silently reciting The Serenity Prayer. Doctor Van Hook watched from his peripheral. She really cared about these patients and this program he thought. He knew the main reason she came on board was the assurance that her husband might be helped. At first, when she had made her offer, He almost declined because of the obvious conflict of interest that would pose. But she was determined and signed an agreement stating she would not get personally involved in any patient's therapy so as to not jeopardize the integrity of the program. From what he knew, her husband was pretty far gone like the others. The doctor remarked,

"The only hope for any of these patients is to find that psychic change that seems to be so elusive."

Milo continued to scream at his unseen torturers. Marie continued to type the messages and they flashed all over the walls like Time Square on New Years Eve.

CHAPTER 26

Pookie woke up. He rolled out of bed. Wait. Bed? White. All white. Everywhere was white.

"Aww man! I died and went to the white man's heaven?" Taking in the scenery, he blinked away the blur. The messages flashing around him hurt his eyes. As he walked around the room, he felt a little woozy from the kidnapper's injection.

"Life is about choices." "Choose life not Death." "God grant me serenity…"

"All right Grandma. Where you at?" Pookie remembered his grandmother. She was the most important person in his life. She had been a powerful woman when she was alive. She always had a positive message for Pookie. God was at her center, and she would recite bible verses verbatim. She also loved Pookie unconditionally like only a grandmother could. Her name was Edith and she would tell him everyday to "Make the right Choices." She would say he could accomplish whatever he wanted in life with faith in God and choosing the right path. Sometimes all that bible junk got on his nerves, but he loved his grandmother. He knew she had just wanted him to succeed. But peer pressure and the street life called to him. Plus, he was a natural born hustler, so he thrived.

Eventually, the drink became his main focus, but he still maintained to eke out a meagre existence. He wondered where all the other missing people were. He stopped short in his exploration of the room at the white refrigerator. Upon opening the door, he gasped. Wow! So much food! He helped himself to some cold cuts. He made a sandwich and added pickles, mustard, tomatoes, and lettuce. It tasted so good! He washed it down with a large glass of milk. Then he found some ice cream. He hadn't eaten rocky road in years.

"I could get used to this." But the hustler in him knew there was always a catch to something this great. This hospital or prison or whatever this was, was too perfect.

"What's the catch?" He walked around the room talking to the walls knowing he was being watched.

"What do y'all want?"

"Why did y'all bring me here?" Marie and the doctor and another technician were in the monitor room watching closely as Pookie questioned the unseen.

"Who the hell are yall and why am I here?" he asked. He was getting louder and more insistent on an answer. His frustration was noticeable to those watching but they would remain silent. Pookie was generally friendly but from the streets and didn't take any shit. He was tough. He had to be to survive.

"What's with all these messages? Are y'all trying to brainwash me? Is this an experiment?" He thought about that for a second. He felt like a rat in a cage.

"Wait! That's it! Y'all experimenting on me!" He followed up this logic with,

"Y'all kidnappin' people, fattening them up, then feeding them with all this bullshit on the walls to see what they do?" He felt proud that he had probably figured out his predicament.

"This is bullshit though, I ain't no damn rat. Let me know when yall wanna talk." All the other rooms had TV's and his was no exception. But the others never even turned theirs on. Yet, Pookie, always more curious than most, did so. Trump was on TV.

Trump was an enigma to him. On the one hand he liked the fact that Trump talked shit and wasn't a real politician. But he was a rich white dude and didn't feel like he did anything for him. Hell, He felt all the black politicians were just like all the rich white ones. They talked a good game, but they were just hustlers like all politicians and ain't done nothing for him or his peeps. They were steady getting richer, while everyone else got poorer.

"All yall full of shit!" He yelled at the TV then shut it off. He took in all the messages again flashing on the wall. Were the people running this place evil or good? Were they trying to hurt him or help him in this experiment? After all, they did kidnap him. He was talking to himself again,

"At least they ain't hurt me." Then he felt it. He rarely felt it because he stayed, for the most part, under the influence of alcohol every single day. The shakes. Alcohol withdrawal. The medicine the doctor laced the food with took longer to work on certain people and sometimes had less of an effect. For the first time in years, Pookie was scared. His hands slightly quivered. In the past, whenever the few times this happened, it was easily remedied by getting another drink.

The only time in the past several months that he hadn't drank was when he slept. A rise and shine drink would keep the shakes away. A drink always made everything ok. That is what he needed right now. It would calm his nerves and give him courage for the day. It is what he needed to hustle. He didn't see any foreseeable hustling anytime soon, but he knew he had to get a drink. Going through complete withdrawals was something he had never experienced. Even when he went to jail, he learned to make "Hooch."

He stayed drunk but he was a functional alcoholic he reasoned. He sat on the bed and popped a coke. He took a big swig, then laid back and closed his eyes. As he opened them for a second, he noticed messages on the ceiling as well!

"Man, yall playing this game tough! He shouted. "This some hoe ass shit!"

He closed his eyes and fell asleep. He dreamed of his grandmother scolding him for hanging out with "those hoodlums" again. "But they ma friends, "Gigi." That was her nickname and she would say, "They ain't your friends. They is trouble and they doing the devils work and if you don't make the right choices the devil will come for you."

"But Gigi I ain't doing nothing wrong."

"Life is about choices, young man! The devil is always waiting for you to slip up!"

His dream changed locations and now he was in the present lying in Dr. Van Hook's facility. He guessed he finally slipped up. He murmured in his sleep, "You were right Gigi, the devil caught me."

The dream awakened Pookie and he thought he heard someone screaming. He called out.

"Who's there?"

Betty heard all the yelling and hoped Milo was okay. She also heard someone that sounded like Pookie?

"Pookie! Hey Pookie! Is that you?" Pookie heard someone shouting from behind one of the walls.

"Who Dat?"

"Hey Pookie! It's Betty!"

"Hey girl! How you doin'?"

"Well, I'm fine considering being locked down in this place."

"Have you met the people that run this place girl?"

"No, not at all."

"Well, the food is sure good though!"

"You are right about that, Pookie."

"Don't touch the black fridge, Pookie!! Bam joined in the reunion.

"Now who's that. Sounds familiar."

"It's Bam, fool! Don't touch the black fridge brother!"

"Bam! I thought you were dead or in jail, brother! And what the hell is a black fridge?"

"I ain't dead, but the black fridge will kill you!"

"Yea, Pookie, The black refrigerator will come soon and will be full of alcohol and drugs and everything you can think of!" Betty's words left Pookie troubled but curious.

"Yea, Pookie and it's fucking awesome!"

"Now who the hell is that?"

"Only the man, the legend, the one and only!" Sarcasm tinged Milo's voice.

"That has to be that maniac, Milo!"

"You know it bro!" Milo's hysterical laughter filled the hallways. Milo was going through withdrawals and the med laced food seemed to have no effect on him.

Pookie's tone got more serious.

"Guys, are you telling me no one knows what the hell is going on here?" Bam spoke next.

"Pookie, listen, this hospital, facility or whatever you want to call it, is some kind of experiment. Like I have been trying to tell you, do not touch the black refrigerator." Betty joined in,

"Yes Pookie, don't touch it!"

"Yea, yea, yea I hear you. Don't touch the black fridge." Milo asked sheepishly,

"Hey, um, can anyone get me anything? These people took my black fridge and I'm hurting really bad." Bam offered, "That's great Milo! You can now make a choice to free yourself from the drugs!"

"Fuck that, Bam! Anything, something, please!" They could hear the desperation in Milo's voice. Pookie wanted to know about the fridge.

"Ok guys what the hell is up with Milo and this fridge y'all keep talking about?" Bam started,

"Pookie…" Betty interrupted,

"It's bad, Pookie! After a few days, the black fridge appears, and it is filled with what at first seems like an answered prayer." Bam jumped back in.

"Alcohol and every single drug you can imagine." Pookie's interest was piqued at the word alcohol.

"Huh? Why in the hell would anyone in a hospital give people all that shit? Yall fuckin' with me, right?" It made no sense to him but the thought of getting a drink sounded great.

"Hey guys? Seriously. Can yall get me a hit a line or anything?" Milo was relentless in his search to satisfy his cravings.

"They really took my shit! My fridge is gone!" Milo was screaming again.

"I'm hurting bad!" Milo opened the white fridge to get a coke and noticed a medicine bottle. He opened it up and saw two pills inside. He thought, what the hell, and popped open the coke and swallowed them immediately. Bam now spoke.

"Look Pookie, you know me. I tell like it is right?"

"Yea Bam, you were always straight up with me bro." So, Bam continued.

"When I tell you to not fall for the black fridge's offerings, don't do it! It's like some kind of test. All the messages around you, see them?"

"How can I not see them fool! They won't stop flashing! How can yall get any sleep around here?"

"Whoever these people are running this place are trying to teach us something. Obviously to change our lives or we gonna die. It's like the signs say; choose life or choose death. It's our choice Pookie." Pookie jumped in.

"So let me get this straight, they are gonna give drugs and drink to see what I will do with it?"

"Yes! Yes! Yes!" Betty sounded excited to share her newfound knowledge.

"Before I came here Pookie, where was I going? Nowhere! My life was horrible! This place has given me a second chance!"

"Fuck that bullshit you sayin' Betty! I need a fix!" Milo was feeling the effects of the phenobarbital and the Ativan slightly and was woozy. He was fighting the desire to sleep with the desire to get high.

"Damn this place! Give me back my fridge!"

"Milo shut the hell up!" Bam was getting mad at Milo's crazed rantings.

"We trying to figure this shit out! Pookie, this is life or death like the walls keep telling you! We have a choice!"

"Yea, my grandma used to always say that shit."

"My mom too, Pookie!"

"But I don't get it. Why would people want to do some shit like this? This shit aint legal! Yall were snatched by that van too, right? Head covered with a hood and stuck in the neck with some shot knockin' our ass out! That's kidnappin'! That's some federal shit, man! Is it the government?"

"I don't know exactly." Every time Bam thought he had this thing figured out, a question would come up that cast him back into doubt. Betty offered her thoughts.

"The government don't give a damn about nobody!" Pookie didn't know what to believe, but whatever this was he knew no one cared about him.

Milo was nodding off thinking to himself. Whatever those pills were, they had taken some of the edge off and he felt a little better. He succumbed to sleep. Pookie was shaking more noticeably now. He clenched his hands into fists. Released and clenched. He shook his hands vigorously trying to make them stop. The knot in his stomach was painful. His vision was blurred and his headache was unbearable. He had already thrown up a few times so he thought another sandwich might help.

"Say y'all, you say there will be alcohol in that fridge? What kind?"

"All kinds!" Bam shouted.

"Don't think about it, Pookie!" Pleaded Betty. "This is your chance to come clean! Me and Bam barely made it!"

"Yea Pookie, I was a goner. Betty too. My life was over I thought. I had given up and I had no hope. I wanted to die but I was too much of a coward to just end it, so I drowned myself in anything I could get my hands on."

"Yea, I know Bam, you were always wasted."

"Right! But then I came here, and something happened. I'm telling you brother something happened!"

"Oh yea? What the hell happened to you, Bam? You find Jesus or some shit?" Pookie laughed at Bam's expense. But Bam ignored the jibe and kept going.

"I changed, Pookie! I don't want to live like that anymore. I changed my mind. I don't want to be wasted. I don't mess with that black fridge, I'm not even tempted!" Betty spoke again,

"Me too, Pookie. I want to do something else with my life! I don't know if I can be anything other than what I've been but now that I'm clean, I can sure try!"

"Listen, Pookie, this place has helped Betty and me.

"This place opened our eyes Pookie, For the first time in many years, we have hope once again!" Pookie was understandably doubtful.

"Man, That's some twilight zone type shit y'all! All I know is I can't find a way out and I need a drink God damn it!"

"Pay attention to the signs, Pookie!"

"Look yall, Like Milo, I'm hurtin' really bad!" Pookie now called for Milo.

"Hey, Milo! Yo, Milo my man!" But Milo was finally passed out. The techs stealthily entered his room, cleaned up and placed more meds in his white fridge.

"What the hell happened to Milo y'all?"

"I don't know," said Bam. Betty offered,

"He comes in and out like this all day and night."

"I need a drink yall! I aint like yall dope fiends! I just drink! That ain't nothing like yall!" Bam laughed,

"Pookie really? You are just like us brother! You ain't got no home. Hell, you sleep at the bus stop sometimes!" Betty tried to reason with him.

"Yea, Pookie. Sometimes you would get a room or shower at the Star of Hope downtown, but you were out on those streets every day with us!"

"Maybe you weren't as bad Pookie but you were just as messed up!"

"No way yall! I just drink!" Like a movie playing in reverse, some of the film was unfocused and full of static. But in Pookie's mind, most of it was walking the streets hustling. His world, His element. Then all of a sudden, the drama started to appear.

He remembered being shot in the leg. He was shot in the arm. Always drunk and occasionally arguing with some fool over a woman. Once he was caught with someone else's lady and was shot at while running away. Bleeding out and begging for help, he had seen people dying in alleyways.

He witnessed heart attacks and seizures from drug overdose. And through his film, He was always drunk. But at least he wasn't a junkie. He wasn't as bad as them, right? He tried to convince himself of this but the more he reviewed his life the more he doubted that premise. He spoke up.

"Man, I played myself. My life is fucked up!"

The doctor and Marie had been listening as usual and were hopeful that the dialogue between them would help persuade Pookie to change. Milo was still passed out.

"What do you think, doctor?"

"Marie, I have mixed feelings. Bam and Betty seem to be on the right path to recovery but this Pookie? What kind of name is that anyway?"

"I believe that is a street name sir."

"Ok, well, this Pookie is in the first stage of withdrawals and the detox meds aren't working as well as I thought.

The next few days will be hell for him and then you know the black refrigerator will arrive."

"I know doctor, I don't think he will make it. But I didn't think Bam would either."

"Right Marie, I think he will drink himself sick. In all my research, alcoholics find it harder to quit than addicts. But only time will tell."

"A couple of more patients than Phase two, right?"

"Yes, Marie. Be patient. We are almost there. I'm so glad you are on board. The other techs and orderlies are just here for a paycheck. But I see your passion for these people, and I know you have a stake in this. I appreciate your dedication and you make my plans much easier."

"Thank you doctor and you're right, I am dedicated to this program of yours. I would do anything to one day have my family back to normal." And she knew being here, helping these people, was the way to make that happen.

CHAPTER 27

Janine had declined another line several hours ago and opted instead to crash on the bed in Blake's motel room. Blake didn't mind, he liked the company. He watched her sleeping peacefully. She was an attractive woman he thought but he loved his wife. X wife. He often wondered how people got to the point of being homeless, desperate and strung out. He was halfway there. His life was like snow on a mountain, creating an avalanche and demolishing everything in its path. He shook the morose images away so he wouldn't lose his buzz. Janine stirred and looked at Blake.

"Are you ok?" Genuine worry in her voice.

"Huh? Um, yea." Blake looked back down at the mirror in his hand. There was blood on it threatening to mix with the cocaine. He jumped up to retrieve a towel or anything to wipe it up and to stop the flow from his nose. Once he cleaned up the mess, he snorted some more and took a drink out of a warm can of beer.

"Are you hungry or thirsty?" Blake asked as he went to the mini fridge.

"I guess I could eat something." Blake got a cold beer and placed a pop tart in the microwave for Janine.

"You don't have to heat it up, I'll take it like that if you don't mind." He handed the cold processed artificial breakfast pastry to her.

"Somewhere back in my childhood I remember eating these. I vaguely remember being happy then. Actually, it's the only time I can remember feeling that way before…" Her voice trailed off.

"I'm sorry, Janine." She started to protest. He knew she didn't like people feeling sorry for her, but he continued.

"I mean, I wish you had not gone through any of those terrible things when you were a kid. No child should have to. My kids did not go through anything bad because," he held his hands up and looked around, I didn't start any of this until after they left for college." She looked away as if lost in thought.

"I know It's affecting them now but… …" This time he trailed off thinking he said enough. She felt his unease and changed the subject.

"This pop tart is great!" She remarked. He took another swig of beer before he said,

"I wish I could eat. I'm wasting away to nothing. What do you think happened to Pookie?"

"Word on the street is he was snatched up."

"What do you mean? By the police?" That statement got Blake worried.

"No, even worse. Aliens!" Blake couldn't tell if she was joking or not, so he waited for a moment. Janine burst into laughter.

"Got you! You should have seen the look on your face!" He relaxed and managed to smile weakly.

"Seriously though, someone told me they saw a creepy white van drive around. Maybe it's the government."

"I don't think so, Janine. Doesn't the government wear all black and drive black cars?"

She thought about that as Blake inhaled another line. One nostril had a bloody piece of toilet paper hanging out. What an awful sight. She was feeling sorry for him again.

"I don't know. Maybe the undercovers are cleaning up the area for us undesirables."

"Yea, I saw on the news when a big event comes to town, they round up all the homeless, give them a little money then drop them off several miles away, so bigwigs and tourists don't see."

"Out of sight out of mind?" Blake didn't reply.

"That's just awful." Blake was too busy chopping up the remainder of his stash.

She continued the flow of the conversation.

"Well, all I do know is that Pookie, Mike and my good friend Betty are gone somewhere, and no one knows where!"

"Right. One after another. They are just gone. Maybe jail?"

"But what they usually get into trouble for can't get them more than a few days locked up though." Blake remembered a news segment talking about no bonds for the poor because bonds were racist and they were letting everyone out quickly and sometimes the same day after committing a crime.

"I don't think so because some people accused of murder were released the same day for little or no bond!"

"Then where the hell are they?"

"I don't know Janine. I hope they are ok." He thought about these people. These rejects, these forgotten ones. They were his family now. Family? He missed his real family. He thought about his kids. Son in the Marines. Daughter in the Air Force. Another daughter in the Army. Good kids despite their loser father. Another child was about to have a kid of their own. He would be a grandfather soon! Wait. His son had a daughter a while back. He was losing track of time and important memories. He had a vague recollection of holding a grandbaby thinking he might drop her. That day, instead of enjoying time with his grandchild, he excused himself, only to lock himself in a bathroom and get high. The best parts of his life were getting lost in the frosty blizzard of his addiction. His children probably knew the extent of his addiction by now. Did they hate their father for all the bullshit excuses he gave them for not showing up for Thanksgiving dinner? Christmas? He didn't even send any cards. A low groan came from deep inside Blake and he grabbed his aching skull and shook it until his mind went blank. Janine snapped her head up at the sound.

"Blake? Are you…" She saw the mirror teetering on his knees and jumped up with catlike reflexes and saved the coke from disappearing from within the fabric of the carpet. Blake, startled out of his mental torment by the movement and saw the quick save.

"Thank you!"

"What's the matter, Blake?"

"Everything! Everything! My life is pointless! I am nothing!"

"Don't say that, Blake!"

"It's true! I've lost everything! My family, wife, children. Everything!" Janine remembered an uncle that talked like that, and he killed himself. She was too young to comprehend the concept of depression and suicide back then but now she recognized the signs in Blake.

"Please don't think like that Blake!" She was pleading with him.

"As long as you have breath in your lungs there is still hope." She thought about some priest that had told her this long ago.

"Don't give up, Blake. Whatever you do, don't give up." Blake lowered his head and cried. Eyes practically too dry for tears from dehydration, only a few fell in his lap. He rocked back and forth on the bed like a child. It looked so pitiful, but Janine sat next to him and gently lowered his head into her lap. She instinctively stroked his hair like only a mother could do and cried with him. In his mind he had already given up. He imagined his wife in all black at his funeral. His children dressed up as well. A preacher reciting bible verses. Why did they do that for the dead? His cries subsided and Janine held him and softly spoke.

"Don't give up Blake. Please don't give up. Don't give up."

CHAPTER 28

"45, 46, 47, 48, 49, 50!" Sweat rolled down Bam's chest. He jumped up from the floor after completing fifty push-ups. He felt surprisingly great considering all that he had been through. Only the huge scar kept him from looking like a Greek statue. It was like a testament to his escaping out of Hades' grasp and given another chance by Zeus himself.

"Hey Betty!" Bam continued to talk to Betty many times throughout the day as a way to ensure her staying sober.

"Yes, Bam? What you up to?"

"Just working out!" Thinking about fighting again!"

"Oh, Bam! I wouldn't want to see you get hurt!" Bam heard the authenticity in her voice.

"Don't worry, Betty. It couldn't be any worse than what I've already been through. Hell, I've died and come back. Fighting in a cage ain't shit!"

"Maybe so, Bam." Pookie stirred. Waking up, he was still a little shaky from withdrawals. He got a soda and some chips and made a sandwich.

Mike had been in the facility eating and sleeping. His mind was so frazzled between the kidnapper's cocktail and withdrawals that he was oblivious to the messages on the walls and the people around him. Until now.

"What the fuck? Bam?"

"Yea? Who is calling my name?"

"It's Mike! I thought that was you! Is that Betty too?"

"Mike! Wow! I'm glad you are, well not glad you are here but it could be worse!"

"What the fuck is this place?"

"A second chance, Mike!" Betty heard the conversation and joined in.

"Hey, Mike! Its Betty!"

"Hey, betty! Oh my God! I've been looking for you!"

"Yea, I've been here getting sober!"

"Sober?" He had heard that word before, but it was like Chinese arithmetic to him.

Pookie decided to greet the new arrival.

"Say fool, it's Pookie!"

"Pookie? What the hell is going on?"

"Man, we locked up bro but at least the food is good!"

"I guess so. But I could sure use a drink or something."

"Me too fool!" Bam felt for Mike in this regard. Withdrawals were awful.

"Listen, Mike. Listen carefully. In a few days, a black refrigerator will appear and what's inside will seem like the answer to everything in this world."

"Huh? What are you talking about?"

"Whoever is running this place is providing alcohol and drugs for us but it's a trick or a test."

"Alcohol and drugs? Why would a hospital do that?" This time Betty answered.

"Because they want to see if we can change. Haven't you seen the signs on the walls flashing all around you, Mike?" At this, Mike looked around. For the first time he saw the messages on the walls.

"What the Fuck?" He got dizzy as he spun around to read. He fell hard but didn't take his eyes off the wall. He read and read. But instead of understanding what the messages were trying to convey he thought of getting high and drinking to alleviate the withdrawals. That is all he cared about.

"Hey guys?" Mike sounded like a scared child. Bam answered first.

"Yea, Mike? What's up?"

"I'm doing bad man! I need a drink! My head is spinning! These withdrawals are killing me!"

"I feel ya, bro."

"Hang in there, Mike." Betty tried to encourage him.

"You gotta stay strong, Mike! Keep reading those words all around you! That's what I did!" She thought as long as he did as she had done, he would be okay, but she wasn't aware of the depth of the demon's pull on Mike.

"I don't know if I can make it guys." Bam turned on his best charm. Mike was his friend, and he wouldn't give up. He couldn't keep what was given to him without imparting it to someone else. The joy he felt wouldn't allow it.

"Mike, all these writings on the wall are there for a reason. I believe these people are trying to rewire our brains. Like behavioral modification or some shit! They are creating a comfortable environment with a strong message then giving us a challenge. A life and death challenge. We have a choice, Mike. To live like we always have and die a lot sooner or choose a life of hope and change!" Betty used Bam's momentary pause to speak.

"Yea Mike, it's not so much the black fridge that will be killing you, but your choices."

"What if I can't resist guys? I am hurting bad!"

"We are too!" Betty shivered at thoughts of the last few days.

"I was hurting bad, but Bam saved me!"

"No Betty, it wasn't me. It was your choices!"

"No, Bam! You encouraged me and I said some prayers I remembered as a kid and the walls spoke to me in a way."

"My mom used to say all this shit on the walls when I was kid. I gave in at first Mike, but my mother came to me in this very room and in that moment, everything made sense!" Bam was talking and getting more excited by the second.

"I know the messages might get on your nerves for a few days but if you don't pay attention then the black fridge wins!" Betty spoke again.

"Mike, listen! Most people will claim they grew up in a horrible environment, either poor, with no education or with abuse and didn't have a chance. But most people had someone, somewhere at one time, say things like this. Telling them about choices. People like us just ignore them and think we know it all."

"Yea Mike, open your mind and really read the words all around you. Mike slowly turned and looked around his room.

"Life is about choices"

"Choose life not death."

"You are worth it."

"Forgive others."

"Forgive yourself."

"Forgiveness is the key."

"Resentment is the #1 Offender!"

Then above his bed, something called The Serenity Prayer.

He remembered that from an Alcoholics Anonymous meeting at the Salvation Army.

"You know guys, all this sounds great, and I even remember some of this shit in my screwed-up head, but I can't get past the part of my brain that says I need a fucking drink and I need it now! That is what I want!"

"Oh, Mike!" Betty pleaded with him. "You can't!" Bam yelled,

"There are so many drugs in that fridge and an endless supply of alcohol!"

"You could die, Mike! We came close in the streets but in here I have no doubt that if I had not stopped, I would be dead!"

"I guess so." Mike sounded defeated. "But this place feels so safe." Betty chose her next few words carefully.

"This place can be your savior or your judge and jury. When that black refrigerator comes and it will come, you'll have a choice. To not use or to give up and face your death head on. I mean, you may not die right away but think about this. In the street, no one has all the alcohol and drugs they could ever want, right? But they chase that desire every day. Doing whatever they gotta do to get the next drink or fix. Because of the limits of money, obviously, they, I mean we, get periodic breaks and get to sleep and rest until the next insane journey. Here, in this place, you'll no longer have the opportunity to chase that elusive, perfect feeling because you will have it! You will be complete. All you could ever dream of is within that fridge, Mike."

As Mike imagined an endless supply of alcohol and drugs, panic attacked his mind like protestors in Antifa rally. He felt excited and afraid at the same time. The anticipation was overwhelming. He knew what they were saying was true. He knew he must not give in but this calling, this urge, took over any sense of what was right and sane in his mind. As far as he was concerned there wouldn't be a battle, he had already lost.

"I don't think I am strong enough."

"You're not!" Bam shouted. "We are here to help you through it all!"

"Yea! And call to whatever and whoever you think will listen! God, Buddha, um, uh, Mohammed? No Allah! Yea that's it! Whoever you choose to call when you need help! And if they don't answer, we will!"

"Whatever you do Mike, you have to gain strength from somewhere because by ourselves none of us are strong enough!" Bam had known Mike for a long time and was not sure he could reach him but wouldn't give up. Betty was in her pink cloud of new sobriety as well, but she thought everyone could be saved, so she continued with her dialogue.

"Mike, out there we were slowly killing ourselves. Slowly but surely. There was no happy conclusion for us. How many people have we seen overdose or shot and killed?"

"Or stabbed?" Bam offered.

"Yea stabbed." Mike couldn't relate to this logic at all.

"Well, I ain't never had anything crazy like that happen to me! I aint like yall!" Mike pled his case but there was no confidence in his voice, so Betty kept going.

"Mike, quit looking at all the differences because everyone is different. Instead look at all the similarities. We all suffer from this deadly problem! It's almost impossible for people like us to stop using! We can't stop killing ourselves!" Betty was so spirited.

"But ultimately, it's up to you to make a choice to stop." Betty finished for the moment to let her words sink in. Up to me Mike thought? Me? I can't do this. All the drugs I want? How could anyone not use in that situation? Mike felt he was standing on a bridge. One direction was heaven and the other was hell. He saw people running, jumping and celebrating an eternity of joy. In the other direction he could see the flames, people on fire, smell the burning flesh and hear the screams of the tormented. And even with all that, in his mind's eye, he was walking away from Heaven towards the eternal furnace. For his Paradise was the never ending high and the torture it brought. Fire and pain did nothing to dissuade him from acquiring that next buzz.

CHAPTER 29

Milo had just woken up and was lying in bed. Every time he stood up, he would puke, so he just rested. He was in full withdrawal mode again. His bones ached from a lack of heroin. The meds they slipped into his fridge had little to no effect. His hands shook and he felt he was losing what little mind he had left. He jumped up to check the white fridge. There were 2 pills. He put them in his mouth and lay back down. He had a plan. He knew there was a way out of this room. There had to be. Obviously, there was a way in, right? Someone was getting in here. Someone was cleaning his room. Someone was getting out.

"I'm losing my fucking mind!" He grabbed the bed sheet and pulled it over his head.

He took the two pills out of his mouth and slid them in his pocket. As bad as he was hurting, he would endure the pain at the prospect of escape. His plan was to feign being asleep, then watch where these people enter his room. He had to get the hell out of there and find some drugs! That is all he cared about! Getting to one of his friend's rooms was the main goal. Finding an exit out of the facility would come later. Come on you bastards, he told himself, hurry up. His mind was racing and going over different scenarios. What happens when he finds the secret entrance? Would they immediately notice? Was he in any condition to fight if necessary? He could not think about that. He must take it one step at a time. He must stay awake and wait. When this was all over, he would make the people responsible pay and pay dearly. He could see the light flashing from beneath the sheet from all the messages. Make a change. Choose life not drugs. How insane that they brainwash you with this crap then give you all the drugs you want! He considered that these people were a special kind of wicked. Sitting back and watching the torture of their patients. He felt like a rat in a maze that was rewarded for finding the cheese, then had the cheese ripped from its jaws only to be made to starve. He was getting sleepy, so he recited nursery rhymes.

Hickory dickory dock

The mouse ran up the clock.

Over and over again with the nursery rhymes.

He must stay awake. He rubbed his legs with shaky hands slowly under the sheet. He was no longer nauseous. But the anticipation had him wanting to jump up and scream for his captors, yet he waited.

CHAPTER 30

Marie was typing notes as Dr. Van Hook observed Milo. He knew he was suffering but reasoned it was for his own good. He wanted to give him every opportunity to choose the right pathway to one day be successful. He wondered if Milo would be another failure in this program. He had no doubt that his program was flawless. The flaw was in the patients' damaged minds.

This was the perfect formula for someone to win the battle of addiction. Or to lose. How many times have these people or anyone else for that matter been offered help for their addictions? There were thousands of programs all around the world created to help everyone in this condition.

People handed out clothing and food. The sick and homeless had a place to go if they wanted to get clean. To find themselves again. But so many took a blanket, a small sack of food, toiletries, said thank you, then continued their journey to nothingness. Sad thing was that no matter how many times people were offered hope they chose the path of misery. It was their choice. That was the one constant in life. Wasn't his son offered ample opportunity to change? He often thought of his son.

That was the main driving force behind all of his work. His son was brilliant. A straight A student and a great athlete. But the occasional partying, that progressed to full blown addiction, was greater. Multiple rehabs. Antidepressant cocktails. The doctor grew to despise the pharmaceutical companies and the Psychiatry field of medicine. The answer by most doctors was a variety of mental diagnoses then medicate. Bipolar? Here's some drugs. Anxieties? P.T.S.D.? Drugs. ADHD? How about some amphetamines! Okay Mr. and Mrs. such and such, we found this seizure medication also works, theoretically, with the condition your child is suffering from. It was like they were experimenting with people. Patients were no better than lab rats.

What was happening is that they were getting people more dependent on drugs. Often the condition worsened. It was insanity to Van Hook. But these were his esteemed peers. He would show them all.

Before he developed this facility, he shared the idea of helping patients get clean with cognitive behavioral therapy and access to real street drugs. He of course left out the whole kidnapping part. But no one seemed to think it was an innovative idea as long as there were breakthrough drugs to try! Not to mention, Pharmaceuticals was a multi-billion dollar a year industry. They thought his ideas were crazy. Called him a quack! So, he retired and created this program.

He found this facility and found some employees that he could manipulate into helping him. He was making up for not being able to save his son and he would make it work at all costs. Even if it meant some would die. He would prove people could beat addiction and choose life over death and do it all without pharmaceuticals! No matter what the consequences of keeping these people captive, he believed his intentions were pure. Only time would tell if the events of the good doctor were noble.

CHAPTER 31

Doctor Van Hook knew it had been several hours since Milo had taken his pills. It was time to send in the orderlies, clean up his room and replenish the white refrigerator. Only a few days of detox and the Doctor figured Milo would be good.

Milo was still fighting sleep and the pain in his body. God, he wanted to scream! He heard a movement. He froze. He realized he was holding his breath and almost passed out from the lack of oxygen. Breathe damn it, he told himself. More movement. He gently pulled the sheet below his nose. He kept his eyes closed. After a few seconds, that seemed like an eternity, he opened his eyes to mere slits and surveyed his room. The refrigerator was moving. Was he hallucinating? Of course! An entrance behind the fridge! He had been too high to figure it out.

The shadowy forms entered the room. He pulled the sheet back over his head and closed his eyes and no longer fought sleep. He was screaming inside at the opportunity to sneak out and find a fix! He didn't think of any possible scenarios after crawling through that exit. Just leaving this room and finding drugs! "Almost there," he whispered. He finally succumbed to sleep.

CHAPTER 32

Blake had fallen asleep with his head in Janine's lap. He had not had any substantial sleep for several days. When he woke up, he sat upright then the dizziness made him lie back down. He stared at the ceiling. He remembered he was out of money and despair hit him like a freight train striking a stalled vehicle on the tracks. Not being able to buy any more drugs didn't bother him as much as the prospect of being homeless. He was paid up on his motel room for a couple of more days. He still had things to pawn. That is the answer. What a low point in his life. Is this what hitting bottom felt like? He knew that you couldn't hit bottom if you didn't stop digging. It probably didn't matter because his hole was so deep, he might not be able to climb out.

"What a loser!" He said aloud. He sat up again and looked around his room. Janine had left. What a sweet girl. She had cleaned up his room. Damn he was starving! He ate whatever he could find, which was one half a sandwich that he washed down with his last cold beer. There were some stale chips, and he ate those begrudgingly. He remembered he had some coke left, didn't he?

Where did Janine put it? He frantically searched the room for the stash. He opened the bathroom sink cabinet and there it was. It was still on the mirror and was enough for a few lines. He mentally made a checklist of his jewelry. The last of his belongings besides the Corvette.

He had not driven his Vette in months and bird shit was caked all over it. It was ironic that this car was once his prized possession. Now it looked abandoned. He did another line and decided to take a shower. As he bathed, he thought about his father's watch. He felt awful that he was about to pawn it along with his wedding ring. He had a couple of necklaces tucked away under the bed too. The watch was the only thing left to remind Blake of his father. It wasn't worth much more than the sentimental value it held but it was a way to keep getting high.

What a scumbag I am, he thought. Fresh out of the shower but still guilt ridden, he snorted what was left of the coke. Looking in the mirror,

"Damn! I need a haircut and a shave!" He found a hat and covered the mop of hair that was still wet. The hat said Trump 2020. He laughed thinking about his dad's passion for politics. His father was educated and extremely articulate and would tell anyone that would listen about his opinion. He ran for office a few times for Harris County Sheriff. He was a retired police officer and with little money and little backing he almost won. In the city of Houston with several million people, he came within 60,000 votes. So, he ran again.

The next time he had several endorsements including the African American policeman's Association, the Mexican Americans Policeman's Association and every city council member. Except one. At one time this man was his father's friend and they had worked together in the past. At the last minute, this man put his name on the ballot.

Almost immediately every single endorsement jumped ship and sided with this new candidate. His father claimed it was racism because he was white, and the new guy was Hispanic, but no one would listen to that line of reasoning. That Hispanic council member won by a landslide and his father gave up running after that.

He decided to back a longtime friend of his for a Constables race. He was a great nephew of a famous Civil Rights champion. He thought for sure this guy would win in an "inner city and urban" election. But again, the man with all the money and all the friends wins. He thought of all the people he knew that talked about chasing dreams, his father was the only one he knew that did. Even though he lost those races more than once, he always told Blake to strive to be the best and never give up. Compared to his dad he felt like a failure.

After that last loss, his father's life was cut short by a doctor's horrible decision to add an extra blood thinner to an otherwise routine hospital visit. He had a stroke and never recovered.

Blake and his family filed malpractice against the doctor and the hospital but because of his already declining health and age, they sided with the doctor. Just another old, sick man at the mercy of a mighty, powerful hospital and the constant drug prescribing doctors.

Blake hadn't gone through that much trauma in his life up to that point. Parents divorced at the age of 8 but he was allowed to go live with his father.

When Blake had slightly experimented with drugs at a youthful age, it was father that helped him get clean before things got out of hand. He was instrumental in Blake's success in business. Ever the mentor and confidant.

He was Blake's best man at his wedding and the best grandfather anyone had ever known. He was Blake's hero. The devastation of his death crushed his spirit. On the day of the funeral Blake got into a horrific wreck. It was when Blake settled the lawsuit for the accident that he dived headfirst into relapse and gave up all hope.

Blake tossed away the memory as he walked out of the motel room. What day was it? What time was it? Hiding in a motel room every day, time does not really exist. Days and nights blend. Life is a hazy blur of forgotten dates and white lines.

Ironically, only the white lines were the organized part of his life now. He stared at his corvette. Under different conditions this car was worth at least $50,000 but he had neglected it. The hood was faded and needed a wash. He shrugged it off and cracked open the door. The smell was stale and of mildew. A spilled plastic cup of cola lay on the floorboard. Would it even start? Luckily, it started right away.

As he drove off, he saw Janine talking to someone in a new Cadillac. Leaning in, smiling and tossing her hair, negotiating a deal. She didn't deserve this life, he thought.

Did he? This was the life he chose, so he figured he did. But to tell the truth, he had blocked any thoughts of the consequences by getting high.

Once again, with the dread of his predicament, anxiety struck him like a tornado in an East Texas trailer park. His motel room rent was due in a couple of days. He would lose his car soon because he wouldn't be able to make the payment. He was homeless, broke and without a car. He wouldn't hit bottom if he kept digging, right?

CHAPTER 33

Milo woke. Room clean, he walked around the room and acted nonchalantly as possible. Inside he was about to explode with excitement. Somewhere through that hidden entrance there would be drugs! At least that's what he hoped. He stopped suddenly. He hadn't noticed the nauseousness in his gut. He stumbled to the toilet and wretched, splattering some onto his clothes. "Damn it!" he said out loud. He grabbed a coke out of the fridge along with the 2 pills, disrobed and entered the shower.

The shower was the only place with partial privacy. It had a swinging door that was below his neck and above the ankles. At least the people running this place aren't perves, he mused. Before scrubbing himself, he pretended to take the pills and took a drink of the coke once again. He went over his half ass plan while showering. Pretend to be asleep and hope once they saw him knocked out, they would look away for a moment. He reasoned they would not pay much attention while he was asleep. He hoped they would become complacent like he had become with his own life. Just going through the motions. Same 'ol same 'ol.

"Nothing to see here officer." The water muffled his words. He dried off, stepped out and put on clean clothes. They had a sense of humor. There was always a change of clothes in his room, but he rarely took advantage of this luxury. His t-shirt read, "I went to rehab and all I got was this lousy t-shirt!"

"Funny guys." He mumbled. "Real fucking funny."

He ate very little because the butterflies would not permit him stuffing himself. He laid back down in the bed and turned off the light. His hands were shaking more noticeably now as he pulled the sheet over his head. He was in agonizing pain deep down in his bones. "Soon," he told himself, "Soon."

CHAPTER 34

Matthew was a technician for Dr. van Hook and his job was like Marie's. The doctor recruited from an emergency room incident. Matthew was in a car wreck and the police suspected he was intoxicated. Van Hook was in the planning stages of creating his facility and was still working in an emergency room. He needed able-bodied participants that were willing to look the other way when it came to legalities; people that were desperate.

Matthew was perfect. Matthew reeked of alcohol and looked drunk. He was slightly slurring his words. The doctor took advantage of this opportunity and approached Matthew. He reminded him of his son. He looked pitiful and like a scared child. Although the doctor and the police assumed he was drunk, that was not enough for the legal system. They needed proof. Usually, a nurse handles the process of taking blood from a patient. The doctor had the phlebotomist cart and the usual tools. Syringes, vials, and a tourniquet as he addressed Matthew.

"Hello young man. I'm Dr. Van Hook. What is the problem tonight?"

Droopy, bloodshot eyes looked up at him. He had seen his son look like this so many times. At this point his son had only been dead a couple of years and he still felt the sting. His heart ached for his son and now for this young man.

"Oh, um, I don't know. Wrecked my car." Words slurring and eyes pleading for help. The Doc closed the curtain, grabbed a chart, and leaned in closer to the patient.

"I assume you've been drinking?" It was more of a statement than a question.

"The blood work will show as much. The police outside will charge you with D.W.I. Then you will be done here, and they will take you to jail." Young Matthew let out a groan. He had a bump on his head and a scrape on his face. The Doc knew it wasn't pain that caused the groan but fear.

"Please, doc," He was now wide eyed and shaking.

"Please, I'm in my 4th year at A and M. I'm going to be an engineer! This will ruin my chance of getting an excellent job! Not to mention my parents will flip!"

Doctor Van Hook sighed. And chose his words carefully.

"Well son, you should have taken that into consideration before. It's my understanding this was a single car accident, correct?"

"Yes sir. I didn't hurt anyone."

"Well, That's a good thing I suppose. Wait. I forgot something. I'll be back in a minute." The doc left knowing the anticipation and fear in this young drunk's mind would help with his plan to manipulate him. Matthew was going over possible scenarios from his parents' wrath to going to jail. He only knew about jail from the movies. He was terrified. The doctor returned to find his patient wiping away tears but trying to hide them. Good. That's exactly what he wanted. Again, he pleaded.

"Doc, please. I'm not a bad person. I drink occasionally, to let off steam when on a break from school." The doctor knew that was a lie most alcoholics told themselves to downplay the destruction their actions created.

"When I'm at school, I'm all business. I get straight A's! Isn't there something you can do?" While Matt was pleading his case the doctor had applied the tourniquet. He stopped short with the syringe and locked eyes with Matt. The memory of his son shot electricity through his core.

"Son, I don't know. D.W.I. is a serious matter. Thousands die every year because of car crashes, and many are because of drunk driving. I see some of those victims right here in this emergency room.

"I'm sorry doc, I really am! I didn't hurt anyone.

"Not this time, but what about next time?"

"I'll stop drinking! I swear!" Another lie. They were always lying to get out of trouble. The doctor chuckled at the familiar statement. How many times had his son said the same thing? The Doc had formulated a plan the moment they wheeled him in and now decided to present his offer.

"Look kid, if I were to possibly, accidentally taint this blood test and it came back negative for alcohol, you would be in the clear. But would that do any good? Oh, sure you wouldn't go to jail. You would go back to school and become an engineer. But it would only enable you. There is no guarantee for either of us you'll stick to your promise. Not to mention I could lose my career, my reputation and possibly go to jail."

"So, what are you going to do, Doc?"

"What I'm going to do is make you a deal."

"What kind of deal?"

"What I'm going to do is provide a negative blood test with the police officers. Now, as to what you are going to do for me."

"Anything doc, anything." The doctor's plan was brilliant and met with open arms by Matthew. He was to finish his last year of college then tell his parents he was taking a one year paying internship and come work with the doctor.

"If you decide not to fulfill your side of the bargain, I will have a vial of the real blood and the proof that you were intoxicated and say I made a mistake and you'll go off to jail. Deal?"

"Yes doctor, yes! Thank you so much!"

"Remember, I will be paying you well and I need a one-year commitment and then you are free to go."

"What exactly will I be doing, Doc?" The doctor detected a bit of suspicion in his voice.

"Relax, Matt. You'll be part of a history making program, and most of all." He emphasized the last part sternly.

"You won't be going to jail." The doctor knew since their relationship started with breaking the law, other unlawful acts would easily be dismissed.

As Matt was reminiscing, he watched the monitors. Some were doing the usual things. Wake up, get high or drink for days, pass out, repeat. A few, he noticed, had recovered and that astonished him. This shit is really working, he thought.

Sometimes, when the patients, in reality prisoners, would not take a break and go to sleep, he was ordered to switch on a safety protocol. This feature was designed to pump an odorless gas into their rooms to make them sleep. The doctor told him they had to give them every opportunity to possibly recover and not sleeping for several days might kill the average person. Watching Milo, he thought his was a hopeless case. But recently, he noticed Milo was taking his detox pills and settled into a somewhat normal routine.

Except for occasional outbursts and asking other patients for drugs, he was doing fine. Matthew had brought a Sudoku puzzle book to work because the monotony of his job was boring him.

CHAPTER 35

Milo lowered the sheet, took several deep breaths to slow his heart from beating out of his chest and eased out of bed. He made his way slowly to the toilet and pulled down his pants and sat down to pee. Still breathing deeply to remain calm, he pulled up his pants and walked to the fridge. It's now or never. If they saw him, he figured he could get some dope and ingest it before they caught him!

He pulled the fridge away from the wall. Since the fridge was only about four feet tall, he had to crouch and feel for a latch or way to open the secret door. He rubbed his hands all around until he felt it. There was a slight indentation in the wall, and he used his fingertips until he heard a soft click and he froze. His heart skipped a beat. He was shaking with excitement now.

The door pushed in and he crawled into complete blackness. He carefully closed the small door behind him but not all the way so a soft glow from his room would lead him back if necessary. Since he could see absolutely nothing in front of his face he slowly and methodically searched with his hands for other entrances. He was in what he could only think of as being a pipe chase. The walls were arms width and had various plumbing hardware sticking in many directions. He kept bumping his head on the metal pipes. So, this is how these bastards keep sneaking in and out of everyone's room.

He found another indentation which told him he found another doorway! Milo pulled the door open towards him slowly. As he did so, he noticed the light was off, but it was not pitch black like the pipe chase, so he began the slow push of the fridge. Was this a white or black fridge? He could not tell yet. Once the fridge was pushed out a couple of feet, he crawled in.

He crawled around until he was facing the fridge, silently breathing so he would not awaken whoever was in this room. His eyes adjusted and he saw it was the white one.

He crawled over to the other fridge and there it was! The Black fridge! He had what felt like a softball size knot in his stomach and it was growing by the second. His bowels were doing somersaults as he was passing gas and he hoped he didn't shit his pants in anticipation of that first taste! He opened the fridge and saw the various baggies and syringes he once had in his fridge. You dirty bastards. I'll show you. The light was dim inside so he could not know for sure what was what, but he shoved as much into his pockets as possible.

He closed the door to the fridge and started to make his way back when he stopped short. He heard what sounded like a child snoring. Was that a woman? Crawling towards the bed, he risked a look. Betty! Big Booty Betty! He felt his loins burn with desire. He had not been with a woman in weeks! He was so tempted to crawl in bed with her but restrained himself. The drugs were his current mission, and he must succeed. He crawled into the entrance, pulled the white fridge into the space, and closed the door.

Clumsily, he made his way back to his room. So far so good. He shut the door and pushed the fridge back into place. He went back to bed, grabbed a towel, pulled the sheet over his head, and waited for "them," his captors, to rush in and bust him with his score. While under the sheet, he took out all his newly discovered treasure and placed it in the towel. After several minutes he knew his clandestine journey went undetected. He got out of bed and turned on a small bedside light. He took off his clothes and with towel in hand, he went into the shower. He turned on the water. Shit! Shit! Shit! Cold! Cold! Cold!

It was such a shock to his body it felt like his testicles escaped somewhere into his stomach. Slowly, the water warmed. He pointed the shower nozzle away from him and carefully unwrapped the towel. He got a better look at the baggies. Coke, heroin. No needles. Oh well, this would do fine. He snorted straight from one of the baggies until it was empty. Some of it spilled onto the shower floor but he paid it no mind. He snorted at least a gram so quickly it took only a minute to hit his brain like eating too much ice cream. He safely covered the stash once again with the towel and set it outside of the shower on the floor and bathed himself trying to look inconspicuous. He was flying high.

Matthew periodically looked up from his Sudoku puzzle only to see everyone sleeping. At one point he saw

Milo taking a shower. Nothing unusual. More monotony. Back to his puzzle. His shift would be over soon. Milo finished his shower and dabbed himself dry with the drug-filled towel doing his best not to spill any.

If Matt had been watching, he would have noticed the strange way he was drying off with a bunched up towel. But Milo didn't care at this point. He felt like a little kid that found a wallet with money in it. He was nervous, scared, and excited at the same time.

His heartbeat was increasing exponentially every minute the cocaine flowed through his bloodstream. The elation he felt was like when the morning sun first hits you and you realize you were still alive after a night of hardcore partying on the streets. Another day in heaven or another day in hell. Either way, another day to get high. It didn't matter what lay ahead for him, as long as he was soaring into space with his cocaine rocket ship. Milo got dressed, slyly removed the baggies from the towel and filled his pockets. He flushed the empty one down the toilet. Now he paced the floors because he couldn't sit still. He was higher than he had been in days. This was too much coke for anyone at one time, even Milo.

His heart was racing like NASCAR on a Sunday along with his brain. Thoughts of his childhood flashed before his eyes. He casually pulled out a baggie and inhaled the entire contents at one time. Damn! He was soaring higher than a 747 and he felt like he was floating. He was zigzagging through the room and started singing to himself.

CHAPTER 36

After haggling with the pawn shop, Blake went back to the motel room. He had decided to keep his wedding ring but pawned his father's watch. He only got $475 for everything! "That sucks!" he had said to the cashier. But he was desperate and took the money and signed the pawn ticket. Maybe he could get the watch back one day? He highly doubted it. Still not hitting bottom yet, he thought. Janine arrived at the motel a few minutes after Blake and helped to brighten his dark mood. He invited her in and she took a seat next to the bed.

"Hey Blake, you all right?"

"Not really. Sold all the rest of my shit. I'm debating what to do with the money."

"How much longer until your rent is due?"

"One day."

"Then that's a no brainer. You need a place to live right?"

"Yea, I guess but that will leave only $175 left to party" He knew how pathetic he sounded but it was too late to take the words back.

"To party? Maybe it's not always about the party Blake." She knew she shouldn't have said that. Blake looked at her like she was an alien. Then he let out a laugh that made her feel uncomfortable. She thought he was laughing at her. She sighed and stood up.

"I'm going to go, Blake."

"No! No wait." He grabbed her arm, then let go realizing it was a little too strong.

"Will you do me a favor?" She knew what that favor was. She sat down on the edge of the bed and sighed again. He seemed so hopeless. She didn't get high every day, only a couple of days a week. She drank more than anything. Like so many others, she considered herself a functional alcoholic. She took care of her priorities first.

"How much?" she asked with a hint of disdain in her voice. He detected it and his squeaky voice said as much.

"All of it." Blake said, handing her the $475. "Wait! I need gas!" He gave her $400.

"But what about your room?"

"I've decided to leave, Janine." She thought he looked sad and defeated. Hair a mess. Unshaven. Patchy stubble of grey and brown on his face. He could use a tan. He looked like a homeless vampire. She almost laughed at the sight, but it was too sad.

He seemed lost in thought, so she asked him,

"Leave? Where will you go?"

"I don't know. But it's time to go." She was incredulous.

"So, you're going to score one more time, get into your car and just leave?"

"I guess so."

"You guess so? Doesn't sound like you have much of a plan, Blake."

"I don't. I haven't thought passed getting high then leaving."

"I don't think you're in any condition to drive anywhere."

"I drove to the pawn shop and back just fine. Don't worry."

"Well, it's just that." She looked down and fidgeted for several seconds. What was she feeling? Was she going to miss him? That was the vibe he was picking up but he didn't say anything.

"It's just that, just." She stood up and walked over to Blake and looked him directly in his eyes.

"There is no one left Blake. Everyone we know is gone. Disappeared. We are the only ones left." Damn, he thought. She really was going to miss him. He started to tear up. He noticed she had a few tears as well. She gave him a tender hug then sat back on the bed.

"What do you want?" He wrote her a list. While she was gone scoring, he made a mental checklist of what little belongings were left. Wedding ring and clothes. Photo album of he and his wife. He had a few shirts and a dirty pair of "For all mankind" jeans that cost him two hundred and fifty dollars. He laughed quietly at the thought of him being the sharpest dressed homeless person. He packed away his toothbrush. He hardly used that any longer. He gargled some mouthwash then threw the bottle of Listerine in the suitcase. Once he was packed, he looked around the room.

This place had been his home for several weeks. He was a little sad and slightly scared to leave. Not because of the comfort or the safety of the room, but because of the friendship he had with Janine. She was the only one of his so-called "friends" that he was certain did not use him. She genuinely cared for him and reminded Blake of his wife. He got lost for a moment thinking of where he and his wife first met. That's it! He knew where he was going.

To a dope fiend, it feels like an eternity when waiting for a drug delivery. According to Blake's watch, it was only twenty minutes. He snorted a line for the road, and she declined his offer for a bump of her own. Then he packed the rest.

"Well, Janine, this is goodbye."

"Can I ask where?" He thought about it for a second.

"Galveston."

"Galveston? Why there?"

"It is where my wife and I first met. It's always been a special place for us, um, me. We are not married anymore, of course, but I would like to take one last trip down there." That last statement set off alarm bells in her head.

"What do you mean when you say, "one last trip?" Blake didn't answer. He just stood there and nervously shuffled his feet.

"Blake? Are you ok? What does that mean?" Subconsciously, Blake knew what he meant. He was broke, about to be homeless, and the dope would run out eventually. That is why he said, "one last trip." But he didn't want to admit anything.

"I don't know what I mean, Janine. I'm just leaving. Going to the beach. Walk through the sand and remember what it was like to be happy." His memory was spotted over the last few years, but he knew when he had first met his wife, he was happy. He had been in Galveston with some friends, and they had got too drunk on the first day to do much of anything. With his addiction not in full swing yet, he decided to rent an electric scooter and ride the Seawall. He had a great physique then.

So, with his shirt off, he set out on his own, leaving his friends to hug their respective toilet bowls. He was having a blast, zigzagging in and out of people taking a stroll in the beautiful weather. Some were yelling at him for coming too close. Then he saw her, on a scooter headed his way. The day he met her, in his mind, was so clear. In this memory, it still seemed like time slowed to a crawl, although he knew he was traveling at least 15 mph. As she got closer, they locked eyes. Her beautiful smile mesmerized him. He was so captivated by her image that they almost collided. As he veered to the right to avoid the collision, they both looked back.

Then it happened. While looking over her shoulder, still with that gorgeous smile, she didn't see the large trash can in her way. She hit it with a loud smack and somersaulted over the receptacle and hit the concrete. "Oh shit!" he remembered shouting.

He jumped off the scooter and it flew off the seawall into the sand several feet below. He could have cared less, "Fuck my deposit," he remembered thinking. At that moment, all he cared about was this beautiful woman. Was she hurt? As he knelt to check on her, she looked dazed and had a bloody scratch on her forehead. Her hands were slightly scraped and on a couple of knuckles as well. He said, "My God!" not out of concern but because of the sheer beauty of this woman. Miraculously, she was still smiling and asked if he was ok.

"Me? Are you ok?"

"Oh yea, I've busted my ass worse than this!" And she gave the cutest chuckle, and he realized she might be a little tipsy. People had gathered around and were asking if she needed any help. One woman with three children in tow, offered a pack of sanitized baby wipes.

"Oh, thank you." Blake accepted the wipes and proceeded to gently wipe her wounds clean of dirt and blood. First, starting at the knees, then each hand. When he got to the abrasion on her forehead, she started talking.

"You're pretty good at this. Get into many scooter accidents?" He looked at her and burst into laughter.

She caught the bug and laughed as well. At that exact moment, as cliché as it sounded, he realized he was falling for her. He wanted to nurse her wounds for the rest of their lives. After she was cleaned up, they went to look for his scooter. Some kids had "found" it and demanded payment for "watching" it for him. He gave them twenty dollars and Blake took her by the hand, then walked off down the seawall. They returned the scooter and popped into a seaside bar that had a pool in it. After removing their shoes, they eased into the water and swam up to the bar at the edge of the pool. He got a beer and she a vodka with "something fruity." The music was pumping through the air in all directions, and they bobbed up and down like two fish dancing in a bowl. The water was cool despite the hot Texas heat. They shared their life stories, laughing and flirting the whole time.

Occasionally, she would kiss him on the cheek at something silly he would say. They drank a little too much, so he called an uber. In the Uber she was all over him. He invited her to his room and she didn't object. It was perfect. Too perfect. She was wasted. Once in the room, she continued her alcohol driven lust. His conscience got the better of him and he told her as much. She had blinked several times to the statements, "we have had too much to drink. Maybe we should slow down." She seemed to "come to" and fell asleep in his arms.

The next morning, she woke up to pee and jumped back into bed. She thanked him for realizing they were drunk and not taking advantage of the situation. She didn't think any other man in his position would have restrained themselves. He admitted that her beauty tempted him, but he wasn't like that. She kissed him long and hard. Then, they made love. Once again, they fell asleep in each other's arms. Janine was asking him something.

"Huh? What did you say?"

"I asked," frustration in her voice, "Will I ever see you again, Blake?"

"I don't know, Janine. I haven't thought much after getting to Galveston. I just want to go to the beach."

"Oh Blake, please be careful." Careful? He thought. His life was anything but careful. Driving to Galveston with baggies full of cocaine was not being careful.

"Blake," she said, grabbing his arm with her tiny hands, "I'll always be here if you need help." He grabbed his suitcase, snorted up the rest of the coke on the mirror, and walked out the door. As he drove away, she watched from the balcony. She thought about what he said, "One last trip."

CHAPTER 37

Pookie woke up with the shakes. He crawled to the toilet and vomited. While hugging the toilet bowl, he couldn't remember the last time he had been this sick. Never, he thought.

He switched on a light and looked around the room. The black fridge had arrived. For a moment, he froze, then his feet couldn't get him to the fridge fast enough. He tripped, stood, fell again and face planted the last couple of feet in front of the ominous black fridge. As he reached for the door handle the messages on the walls seem to come alive.

"Make the right choices."

"Forgive yourself"

"Forgive myself?" Pookie was talking to himself again and was confused.

"Forgive me? For what? I ain't done shit, fool! Yall trippin'!"

He knew the messages were trying to help him like his grandmother from the grave, but he couldn't resist the calling of the fridge. When he opened the fridge, he was in awe of the assortment of liquor and drugs. He grabbed a forty ounce bottle of Ol' E, his favorite, and drank half of it down in one breath. He felt like someone that had crashed landed in the Sahara and had not drank water in days. This was his lifeline. He was starving for the drink. He finished the bottle in less than a minute.

Before he could catch his breath, he twisted open a bottle of Mad Dog 20/20 and pulled a huge swig. He lay back down on the floor in front of the black fridge and let the alcohol warm his bones. After several minutes the shaking stopped. He felt like a new man. While lying on his back, he realized the messages were above him.

"Yall crazy! Let me enjoy this in peace!"

"Choose life not death."

"Hey Pookie! Whatcha' shoutin' about?" Bam had heard Pookie yelling and was concerned. Betty heard the commotion too and was curious.

"Hey Pookie, the black refrigerator should be there by now, please don't open it!" Betty sounded worried. Pookie crawled to the wall to hear better. He started to laugh. He laughed for a few minutes straight. Mike got up and chimed in.

"Hey guys, I think he's drunk." Up until this point, Mike had only drunk a little. He had been trying to hide that fact from the others. The urge was too strong. He would wake up, drink a few beers and a shot of whiskey, then fall asleep. His alcohol maintenance program was working, or so he thought. Now, hearing Pookie drunk and laughing it up, the desire to get high consumed him.

"Man, I feel like myself again." Pookie managed through his laughter.

"Fuck what these people be sayin'. Life's about doing what the fuck you want. This is a free country! And these people violatin' all that shit!" He was too drunk to be angry, but his tone let the others know he was serious. He continued his rant.

"But as long they payin' for it, I'll oblige them!" He laughed some more and kept drinking.

"Betty," Bam called for her.

"Yea, Bam?"

"I think we lost him!"

"No Bam! He still has a chance to get it right!"

"Maybe so Betty, but.." Mike interrupted.

"I can't resist any more guys! I'm going in!" And with that, Mike shut

out the words on the walls and the protests of the others. He opened the black fridge, but this time he didn't grab a bottle, he reached for the cocaine. He stood there, staring at a bag of white powder, holding it up to the light. Mike gently caressed the cocaine in his hands like it was a priceless artifact or a rare antique and he was afraid of damaging it. As Mike poured the entire contents on to a side table, he said,

"Holy shit! That's at least an ounce!" But before he could partake in the God send, he felt that familiar rumbling deep within his bowels. He ran to the toilet as he was shitting his pants. Barely wiping, he jumped up and tripped over his pants that hung around his knees. He shook out of his jeans and ran half naked to the coke.

He buried his face in the already chopped up powder and snorted half into each nostril until he choked.

The coke hit his brain like a bolt of lightning in a thunderstorm. Thunder was in his chest from the pounding of his heart. The symphony of the storm playing in his body was the music of his soul. How he had missed the sweet melody. He stood up too quick and braced himself on the wall. This place was crazy. They even provided metal straws to snort with. At the first two lines he felt guilt and shame. After several more, he was numb to the world around him. He didn't notice the signs flashing anymore. Questions raced through his mind like the cocaine racing through his blood. Why would people do all of this? Experiment? Torture? Government? Mad scientists? Aliens? Whoa. I wonder if they are aliens. That's crazy, but this place was too.

There were so many drugs to choose from. He walked to the fridge, got a beer and a shot of whiskey. He downed the whiskey and walked back to the coke sipping the beer. He could hear his friends through the walls, but he ignored them. He wasn't strong enough to resist and all these messages were bullshit. How could anyone that was offered all the free drugs and alcohol they could ever want, while in a safe and comfortable environment, resist? Why would they choose the right path? What was that? Did he hear music? Was that Nirvana? Wait, that wasn't music. It was someone singing.

"Hey guys, Yall hear singing?" Bam and Betty heard it too. "Yea," Bam answered. "That's Milo tripping again, I think?" Mike said,

"Didn't he say they took his black fridge away?"

"Yea, and he's been quiet for a few days." I wonder what he is tripping on." Pookie was drunk and oblivious to his surroundings and was singing to himself as well. It was his favorite song by Earth, Wind and Fire.

"Do you remember, Remember the time, September." He was slurring his words, but to him, he was a superstar. Pookie was dancing around the room with another forty and he was in heaven. All the answers in the world were in that bottle. All his problems were washed away with that drink.

CHAPTER 38

Matthew was watching the scene unfold before him and was curious. This was not Milo's normal routine lately. What in the hell was he doing? Marie walked in to take over the shift. Dr. Van Hook would soon follow. Marie was so beautiful to him. She was in her late 30's early 40's but still gorgeous to his twenty two year old eyes.

"Marie, look at this." She walked up to the screen following his gaze. Milo was walking around in circles singing.

"What is that he's singing?"

"Nirvana, I think."

"That's right. Smells like Teen Spirit." Milo continued his aimless pacing and singing.

"A mulatto, a mosquito, YEA!" He was playing air guitar and making sounds with his mouth, then switched to air drums still mimicking the sounds with each instrument. His "head-banging", like he was in a concert, was not the strange part to Marie. What struck her as odd was the clumsy pacing and the heavy breathing. Like he was speeding up but running out of gas. He sounded like he could not catch his breath.

"Have you watched him all night Matt?"

"Um, yea, of course. He just woke up and took a shower then started acting weird."

Suddenly, he stopped mid song, grabbed his chest, and collapsed.

"Oh shit!" Matt shouted. "What happened?" Dr. Van Hook walked in as Milo collapsed.

"What the hell is happening? Marie? Matthew?" Matthew stammered.

"Sir, um I think Milo is having a heart attack?"

"What? How?" The doctor shouted frantically. Marie offered.

"I don't know, doctor." The doctor went into action fast.

"Get someone in there now! No wait! Matt?"

"Yes doctor?"

"Come with me. Marie, turn off the lights in his room." The doctor and Matthew made their way through the hallway to his office, and the doctor quickly stepped inside to retrieve something from the medicine cabinet. Then they went to the pipe chase to the patient's rooms. They crawled to Milo's secret entrance, opened the door and pushed the refrigerator out of the way. Dr. Van Hook had given Matt two syringes. One of morphine and one of adrenaline. They both used pen lights to navigate Milo's darkened room and they looked like two cat burglars tip toeing to his motionless body. The doctor knelt beside Milo and checked his pulse. Nothing!

"Adrenaline." The doctor said in a demanding whisper. Matthew gave him the syringe. Van Hook took off the safety cap, held it up and gave it a couple of taps to make any bubbles rise to the top. He squeezed the air from the syringe, then slammed it into Milo's chest. Mathew was already handing the doc the other syringe while reaching to grab Milo's shoulders.

Milo's eyes popped open, and he sat upright with a gasp. He looked like a corpse sitting up in the middle of a funeral. It scared the hell out of Matt, but he pushed Milo back down as the doctor injected him with the Morphine. Milo felt high one moment then everything went black again. Hands were on him as felt stinging and his chest hurt. He knew that feeling. Oooohhh, warm. So warm.

"Morphine." He managed to mumble. Silence, and he was still once again. Crisis averted.

"Thank you for your assistance, Matthew."

"No problem, doc."

"Now, I wonder what happened. Please shine the light on him." Matthew complied. The doctor examined Milo, not like a doctor but like a detective at a crime scene. He went through his pockets and found several baggies of different narcotics.

"How in the hell did he get all of this Matt?" The accusation was clear in the doctor's tone. Matthew stuttered.

"I-I-I-I Don't.."

"Don't give me that shit, Matthew! Haven't you watched the monitors all night? That is your job, you know."

"Yes, doctor. But I didn't see anything out of the ordinary."

"Well, he got this junk somehow. I don't believe he held on to this stash and didn't use until now." Marie was wondering where the drugs came from as well. She watched Pookie roll around on the floor singing. He seemed so happy. Most drunks appeared that way. But she knew many of them were drowning in their misery. Covering up their pain and searching for relief from a life they couldn't bear.

"Pookie! Pookie! Pookie!" Betty was shouting. Bam called to her.

"It's too late, Betty! He's gone!"

"No!" Betty pleaded with Pookie.

"Pookie please!"

Dr. Van Hook and Matthew searched Milo's room top to bottom looking for any evidence that would point to the source of the drugs. The doctor knew they came from somewhere else other than Milo's room, but where exactly, they had not a clue.

"It must be … No." The doctor knew what to do.

"What, doctor?"

"Come on, Matthew. We must review the video footage." Mathew's heart sank. He knew it was his fault, and his complacency created a window of opportunity for Milo. Matthew felt his world slip away. Would he lose his job for this? Or worse yet, would the doctor expose his D.W.I.? He would lose everything. He followed the doctor back to the monitor room where Marie was already searching the video footage.

"Doctor?" Marie started. "You need to see this."

CHAPTER 39

Janine walked back to her room. As she entered, sadness clouded her mind like a storm ready to shed its rain. And like the rain, her tears fell while lying on the bed. Everyone was gone. There were still people at the motel that she knew but the ones in her circle had all disappeared. Pookie, Mike, Betty, Bam. Hell, even Milo. Always a little crude but he was still in the circle. Blake was the only one that she knew where he was or at least, where he was going. What happened to everyone? Would she disappear like everyone else? Her mind ventured towards their death.

"What an awful thought." She said out loud. But she knew it was possible. She let her mind drift to Blake and every nice thing he ever did for her. Getting her food. Paying for her room a few times when business was slow. And what was so incredible, he never wanted anything in return. Who does that? Blake does. Did. A good man. She stood up and looked in the mirror. Oh my God, she looked awful! Hair, wild and crazy. Eye shadow and mascara ran down her cheeks. She looked like a rock star after a concert! She jumped in the shower and scrubbed her face. Washed her hair, then she just stood there, eyes closed allowing the warm pellets of water to massage her body.

She loved the peacefulness of these moments. Here, in this isolation, she could dream of a world that would never exist. A world where she had someone like Blake to come home to. A home where she could raise a child or children? Somewhere she could make dinner for her family. They would sit around the table and smile and joke and eat. A home and a family that she would never know. But she could dream. She dried off, then dropped the towel on the floor and starred in the mirror once again. She was thin but not crack head thin. She still had curves. She was a healthy size 3. Stomach was flat and her breasts were still upright and perky.

"I could make a man happy." She laughed as she said this to the mirror. Because she often made a man happy with her profession. But that's not what she meant. She still believed she had enough love in her broken heart to have a meaningful relationship. The problem was, where would she find one? More than that, where would she find one that would forgive her past? A past?

In reality, it was her present. But if she was to clean up and go straight, could someone love her? Was her heart too damaged to love herself? That was the biggest question. She had so much resentment inside that only alcohol and drugs could suppress it. How could she heal the pain of childhood trauma? She had none of those answers. She wished Blake had invited her to Galveston. She would drop everything and gladly go. Maybe she could have helped him get over his wife. She would love to try. She never met a man like him before.

"And never will again." She felt strange talking to her reflection, so she proceeded with her prep for the day. She dried her hair with her cheap hair dryer. She could not use it very long as the handle always got too hot. She brushed and sprayed it into place with Aqua Net. That stuff didn't smell that great, but it kept her hair in place for hours and held up to the physical activity her job demanded. Next stop, make-up. She liked earth tones. She never understood women that used blue, greens and purples. They looked like those old movies about Egyptians and mummies coming to life. She remembered Elizabeth Taylor in one of those movies.

She was the only one that could pull that color combination off because she was so incredible. She was Janine's favorite actress and she thought Elizabeth was the most beautiful woman in the world, ever. And these women on the streets? Well, they were not. Zombies with make-up. That made her giggle. She knew the only reason she didn't look like them was because she didn't smoke or shoot drugs.

Also, she made sure she went to sleep at least every other day. The other prostitutes were up for days on Meth or shooting heroin. She drank and occasionally snorted cocaine. The girls that had pimps were kept on a short leash with easy access to as much as they wanted. So much so, that they were enslaved by the debt.

Now that her face and hair were presentable, she opened the mini-fridge and grabbed a wine cooler. One giant gulp and it was gone. Before the alcohol hit her blood stream, she opened another and took a sip. She wasn't that hungry but would need her strength, so she grabbed an apple. Time to pick an outfit. She didn't wear the typical street clothes of her trade. Shorts up the crack of the ass exposing fat and dimples, she never understood that. Tits hanging out. Well, she understood Betty doing that. Those breasts were huge! She always wore a modest dress. It was always tight but came to mid-thigh with only moderate cleavage showing. After all, she was just a B-cup. And all of this worked. Her persona was a hit. She scored more "Johns" than anyone and charged more and did less. Some of the girls didn't even require condoms.

Janine grabbed her third wine cooler, checked herself in the mirror one last time and walked out the door. Her sex for money life was so routine. The alcohol helped to numb her to the disgusting parts. She had several regulars. Married men that were not happy at home. A few single Firemen and Police Officers with crazy long shifts and no time or desire for relationships. But occasionally, she would get a "jerk" that wanted more for less. She could usually spot them by the car they drove and would ignore them or wave them off. Some would even try to "back-door" her. And all for only a hundred dollars! That was her minimum. Some of the girls charged one half for that. As she walked through the parking lot sipping her cooler, Blake came to mind again.

She shook him away because she had to concentrate on work. She walked down the sidewalk. It was 7 p.m. The light of the day returned to its home over the horizon to allow the night to roam free and hide the adventures and horrors that awaited the City of Houston. Crime was steadily climbing in this once beautiful city.

People would commit murder and be let out on bond, only to get out and rob or kill someone else! Who are the people in charge? She didn't worry though. Nothing bad ever happened to her. Well, one time a guy got too rough, so she gouged one of his eyes and ran away. Another time she was given two counterfeit hundred dollar bills. Now, she kept a pen that checks for that in her purse. A clerk at a convenience store gave it to her because he was one of her regulars.

She had the usual playful bounce in her gait as she walked. That was another reason people chose her over the stumbling zombies that were wide-eyed with chicken head like movements. It was a sad sight but still made her laugh inside. She didn't see the white van pull up behind her. Neither did she hear the sliding door open. But what she did hear was shuffling feet on top of leaves on the sidewalk. She started to turn around, but she was too slow. The hood made everything go black as it did for everyone else. She felt the sharp prick in her neck as her tiny form was carried into the van. Her kidnappers placed her down softly on a bed of blankets. Sleep took over as she muttered to herself,

"See you soon guys."

CHAPTER 40

Mike did two more lines and chugged another beer. "This place is awesome. Fucking awesome! I never want to leave!" He walked around the room for a minute trying to avoid looking too long at the annoying messages on the wall. His thoughts were like the mall on Black Friday. Chaos. Out of nowhere, he started to feel different. He went over scenarios of doctors coming in and taking him into a room. They were poking and prodding him with numerous instruments. He hated doctors. They always told him to get help and stop using. He wasn't that bad. He wasn't like Bam or Milo.

Nothing that bad ever happened to him until his little heart scare and now this place. He started to get paranoid, which was unusual for him. Most people that he partied with got quiet and peeped out the windows. They would see and hear things that weren't there. He never saw the "Shadow People" that so many addicts swore were coming for them.

He remembered people saying, "Be quiet! The police are outside! They're coming in any second!" He would laugh at these people and tell them to shut the hell up and enjoy their high. If they persisted, he would get pissed off and open the motel room door and scare the shit out of them. One time a buddy of his was staring out the window so long he decided to play a prank on him. They were partying in an abandoned house. So, while the guy was staring out of the window, Mike snuck out of the house and crawled outside through the grass under the window. After a couple of minutes, Mike jumped up and screamed.

Upon seeing this, his friend turned pale, passed out and his heart stopped. The others in the house freaked out and ran away. Mike had to perform C.P.R. on him until he woke up. Mike was laughing the entire time. Blake wasn't like that. He would just sit there and opine about his wife. Damn! What a lucky S-O-B! He had it all.

Mike had it all once too. Mike started jerking his head back and forth, expecting mad scientists to come into the room and carve his brain up into little pieces and dissect it to see how he thinks. He looked like a chicken looking for worms, eyes locked open. He began to talk to the voices that weren't there.

"No! Leave me alone! What do you want from me? You can't have my brain!" All this fear and paranoia did not deter him from using more cocaine. The images on the walls seemed to blur into new messages.

"If you don't stop you will die!" Wait, that wasn't the message before.

"You're choosing death."

"Death awaits you."

"You are killing yourself."

"You are dying." The messages blinked, blurred and morphed into more ominous meanings.

"No one will mourn your death." Would anyone mourn him? Where was his family? Did they even care? He had not heard from them in years. The thought of him dying and no one showing up to his funeral caused his heart to sink and a pitiful knot filled his stomach. The oppressive and morose thoughts took over his mind.

The sadness was so overwhelming he dropped the straw. His life of waste, worthlessness and debauchery began to play in reverse at high speed now. The images appeared on the wall in front of him like a movie. His life on film. He watched at the sheer squandering of his life, and it weighed him down like the Great Deluge he read about in the bible as a child. He was drowning in the devastation of his life. It was too much for him. He felt his mind snap in two. He stood up rapidly and screamed,

"No! I'm sorry!" To whom he was talking to, he had no idea. The shouting and the speed in which he stood, caused him to get dizzy and temporarily lose his sight. He fell into a clump on the floor spilling the cocaine all around him. Lying there, looking dead, it was as though a drunk C.S.I. Investigator tried to chalk up a murder scene. He sat up and brushed off the white dust. Next, he stood up slowly and sat on the bed. He looked at the images on the walls once again. He read a small paragraph that he had not noticed before. The Serenity Prayer? For some strange reason he was inspired to read aloud.

"God." Did he believe in God? He continued to read.

"Grant me the serenity to accept the things I cannot change." As he recited this timeless prayer, a light shone all around him. The hairs on his body stood up straight. He felt weightless as he said the last line of the prayer.

"And wisdom to know the difference." He cried. He bawled like a baby that didn't get their way. His body seemed to convulse. He felt every hurt, every pain and every negative thing in his life wash away with his tears. He couldn't hear anything except for his heartbeat, and he was blinded by the tears. After a few minutes the barrage subsided. He stood up feeling lighter and clear-minded. Sane. He studied the words before him. He shouted to the world.

"I choose life not death!"

CHAPTER 41

"**M**atthew!" The doctor was furious. Matthew and Marie were in shock.

"How did you miss this? This is unacceptable!"

"Doctor, I, I, I. I, Um." Marie could not believe what she had just watched.

"Rewind it and play it again, Marie."

"Yes, doctor." Marie restarted the video at the beginning. Milo was in bed and covered by his sheet. He lowered the sheet, got out of bed, then used the restroom. He walked to the white refrigerator and

pulled it out.

"Stop there, Marie."

Doctor Van Hook pointed at the screen and glared at Matt.

"How did he know to do that? And how in the hell did you not see this?" He raised his voice while simultaneously poking the monitor.

"I don't know Doctor."

"Did you step away for a moment?" The doctor continued in a patronizing tone.

"I mean, everyone has to pee, right?"

"But we all know to make sure a tech is here at all times, right?" Marie added.

"Well, um." Matthew looked defeated.

"Rick called in sick, Doctor."

"So, you were here, all alone for your shift?" Marie cut in.

"Matt! You know you are supposed to call one of us in the event someone doesn't show up for work!" The doctor spoke, sounding more stern by the second.

"There must be two technicians on duty at all times, now you see why." The doctor looked at Marie. She could see the anger in his eyes, but also the fear. It was a side of him she had not seen before. The doctor liked to be in control and ran the facility like a battleship. Everyone had their job and there was a contingency plan for every situation. Except this.

"Continue the video, Marie." There was Milo, Probing the wall. He found the spot to open it and crawled in.

"Okay, that's where we lost him." Marie looked to the doctor for further instructions.

"Right, there are no cameras in the pipe chase."

"What if we note the time when he goes in then check all the other patient's video footage?"

Matthew was trying to be helpful to atone for his sin.

"Okay, Matthew." The doctor stared directly at him. "Whose video shall we look at first?" The patronizing tone had returned. Even with the doctor's attitude, Matt felt like Van Hook was offering him a chance to redeem himself.

"I would see whose room is closest to his and watch their footage?"

"And whose room is that, Matthew?" Again, Matthew could sense the disdain the doctor was feeling.

"Um, Betty, sir."

"Good Matt, Marie, pull up that footage please. Marie was already looking for the exact moment on Betty's video feed. After a few seconds of watching Betty's video, her refrigerator pushed away from the wall and Milo crawled through. He crawled to the black fridge and stuffed his pockets.

"Stop the video, Marie." Dr. Van Hook sighed deeply. He walked around the room. Marie had never seen the doctor not able to come up with a solution to a problem right away. As far as she was concerned, he was a genius. His philosophies on addiction, as well as this program, were brilliant. These patients, seemingly hopeless, on a deadly path of destruction, were being healed. Now, watching this video, she had doubts. The doctor finally spoke.

"First of all, we need to administer sedatives through the ventilation ducts to all of the patients. Then, we enter their rooms one by one and remove the access to the pipe chase from the inside.

"What if a tech accidentally locks themselves inside during clean up?" Matthew asked a very logical question, Marie thought. But the frustration in the doctor's voice said otherwise.

"They can communicate via their earpiece to the control room and ask for assistance." The condescending way the doctor spoke to him caused the air in the room to fill with more tension. Matthew lowered his head and answered in a childlike way,

"Yes sir. I understand."

"Play the rest of the video, Marie." They watched with fear as Milo slowly crawled to Betty's bed. Marie let out a gasp and her thoughts went wild. Would he hurt her? Would he…. After several seconds, Matthew realized he was holding his breath and let it go when Milo crawled back to the fridge. They watched him go through the secret door, pull the fridge back into place and disappear from the screen. Matthew knew it was his fault. He thought again of the prospect of being fired and the vial of blood coming to light. He was reminded of a church song, "There's Power in the Blood, Power in the Blood."

"Doctor, I" he started, but was rudely waved off by the doctor's hand and penetrating stare. Doctor Van Hook looked past Matthew. Marie noticed. So did Matt. They both followed the doctor's eyes to the corner of the room at the end of the desk that held all of the monitors. There, lying on the desk, was a Sudoku puzzle book with a pencil on top. It was open to a half-completed page. Van Hook walked over to it and stood, contemplating. He turned suddenly and faced Matthew.

"Need I tell you the gravity of the situation?" It was a rhetorical question and Matt knew it, but he was too scared to answer anyway.

"And need I ask if this!" He said as he shook the book in the air. He didn't finish. He threw it on the floor and walked out of the room. The door slammed and a painful silence followed. Marie spoke first.

"Matthew, use this as a learning experience."

"I am so screwed!"

"No." Marie continued. "It will be okay."

"You don't understand! The doctor has a vial of my blood that proves I was drunk and crashed my car!"

"What?"

"Yea! And he is holding it over my head! That's the real reason I'm here!"

"Are you serious?"

"Yes! I don't believe in any of this bullshit!"

"What?" Marie was shocked at the confession of the young man.

"And I've been doing my own research into this "addiction" thing." He used air quotes at the word addiction.

"The American Medical Association states that these people," he made a sweeping motion towards the bank of computers.

"Have a disease. Everyone that suffers from this problem has a fucking disease!" So, forcing them, illegally I might add, is tantamount to torture!"

"Matthew, I don't think…" Matt cut her off.

"I mean, we are committing multiple felonies here, Marie! And kidnapping is Federal!" Marie thought about what he said. She knew it to be true, but she would do anything to possibly restore her family. But she hid this motive from him. Instead, she spoke carefully.

"You're right, Matt. But take into consideration the fact that although his methods are felonious, they work."

"Not for everyone, Marie."

"Look at Bam and Betty, My God! Have you read Bam's profile? He was probably the most hopeless!"

"Until Milo you mean?" Matt said sarcastically.

"Well, yes, that is a setback, but we shall work through it and do our best."

"Marie! People could die! Hell, we have two bodies in the cold storage in our basement, don't you remember?" Dr. Van Hook disclosed to her that one week before she was hired there were two casualties. The first two patients were prostitutes. Both in their 40's. They had been on the streets since they were teenagers. They were intravenous drug users and had H.I.V but despite being rescued when brought to the facility, their addiction was too far gone, and they overdosed. Although haunted by this, Marie knew she was too invested in the program to leave. She would see it to the end. No matter what. Sometimes, her thoughts drifted off into worse case scenarios of the F.B.I. storming the hospital and leading her away in handcuffs. The most terrifying vision of all was if her husband was a patient and succumbed to the calling of the black refrigerator. She could see him lying in the all-white room. Eyes opened with a death stare. Heart to never beat again. Her daily prayers and daydreams of her husband being cured kept her mind off the fear and setbacks. Matt was speaking as she was lost in her mind's eye.

"Huh? I'm sorry, what Matt?"

"I asked what you are going to do, Marie." Marie pondered for a moment before speaking.

"I'm going to do my job and help these people, including Milo, to choose." She stopped abruptly at that word. Her eye caught Milo stirring on the monitor. Matt followed her gaze. Milo sat up and screamed. Blood curdling, like a B-rated horror movie.

"No! No! No! No! You took all my shit! Noooooo!"

CHAPTER 42

The van pulled up to the building in the warehouse district of downtown Houston. The sign read, Van Hook Manufacturing. Dr. Van Hook and Marie were waiting outside at the back loading dock.

"Marie, this is the next to the last delivery of the target area. After that, Phase two. The door to the van slid open and the kidnappers appeared. The doctor called these men "contractors. They were local criminals he employed to do the "snatch and grabs." They carried Janine and gently placed her in the wheelchair. She was still unconscious, so they strapped her in. Dr. Van Hook checked her vitals. The leader held out his huge hands.

"Hey doc." He pointed one finger at the other hand gesturing payment. The doctor gave him $10,000 in hundred-dollar bills still wrapped in a bank band.

"There is one more patient to acquire then we will go dark for a while." Van Hook handed him a folder containing information on the last target.

"Oh yea? That's a shame. This job is easy and so is the money!" At this, his goons laughed and so did he.

"Well, you got my number doc." They jumped in the van and drove off. Janine was wheeled into her room. In addition to the secret entrance behind the fridge, there was one located behind the bed. The entrance was larger because the patients were brought in by wheelchair. Once inside, the patient would be placed in the bed and the bed pushed against the secret door. The doctor and Marie exited behind the refrigerator into the pipe chase. They walked back to the control room.

"Doctor?"

"Yes, Marie?"

"What are we going to do about Milo?"

"Good question." It's too early for Phase two. So, let's focus on Janine first and keep giving Milo detox meds and extra sedatives and go from there. He'll get tired from screaming eventually."

CHAPTER 43

As Janine stretched and gave a big, mouthed yawn, her eyes slowly opened. She sat up and surveyed her surroundings. What was on the walls? She eased out of bed; her vision was slightly hazy, so the words were hard to read. She steadied herself on the nearest wall and read aloud.

"Acceptance."

"Forgiveness."

"Choose life."

"Don't give up." She was startled by a scream.

"Damn you all! Give me my shit back! Now!!" Then she heard others.

"Milo, it's going to be okay!" Was that Bam? Then Betty.

"It's not over yet, Milo! You've still got a chance!" Betty. Yes, that was Betty!

"Hey, Betty! Betty! It's Janine!"

"Janine!" Betty was filled with excitement. She had not seen her best friend for several days.

"Janine, you're here!"

"Yes! Yes! I'm here!"

"Damn girl!" Bam joined the reunion. "Took you long enough!" At that, laughter broke out in unison.

"Fuck what y'all sayin'! This is bullshit!" Milo was still pissed off and going through withdrawals.

"Yo, yo, yo, yo!" Pookie joined in.

"Is that Janine?"

"Who's that?" Janine asked.

"Well, the angry one is Milo and the other is."

"Pookie, girl! What's up?"

"Hey, Pookie!"

"Glad you could finally make it!" They all laughed again.

"So, what is this place guys?" Betty was the first to attempt an explanation to Janine.

"Well, this place is either heaven or it's hell. It all depends on your perspective."

"Don't forget your choices!" Bam continued.

"You see that white refrigerator, Janine?"

"Yea, Bam?"

"Well, open it!" Janine walked to the white fridge and complied with Bam's instructions. She was awestruck at the variety of food to choose from.

"Yogurt!" Janine exclaimed. She sounded like a child. She had not eaten any sort of quality food in years. She found a spoon and ate while Bam further explained the situation.

"That white refrigerator is all the food you will ever need. While we sleep, it is magically refilled!" Betty countered.

"Not magically, but someone is doing it." Bam was focused on warning Janine.

"Look, Janine, you have to be prepared for the Black fridge."

"Huh? What is that?"

"Pay very close attention to what I tell you because your life depends on it. On the fifth day, you will be going through withdrawals and then it appears."

"What are y'all talking about guys? What the hell is going on? Janine was feeling frightened and confused and on top of that, she needed a drink. Bam was still trying to get through to her.

"The Black refrigerator is death in a box. It will seem like the answer to your prayers. Within that box is everything you crave. Whoever these people are know what we want, and they place it inside."

"Guys, y'all are freaking me out!" Betty took over.

"Janine! We are trying to help you! They put alcohol and drugs in the black fridge!" Mike had been listening and wanted to share his experiences with her in the hopes of deterring her from giving in.

"Hey, Janine! It's Mike! You must listen to us! That black fridge will kill you! It almost killed me! I gave in and it was hell getting back!" Bam heard his share and was hit with a feeling of triumph.

"Mike! Thank God! We thought we lost you!" Mike ignored Bam and continued to talk Janine off the ledge.

"Janine, the temptation will be overwhelming, but you have to fight it!"

"Mike, I'm really scared. This place makes no sense. Great food. Comfortable room. We have been kidnapped!

And now they are going to bring me drugs? What the hell! Also, it seems like everyone from the motel is here!" Mike was now pleading with her.

"I know it makes no sense, Janine. But, whatever you do, do not touch the black fridge!" Betty took over.

"Janine, look around you. Those messages are there for a reason. Whoever is running this place wants us to pay attention. We don't know if they are trying to help us or hurt us but either way, they are offering us choices. We are responsible for all our choices!" Mike took Betty's pause as a sign to talk.

"Yea, Janine, look at the messages. I was too drunk and too high to get it before. I didn't even care. I couldn't focus on anything else but another drink or another line." As Mike shared his story of a miraculous intervention, she walked around the room and read the walls. Thoughts of a video horror game came to mind. But why would someone do something like this? She had seen many of these messages in jail. She went to a meeting just to get out of the cell block like most people when incarcerated. There was coffee, and someone from the outside world would share how they recovered from a seemingly hopeless state of mind and body. She barely listened. Now, the words from that jailhouse meeting flooded her mind and echoed on these walls. Mike was still babbling about how great he was feeling. Pookie was laughing hysterically, and Milo was shouting,

"I'll kill you when I get out of here, do y'all hear me!" Pookie couldn't take Milo's hysteria any longer.

"Shut the hell up, Milo! You fuckin' with my buzz fool!" Janine directed her question to Betty.

"Betty, have you met the people running this place? Is this a hospital or a rehab?" Pookie answered first.

"This is a party, baby!"

"This is hell run by Satan himself!" screamed Milo.

"We don't know exactly." Bam said. "As far as we can tell, whatever this is, it's a second chance at life. It's a choice. You have a choice, Janine!" Betty spoke next. The gravity in her voice was unmistakable.

"See the messages? Choose life not death. Choose the right path. All of that is to offer you one way or another. It's up to you."

"But why give us drugs? Janine was lost by the insanity of the situation. Fear gripped her like a vise.

"It's like a final test, I guess." Bam stated. "Most of us failed that test, including me. I used, then had a vision of my mother. I don't know if it was real or a hallucination, but it was enough for me to finally understand and stop."

"This is crazy guys!" Janine was astonished.

"Yes, Janine. And all this craziness, we believe, is designed to see what we will choose. I guess they want to strengthen our minds. Think about it. We're made comfortable, bombarded with information. Then given two choices. The white fridge with good food. Or the black fridge, same shit we are used to, misery and inevitable death!" Betty hoped she was getting through to her friend.

"Hey you, fuckers! Milo was lost to the pain of withdrawals. It was tearing his mind and body apart. He had already ransacked his room looking for an exit, but he concluded they must have sealed his way out. He decided to let the others in on his secret.

"Hey guys! I found a way out! It's behind your refrigerators! I made it out and was in Betty's room and got drugs from her fridge. These people must have figured it out and sealed up my exit and took my stash!" Betty was mortified.

"Wait, what? Back up to the part where you said you were in my room." But Bam interrupted her.

"He said there is a way out, Betty! Everyone check!" As they all scrambled to find an exit, Dr. van Hook and Marie watched but were not concerned. They knew they couldn't escape. All inside access was removed. It was an oversight that was fixed before something worse occurred. Pookie was singing again.

Burn rubber on me, Charlie. Oh no, no, no.
You told me to go up the block
To get you a strawberry pop
When I came back to the flat
You had burned rubber out the back
I went to closet and saw no clothes
All I saw was hangers and poles
I went to the phone and called your mother
And told me that you had burned rubber on me, Charlie,
Oh no, no, no, no, no, no, no, no, no, no, no.

Bam lifted the black refrigerator above his head and threw it across the room. The crash echoed through the facility.

"Don't worry, Marie, they'll give up eventually."

Janine just sat on the bed drinking a coke taking in all that she learned since she woke. Messages on the wall. Colored refrigerators. Drugs and liquor. All her friends were here. Did Blake make it here too? She hadn't heard his voice chime in with the rest. She could feel the need for alcohol through every cell of her body. She didn't think she would have an issue with the drugs, but the alcohol, that was a different story. She had been drinking since she was 13. Her coping mechanism for a traumatized life. A message on the wall caught her eye.

"Forgive others"

"Forgive yourself."

Milo screamed.

CHAPTER 44

Driving while looking in the rearview mirror, not looking forward, is a special skill reserved only for those high on cocaine. Blake wasn't a paranoid guy, but he was on his way to Galveston with a few grams of cocaine and that made him hyper-vigilant. The past several weeks played out in his mind. He knew all his choices had led him to this moment. Before, he was able to bury deep thoughts of being broke and homeless.

But now, the burial site was being exhumed and he cursed himself. He was no idiot but the stuff he did was stupid and insane. He knew he had issues with drugs but didn't think he was that bad. Up until now, he wasn't poor, wasn't living under a bridge and didn't rob or steal. So, he wasn't that bad right? Not like real druggies and criminals that shoot dope and rob people. But every time things got worse, he would lower the bar until he was limbo dancing with the Devil in Hell and even the Devil was scared.

"Oh shit!" The flashing lights interrupted Blake's deep reflections. He didn't see the police car until the lights were on. The cop was coming up fast from behind. Blake slowed down and started to pull over. His heart was beating so hard and his head pounding like a bass drum in a high school band. The sirens were silent to him as he was focused on all the bullshit he would tell the officer. The red and blue shone all around him as the police car was within a few feet. As Blake was pulling on to the shoulder and applying the brakes to a crawl, the cop suddenly accelerated and veered around him, nearly clipping his rear end. He drove off, obviously to another call.

"What the fuck?" Blake hyperventilated then, passed out. Somehow, he had put the car in park and awoke with his eyes darting in every direction. All clear! He put the Vette into drive and continued his journey to the beach. Galveston, where it all started. Where his life began to have meaning. Where he met his wife. X wife.

This place was so enchanting to him. He crossed the long bridge to the island and stopped at a McDonald's to piss. He wasn't hungry but bought a coke because his throat burned from the cocaine draining from his sinuses. His face felt numb as well. He walked into the bathroom and closed the stall door. He dropped his pants and pretended to take a crap. He dug into his pocket and pulled out one of his baggies. He dipped his key in and brought it to his nose.

The door to the restroom opened. Footsteps. He froze. Someone was at the urinal. They let out a huge fart that sounded painful. He was too scared to laugh. Now they were washing their hands. Gone. He gasped. He had been holding his breath and spilled the bump on the end of his key.

"Damn it." He whispered. He dipped for another and sniffed. Dipped again, sniffed. Several more times until he used up a gram in a couple of minutes. He tore open the baggie with excitement like a child on Christmas day. He licked the baggie clean and dropped it in the toilet. He sat there for a minute more waiting for this fresh introduction of accelerant to hit his system.

Mmmm. There it is. Renewed by the overload of endorphins, he jumped up, pulled up his pants and shot out of the stall. Holy shit. The image in the mirror was unrecognizable. His once 175 lbs frame was now 140 lbs. Eyes bugged out from a combination of starvation and too many drugs. Eyes dilated, and the once hazel color hidden by black. Dark circles plagued him as well. He had never grown a beard but now it was a white and brown patchy mess. Didn't they have dye for your beard? He chuckled at the thought. He had to fix a shitload of problems in his life before he worried about his appearance. He realized he smelled bad. More than that, he smelled like a Pasadena refinery at four o'clock in the morning. If no one saw his Vette, they would have thought he was a homeless junkie. Wait a minute.

"I am a homeless junkie." He said to his reflection. "A homeless junkie loser!" He walked out of the bathroom and got into his car. He sipped his soda and felt better now that he was high as hell. But the enormity of his situation was weighing him down. Only one solution. Get drunk and do more drugs. That's the answer! How crazy his rationalizations were. Maybe he could rent an electric scooter like the first time he met his wife. Or he could walk up and down the Seawall. The dashboard read 101* so forget that.

Once he got to Seawall Boulevard, he turned right and drove further. He pulled over in a Jack in a Box parking lot and fished the rest of his stash out of his suitcase. He was careful to look around for cops. He went inside the restroom to repeat his previous task. This time he was uninterrupted. He sat there for at least 30 minutes trying to plan his day, but his racing thoughts kept driving around the endless track of confusion in his brain. Damn, he was fucked up. He took another bump. He started to stand up but realized his legs had fallen asleep.

"Shit!" He managed before he fell back down on the toilet. He unbent and bent and rubbed his legs until the feeling returned. He stood, disposed of his baggie and left. He returned to his car and once started, he allowed the air conditioning to cool his overheated body. He was sweating so much, and he needed to slow his heartbeat. Too much coke. He needed alcohol, he reminded himself. That will slow down the speed in his blood so he can do more!

He drove to a familiar bar that he and his x-wife frequented. This one had an outside pool. They had so many wonderful memories there. It takes a special kind of crazy to lose such an incredible woman. He wasn't the first man to let a woman slip away. Slip? No, he drove her away. Truth be told, she should have left long before things got out of hand. But she endured his torturous treatment. She tried to reach him even as she was leaving. She had said to get sober, and she would return. But the alcohol and the drugs were more important. He tossed away the unhealthy thoughts and ordered a drink. Good thing he had on sunglasses so the bartender couldn't see how wasted he was.

He looked out of place. Everyone wore shorts, some patrons had no shirts. Women in various styles of swimwear. He was fully dressed in jeans and a button-down shirt. No matter. He downed the beer and ordered another one. He found an open spot at a high-top table with an umbrella and made a beeline for the shade. Once seated, he finished the beer and asked a waitress for a shot of whiskey with a third beer as a chaser. He was starting to feel drunk. Much better now. Time for a bump! He did a few in the bathroom and returned to his table. Ordered another shot and another beer. The music was playing some 80's hit song,

Come on Eileen,
Oh, I swear (what he means)
Aah come on,
let's take off everything,
That pretty red dress
Eileen (tell him yes)
Ah, come on, let's
Ah, come on, Eileen, Please

His wife loved that song. She would grab his hand and want to dance to it, even though she didn't know how. But when they were hip to hip, they moved magically in perfect sync. The memory brought a smile to Blake's face. As he got up to go to the bathroom again, the combination of drugs, liquor, and heat must have been too much. His vision clouded and he fell, face first on the concrete shattering the bottle of beer in his hand. When he came to, people were asking him if he was okay. He sat up slowly, against their wishes, and saw that he was bleeding. Someone offered him a napkin and he wiped the bloody abrasion on his face. Someone was calling an ambulance, which meant the police! Shit! He had to go! Blake, pull it together now! He stood and steadied himself with those around him and walked to the bar. He retrieved his wallet from his back pocket and used a credit card with a small remaining balance to pay his tab. He headed to the exit as the paramedics were coming in. He ducked his head and passed right by.

Blake went back to his car and tried to catch his snap. The A.C. felt good while he decided what to do next. He was in no condition to drive, so he watched the ambulance leave and walked to another bar. Once again, he found a restroom stall and snorted until the intoxication was erased by the cocaine. He came out of the restroom a new man! He smiled and even greeted a few people. He bought a beer with the little money that was left on his card.

Later in the restroom, he met a few guys that were hip to the fact that Blake was high as a kite. Most addicts can identify each other in some mysterious way. They asked him for a bump, and he was too high to care and welcomed the company. He shared his stash and made new friends.

They bought Blake beer and he listened to all their bullshit stories. As long as they were buying, he would have fun. Plus, he had plenty of coke to keep the party rolling. At some point, Blake blacked out and left the bar. He was wandering around the Seawall oblivious to his surroundings. The next thing he knew, he was sitting on the Seawall, feet dangling over the edge, facing the water and heard sirens. Lots of sirens. Police. E.M.S. Fire. How could he differentiate between them? Why were these sirens playing this God-awful symphony in his head? Where were they going? Why were they getting closer?

CHAPTER 45

Milo was blinded by rage and continued to destroy his room. The walls were blood stained from his knuckles. He tried to punch through, but the walls were made of something stronger than his will. Bloody shadows were cast from the flickering messages. Some were broken. He thought of drunk fireflies on a mission to drive him insane. But he was already there. Crazed from having made it to the addict's heaven and tasted its glory, then having God's sweet ambrosia ripped from his lips. He was like a wild animal when first imprisoned in a cage and looking for any opportunity to tear his captors to shreds and devour them. He was shaking uncontrollably, and he sounded like a banshee when he roared. His shrieks echoed eerily through the halls.

"I will kill you all! Do you hear me?" The others did their best to block him out. His mind was screaming with alternatives of escape. There had to be another way. Think Milo, think. But it was hard to concentrate on anything because his head throbbed like he had been kicked by a mule.

He was not used to suffering through withdrawals this long and threw up several times in the last hour. In thirty years, he had experienced it twice. Once in jail, and this place. If he tried to explain the pain associated with withdrawals, he would say it felt like someone was inside his body with a sledgehammer trying to beat their way out. Smashing every fiber of his being in the process, he thought it was worse than death. He knew his captors were watching, so he raised his bloody fists in the air and gave a horrifying scream.

Dr. Van Hook was watching Milo while Marie typed away. She stopped to watch the monitor.

"What are we going to do, doctor?"

"At this point Marie, all we can do is wait. Mr. Milo is going through extreme withdrawals and is exhibiting violent tendencies. His aggression should subside in a few days. I hope."

"As long as he lives through it, doctor."

"Um, yes. I believe he will. Most addicts have put themselves through so much punishment that their evolved resilience is remarkable." Marie recalled her husband seeming to bounce back from a bad relapse only to succumb to the cravings again and again.

"Do you think we should monitor him more closely after his heart attack?"

"Yes, Marie. And if he has another one, we will have to place him in our emergency room."

"Under restraints, right?"

"Of course, Marie. Of course.

"I'm worried about Milo guys." Janine was listening to the destruction and his ear-piercing screams.

"Janine." Bam tried to console her.

"Don't worry about Milo. We tried to help that fool. He made his choice."

"Like we all have." Shouted Mike. Betty joined in.

"Guys don't do that! We all have to help each other!"

"He doesn't want our help!" Mike was adamant about Milo giving up and that there was no hope for him. Bam agreed.

"He's right, Betty!"

"Isn't there anything we can do?" Janine was such a caring person, that's why Betty loved her.

"He can make it through this, but he will have to make the choice for himself. We can listen and offer support, but he must choose the path." Betty and the others had learned much since their stay in the facility and Janine sounded willing, so Betty continued.

"He must kick the drugs and put down the bottle. Although it seems they took away his black fridge, he is still craving and not wanting to listen to us or the messages. Without hope, we can talk until we are blue in the face, and it won't matter." Pookie was slurring his words as he spoke.

"H-h-o-ope? I h-o-p-e they never run out of Mad Dog 20/20 cuz' this shit be hittin'!" Pookie's drunken laughter caught everyone off guard. Mike was concerned for Pookie.

"Say, Pookie? Leave that shit alone, man. We got a chance to do something different. This place is giving us a choice."

"I know that, fool! My choice is to kick back and enjoy myself!"

"Come on, Pookie!"

"No, fool! Listen, the food is great, and the liquor is free! What more could a brother want?" The question was, of course, rhetorical. But Betty offered an answer anyway.

"What more, Pookie? How about freedom from the prison of our minds! I don't think they will keep us locked up forever. But if we don't choose a new way to live when we get out? We will continue to be trapped by our addictions! More, you ask? The more is the chance to finally enjoy life without being messed up all the time! Live without killing ourselves!"

"Yea, Pookie, I haven't felt this good in years!" Bam took over.

"In retrospect, I haven't felt anything because I've been numb! I have been killing myself to kill the pain! Now, I only want to live, fool. The pain isn't my focus. Besides having less pain to deal with, I focus on hope." Pookie was incredulous.

"Hope? What you hoping for? You gonna get out and get a good job? Get a good woman? Shit, you been on the street almost as long as I have and you ain't gonna get nothin' you hope for, fool!"

"Maybe, maybe not. But at least I won't be screwed up. And that is the first step." Mike jumped back in.

"You gotta close that fridge first bro and start thinking. Pay attention to the signs. Milo may be too far gone but you're not."

"And we are here for you, Pookie!" Betty said.

"Man, this is all I know. This is all I know." Pookie continued to drink.

Milo had blocked them goody two shoes out of his mind. He was grinding his teeth and was fully clothed in the shower. The water was cold, but he didn't mind. The cold helped to soothe the pain deep in his soul.

As the water ran down his face, he reviewed every single memory he had since he first arrived. Secret entrances. Refrigerators. Someone had come in. Someone had gone out. How would they come in again? They had to refill the fridge at some point. How did I get in here in the first place? Drag me through the pipe chase? That doesn't make sense. There has to be another way in and out of here. He heard the others search for an exit only to give up after a few minutes. Now they ignored him, so he returned the favor. In their defense, he remembered yelling some crazy shit. Fuck them. He didn't need them anyway. He didn't need anybody. All he needed was to get high.

"I don't need anyone." He muttered to himself.

CHAPTER 46

"**M**ilo has seemed to calm down, Doctor." Marie was watching the monitor in Milo's room.

"Yes, Marie. What do you think of the other's progress?"

"Well, doctor, I think it is amazing! They are coming together in support of each other. They are showing genuine concern. They are from different backgrounds but brought together by addiction and now they are being delivered by your program. I am so hopeful for….." Her voice trailed off. She was hopeful for them but what about her husband? Could this program save him one day? Or would he be lost like Milo. Or worse, would he die like the first two patients? Dr. Van Hook must have read her mind.

"Don't worry, Marie. We'll do our best for your husband. Sooner or later, we will find him. He will have the same opportunity as the other patients to choose. I Hope he chooses life."

"But what if he…." She didn't finish her sentence. Instead, her frightening thoughts took her to a dark place. She imagined her husband overdosing in an alley. Then she saw him wandering the streets homeless. Another nameless face having a psychotic break, doomed to live in psychiatric hospitals and die in the streets. A man with no hope and no destination on this Earth. On a journey to misery and death. She shuddered.

"I hope we find him, Doctor."

"We will, Marie. We will."

CHAPTER 47

Sirens reaching a crescendo helped Blake return from his blackout. They stopped, and his blurry vision allowed him to slightly watch the waves gently wash ashore. People were on the sand thirty feet away standing, staring. Are they staring at me? Blake felt pain. A stinging feeling on both forearms. He looked down and noticed what appeared to be a piece of a torn beer can in his right hand.

"What the fuck?" Blake shouted. The piece of jagged aluminum beer can was covered in blood and so were his arms. The blood was staining the concrete where he was sitting. He dropped the makeshift knife and looked at his arms. There were several slashes across his veins from elbow to wrist. The blood looked as if it were filling his palms. Terror filled his soul and he slowly stood. He turned around to the sight behind him. People, everywhere, standing in the middle of the street. Some were holding cell phones, some holding their children. The ones with no conscience filmed the social media event of the pitiful man bleeding profusely from each arm. Eyes wide with fear, Blake looked like a man interrupted during an attempted suicide. Not by those that wished to help but those trying to get a million views on the internet.

Some even covered their little one's eyes. Blake did not notice the police officers, paramedics and firefighters approaching from either side. Blake managed to speak.

"It's not what it looks like, I mean I, I don't remember anything. I wasn't trying to…" He faltered. It was absolutely what it looked like. Except he wasn't aware of what he was doing during his blackout. A common occurrence for thousands of alcoholics and addicts. They check out from the here and now and travel somewhere in time while their brain switches to auto pilot. Then the real fun begins. So many end up in a D.W.I. fatality. The statistics are staggering.

"Take it easy, buddy." One of the officers was talking to him trying to get closer. As the officer took another step, Blake's fight or flight instinct kicked in and he leaped off the Seawall. The Galveston Seawall was built after the deadliest hurricane to hit the Texas coast in 1900. It was there to help block storm surges from taking lives and flooding the businesses across the street. In mild storms, it often worked. The wall was the outer edge of the street facing the ocean and was approximately eight feet high above the sandy beach. He landed and rolled, then jumped to his feet and ran. He turned to see his pursuers run a few feet to the concrete stairs. Why didn't he take the stairs?

"Dumbass." He mumbled to himself. He kept running until he came to a jetty, a giant outcrop of stones protruding from the beach about 300 feet in the water. People were watching the waves crash against the stones. Some fished while others watched the scene unfold. They had heard all the commotion and retreated to the outer edges of the jetty to let Blake run by with his posse in pursuit. A few officers slipped and fell on the wet stones and cursed and yelled for him to stop. The people on the outer edges were helped back to shore by the firefighters. As far as the police knew, the call on the radio said some homeless man was cutting his wrists while singing "Come on Eileen." They only wanted to help. It was almost funny, but not to Blake. He was terrified and just wanted to get away.

"Stay back! Don't come any closer!" Blake had his hands up like he was a sorcerer with special powers to stop the police from taking him into custody. It seemed to work for the moment, and they froze in their tracks. The officer closest to him spoke in a firm but gentle tone.

"Hey, buddy. It's okay. We are here to help. Let us help you."

"Stay back!" He shouted once again. They took another step toward Blake in unison. Now, they were holding up their hands.

"It's okay. Relax. We are going to get you some help.

"I said stop or I'll jump!" At this the officers froze once again. They shared a look among each other. A couple of E.M.S. had joined the group of police and tried their best.

"Hey, let's stop that bleeding for you, then talk. What do you say?" Blake looked down at the inside of his forearms. Bloody cuts with white jagged lines. Damn, that is going to leave some ugly scars.

"I said stay back or I'll jump!" Another paramedic spoke,

"Look, it's only water. It won't hurt you, but we are concerned about those cuts. Let us stop the bleeding and if you want to go swimming after that, no problem." At that last comment the nearest officer tried to grab Blake. Blake sensed the action and jumped off the edge of the jetty. Even though it was 100* outside, it was shockingly cold when he hit the water and submerged. He broke the surface with a gasp and choked on salt water. Even though he had been up for days, he was able to swim. About a mile out from shore he noticed a buzzing sound. Two jet skis were approaching and there were lifeguards on surfboards. What was this a Baywatch rescue? No pretty girls? He laughed at this and choked on salt water again. In the middle of his coughing, a lifeguard jumped off one of the jet skis and tried to rescue Blake. The problem was, Blake didn't want to be rescued. Blake avoided the capture and submerged only to reappear several feet away. His rescuers had formed a circle around him attempting to corral him. He submerged once again and popped out of the circle.

"Stop trying to grab me!" He managed with mouthfuls of water. They reached for him, he submerged. Reached. Submerge. From an observer above, this must have looked like some kind of twisted game of "Whack-a-Mole." But the mole was too elusive. The lifeguards, seeing this was going nowhere, decided to talk to Blake.

"Say, dude. What's your name?" Blake stopped and tread water.

"Blake, now leave me alone!"

"He'll get tired eventually." One of the lifeguards said to his coworker. Blake overheard and spoke.

"That's what you think! I used to be on a swim team!" Another lifeguard offered.

"We can see that! You're in pretty good shape, dude!"

"You got that right! Now leave me alone!" Blake resumed his swimming. The water was calmer a mile offshore. An occasional mild swell lifted him and the lifeguards a few feet before setting them down gently.

"Where are you going, Blake?"

"See that oil rig out there?" A lifeguard responded.

"That's like ten miles away, bro."

"I know but I can make it!"

"I believe that, but you should let us help you first."

"I don't need help from anyone, now leave me alone!" Blake's swimming impressed these seasoned lifeguards, and even on surfboards, they were hard-pressed to keep up. The ones that had previously ditched the jet skis swam back to retrieve them. They headed out further to create a blockade in the hopes of stopping Blake.

"Hey!" One of the lifeguards spoke with real concern in his voice.

"Did you know that sharks can smell blood in the water with a ratio of one part per billionth?" Blake stopped cold in the water.

"Oh shit. I didn't think about that."

"Yeah, we are out here over two miles now. Let us help you, buddy. In reality, we are all in danger. We just want to help." After a minute or so of treading water, the lifeguards patiently waiting, Blake pondered his options. Go to jail for being a psycho, terrorizing beachgoers, or eaten by a hungry shark.

"Shit!" Blake shouted. Although subconsciously Blake tried to kill himself, the thought of being torn to shreds by shark teeth did not appeal to him. No matter how shitty his life was.

"Okay, okay. But I'll swim back by myself. Don't try to grab me!"

"Okay, bro."

"Yea, you got it!" Relieved, they all agreed, and in unison, they turned and began the two and a half miles back to the beach. About halfway through, Blake ran out of adrenaline and began to fatigue. He tread water once again and called out to the nearest lifeguard. The lifeguard stopped and turned around on the surfboard and asked,

"What's up?" Blake had been eyeing the red flotation device strapped across his back.

"Do you think I can hold on to that floaty thing and you help pull me?" Embarrassment in his voice.

"I'm getting a little tired now."

"Sure, bro." He tossed it several feet between them, and Blake thankfully grabbed hold.

"All right, here we go." The lifeguard began to pull him behind his surfboard like a tow truck would pull an old broken down car on the side of the road. Blake kicked his feet to help along. He was so exhausted, the only thing keeping him going was his pride. More like pseudo pride. His lungs were screaming, and his breath was labored as they were only 100 yards from the shore. He realized he had stopped kicking. The young lifeguard didn't seem to notice and continued his tow, all the while conversing with his comrades about the upcoming parties on the beach.

"Yea, bro, Natalie really wants me, and we are going to get drunk tonight!"

"Dude, she's so hot!"

"Tell me about it!" When Blake realized he could stand, he did so and noticed there were more than a dozen police officers waiting along the shoreline. They were standing just shy of the tide so their shiny boots wouldn't get wet. Most of them looked formidable with their hands placed on their hips. They removed everyone from the immediate area, but the crowds formed around the outer perimeter. Blake could see hundreds of people gathered on the Seawall catching a glimpse of the police chase. Someone from the crowd shouted, "World Star!"

He saw a couple of news cameras and a helicopter was directly above him. An old James Cagney movie flashed into his head, "Top of the world ma!" Yea, now he was famous, but not for anything worthwhile. This must be what hitting bottom felt like. He slowly eased closer to the edge of the water. Out of the corner of his eye he spotted an ambulance a couple hundred yards away on the Seawall. He bolted and ran as fast as he could for the ambulance. Cops were confused for a few seconds wondering where in the hell this nutcase was going. They ran after him. He took the concrete stairs two at a time and practically flew into the back of the ambulance. He startled the E.M.T.'S sitting inside.

"What the hell?"

"I'm sorry, help me please!"

"Oh, you're the guy that," The medic's voice trailed off, but his eyes silently spoke as he focused on the fresh cuts to Blake's arms.

"Yea, I'm him." Head hung low in shame. Blake took a peek out the door like a rabbit looking for a pesky fox. Shit. They were coming for him. Well of course they were coming, stupid.

"Can we hurry and go to the hospital?" The medic seeing the fear in Blake's eyes said,

"Look buddy, everything is going to be okay. Those cops are not going to hurt you. I mean, as long as you are not violent. You're not violent, are you?"

"No, no, no I'm not."

"Okay. Good, just cooperate with us and let us get this i.v. started and get your wounds cleaned up." They took his silence as compliance.

"What did you cut yourself with?" Blake looked down again. He looked like a shamed puppy that made a mess on the floor.

"Um, I think a ripped-up beer can?"

"I see, those ain't pretty but I don't think they'll need stitches. The bleeding looks about stopped. They'll still scar something awful though. The other E.M.T. spoke.

"But don't you worry, we'll take good care of you." As they were taping the i.v. needle to his arm to prevent jostling enroute to the hospital, a large black police sgt. appeared in the doorway to the ambulance. He was obese and did not appreciate running in the summer heat several hundred yards in the sand, then up a long flight of stairs. The scowl on his face said as much. He was trying to talk but couldn't seem to catch his breath. One of the medics, seeing the Sgt. in distress, jumped out to offer him aid.

"Are you okay, officer?" The officer, annoyed, pushed away and approached Blake more closely. He started to speak through gasps of air.

"What…is..(gasp)..   the…deal?...Why..(gasp)..are you …..(gasp).. running?" Blake was a little frightened and didn't know how to answer.

"Hey, Sgt., could you give us a minute to attend to his wounds? He's compliant and poses no threat at the moment.

"Yea, okay." The Sgt. Stepped back and used this pause to catch his breath. Blake thought the officer was going to have a heart attack. Great, now I've killed a cop! The sgt. did not avert his gaze the entire time and his hand rested on his holster as if to say, "Try running again and this bullet will catch you." But Blake was done, and he knew it. His running was over. Not just from the law but from himself. From life. He felt defeated. The cop finally caught his breath and his tone changed to a more formal, almost gentle tone.

"Son, what's going on with you today?" Blake took a moment to reflect on the time prior to the blackout then the moment he "came to" on the Seawall. He thought about his wife leaving him and it was too much for his fragile psyche to handle. He began to sob. Barely coherent, he told his story. Starting with his wife leaving him and diving headfirst into his despair. He, of course, downplayed the drug and alcohol use for fear of legal trouble but hinted at a little "partying" to cope. This pitiful explanation went on for several minutes until the sgt. had heard enough and held up his hands.

"Okay, okay, son. Look. Look. Calm down. Stop crying. It's going to be fine." Blake's rant subsided and he continued.

"Seeing how you didn't hurt anyone, although you did scare the hell out of plenty of tourists. You seem harmless, except, well, to yourself. So, I'm not taking you to jail."

"Oh, thank you, thank you!" Blake managed.

"But." Oh, here it comes. The "but" Blake thought.

"But, I am taking you to a psychiatric hospital." He paused to see Blake's reaction.

"Now, you could protest and even go to a hearing in seventy two hours to plead your case against being committed because that is the law. But you pretty much showed you need help here today. So, why don't you let me help you?"

It didn't take Blake long to think this offer through. Go to jail or to some place to get help and a decent night's sleep. Safe and sound from his own destructive tendencies.

"Okay. Thank you, officer. Thank you." Blake lay back on the gurney and closed his eyes. The hum of the diesel engine soothed him as he imagined the journey to a heavenly destination. That's where his mind took him for he had literally been to hell with the devil inside and rescued by Baywatch. He laughed and one of the medics turned to look and whispered to the other,

"I think he's lost his shit."

"Maybe so. At least this one is not trying to kick our ass like the last one."

"Yea, right. Hopefully the doctors can reach this guy."

"Maybe." Blake couldn't hear what they were saying. All he could hear was his wife, x-wife telling him to, "Choose me or the drugs."

CHAPTER 48

Janine was shaking. Like the others, her head hurt but she had only thrown up once. She sat up in bed and the hairs on the back of her neck stood up. The black refrigerator. She couldn't move. Her being frozen was a good thing. Eventually, she would need to get out of bed and use the restroom, eat, shower, etc. She got out of bed and tried to occupy her mind. She got a coke and ate some yogurt, then made a sandwich. She jumped in the shower and let the warm water trickle down her petite frame. Her mind wandered. She pictured Blake washing her back. She saw him driving away to Galveston. She scolded herself for not asking to go with him on his trip. He might have said yes. She envisioned walking hand in hand on the sandy beach. Barefoot, smiling and singing. She sang out loud.

She says we've got to hold on to what we've got
It doesn't make a difference if we make it or not
We've got each other and that's a lot for love
We'll give it a shot
Wo-oah We're halfway there
Wo-oah Livin' on a prayer
Take my hand we'll make it I swear
Wo-oah Livin' on a prayer!

Bam, Betty and Mike joined the chorus. Janine started crying as she got out of the shower. It was a soft, weak cry so the others didn't hear.

"Don't stop girl! That was great!" Betty always enjoyed Janine's singing.

"You've got such a great voice, girl!"

"Yeah, she does!" Mike agreed. Mike was still singing Living on a prayer. Milo screamed.

"Shut the hell up assholes! Bon Jovi sucks! Give me some Black Sabbath, bitches!" Bam shouted back.

"Shut the hell up, jerk!" Janine was standing in front of the black fridge. Although the towel was draped around her, she was still dripping on the floor. She closed her eyes and imagined what was inside. Wine coolers? Her favorite. Beer? Close second.

"Janine? Janine?" each of her friends were calling her name.

"Are you okay, Janine?"

"The black fridge should be there by now. Please study the messages!"

"They will help you and so will we!"

"Keep talking, Betty." Bam knew the importance of having people in your corner. When he was a professional fighter, he had people he could count on to give him advice on how to beat his opponent. The opponent this time was Janine's cravings and the black fridge. He felt this worked the same way. Inside the Black fridge wasn't the real opponent though. Drugs and alcohol weren't the real problem. Using was just a symptom of a greater issue. Those without addictive natures found this concept impossible to comprehend. Just stop using they would say. Quit. Give it up. For them it was simple. For addicts and alcoholics, the opponent was themselves. The fight was in their mind. That is why doctors declared this a disease. But how do you fight yourself? More than that, how do you win? The mind of an addict says it's not that bad. I can stop anytime. Or, I won't use that much this time and I'll just drink a few. Most of the time it ends up in disaster. The battle of the mind is the greatest war mankind has ever fought. And until each and every one chooses a different path; the path of destruction is the road most traveled. Bam studied the messages on the walls. His daily ritual. Like his daily physical routine, he exercised his mind. He read the information that was provided day and night. It fed him on a deeper level than any refrigerator full of food or drugs could. And most importantly, he had people in his corner. This Motley Crew of misfits that were his friends, were his lifeline. They supported him. They supported each other. Now, Bam was speaking to Janine.

"Hey, Janine! I know it's rough and you're probably going through the shakes or nauseousness or headaches. Hell, I had all three when I first got here! But we are here for you. Choose life. Choose joy. Let your past go and whatever has your mind thinking you need that shit to cope. Life is about choices, Janine! Up until this point, our choices sucked.

Our wrong paths are most often chosen because of pain and resentment. Not so much the physical, but the mental stuff we've been through. We have numbed ourselves so long with chemicals it's the only way we know. But the good news is we don't have to live that way again! This is your chance to live. To feel alive for the first time in years! I mean, you're alive. You woke up. You're breathing, but right now all you can think about is using. That's not living. That's surviving another day of misery by drowning your problems so you don't have to feel. But in life we must feel! Love, pain, joy, sadness. All of it!

By yourself the task is daunting, but with each other, we can win! Pookie was listening to Bam's inspirational speech and started laughing.

"Man, Bam, you sound like one of those late-night info-mercials! It was good but still sounded like bullshit! But still makes sense I guess." Mike shouted at him.

"Shut up, Pookie! You may not care about nobody, but we are trying to help!"

"Fuck all of you! Give me some shit!" Milo was in full withdrawal. Since he woke from his heart attack, he was bouncing off the walls. He was shaking uncontrollably and the need for heroin had his bones screaming for more. The doctor prescribed suboxone, a med for heroin users, and it was in the white refrigerator. It wasn't enough to numb the pain. He hurt so bad he couldn't read the messages on the wall.

"Go away, Milo!" Bam was angry that Milo had interrupted his heartfelt speech to Janine. Thoughts of his mother and the helplessness he felt while holding her lifeless body charged him with the desire to help those with his affliction. After his mother's death, he had done so much damage to the remainder of his family that the need to make amends was overwhelming. To anyone and everyone. Somehow, he forgave himself and God. God, for taking his mother. Focusing on the good memories of her helped in his healing. He did all of this with finding gratitude. A recurring word that flashed before his eyes. That word is impossible to practice for an addict that lives on pain and resentment every day. Those two feelings are nutrients to a person that needs to survive being imprisoned by their own mind. But once they deal with those destructive feelings, they are paroled from the barbed wire cage that they themselves built.

"There is a wayout, Janine." Bam continued the attempt to reach her.

"The way out is making a choice. As long as you have breath in your lungs, you can choose."

"Choose, Janine!" Betty implored her.

"Choose life!" Mike joined in.

"You can do it girl! Let all that bad shit you feel go and choose!" Janine was still standing in front of the black refrigerator. Still shaking. She threw up on top of the fridge, wiped her mouth and chin and cried. Her silent cry wasn't for sadness but for fear. She was terrified. What lay behind the door of this fridge had been her answer to all of life's problems. Everything could be washed away in her mind that reminded her of the pain she felt. Even if it was temporary. Anything was better than guilt, shame and worthlessness. How does she let that go? How does she forgive the horrible people that ruined her innocent childhood? She turned around for a second and looked above her bed. The Serenity Prayer was brighter than usual. Marie, of course, had been observing and turned up the brightness of the lights. Janine read silently.

"God," she stopped believing in God a long time ago.

"Grant me the serenity." She lost her train of thought. The siren song of that black refrigerator was calling. The sound was so beautiful to her mind. As she faced it once again, she said out loud,

"I'll just have one drink. Just one to calm my nerves. I can do that." The mind's ability to blatantly lie to an addict is so terrifying because ninety nine percent of the time, the addict believes the lie. Janine opened the black fridge.

CHAPTER 49

Blake was helped to his room in the Psychiatric Hospital. He had a roommate that was standing in the corner facing the wall. He was talking to himself. At the sound of Blake sitting on the old spring mattress, Blake's roommate turned abruptly and looked upon the new arrival.

"It's the Monkeypox. "Blake was confused at this topic of discussion.

"Excuse me?"

"Monkeypox, you know. First it was Covid, now Monkeypox."

"Uh, huh." Blake was trying to stay neutral, not knowing where he was going with it.

"It's the government, man!" Blake's new companion was about five foot two, short by any standard for a man. He was bald and had huge eyes that were wide and exaggerated as he shared his thoughts on the world's conspiracy theories.

"You see, they want to instill fear in us, man." He talked like a 1960's hippy.

"It's a way to control us! Scare us into submission! But I'm onto them! That's why they locked me up here. They say I'm crazy! Paranoid. But I know their game!" Blake didn't know how to answer this obviously distressed man.

He wouldn't necessarily say he was crazy, which was a derogatory word in this day and age, but after all this was a psychiatric hospital. The man clearly had mental issues. So, what did that say about Blake? He was right here along with him.

Yes, Blake had problems, but was he crazy? What he did was a little crazy, but he blacked out right? Yes, of course, I was blacked out, he thought. Replaying the events that led up to this disturbed him. They had bandaged his self-inflicted wounds and gave him a little morphine to calm his nerves. He was still buzzed from the narcotics, but it was a welcome change from all the cocaine and booze. He was brought out of his thoughts by his roomie's question.

"Uh, I'm sorry, what was that?"

"I asked what you did to end up with all of us crazy folk." Blake didn't answer right away. Seeing the hesitation, he introduced himself.

"I'm Joe." Blake took his hand.

"Blake." Joe looked at his bandages.

"Oh, I see. Life got pretty tough, huh? That's the government! I told you! They want us to be angry, scared, depressed and at war with other countries! War with each other and at war with ourselves!" Joe seemed animated now. Like a surreal cartoon character. Maybe a bald Yosemite Sam. He was walking around the room waving his hands, getting louder by the second.

"I'm telling you. They tried to push you to the brink, but you survived! You survived! You must not let them get to you! You must fight the urge!" At this, Joe grabbed

Blake's shoulders. He had to reach up to do so. He started to shake Blake. The nurses heard Joe's elevated voice and recognized the beginnings of an "episode" as they liked to call it. A large nurse walked in followed by an even larger orderly.

"Joe! No touching the other patients! You know the rules!" Joe continued his rant but let go of Blake and faced the nurse.

"I'm trying to warn my new friend! They tried to kill him, but he survived!" Joe slowly backed up as they got closer. The nurse and her co-worker looked like predators in the wild stalking their prey. Joe was walking backwards while darting his head side to side trying to find an escape. The prey, with nowhere to go, did what any animal backed into a corner would do. Scared and feeling threatened, he attacked. The speed at which Joe sprang into action was superhuman. He jumped up and landed in the nurse's arms with such force that she tumbled backwards knocking down the six foot 300 lb. man behind her. Her shriek combined with Joe's battle cry, alerted the rest of the staff.

He was all over them snarling and clawing like a wild animal. It must have been a requirement to work there to be so massive because three more orderlies with the appearance of NFL lineman stormed into the room. The last one to enter held a formidable syringe. Blake retreated to his bed, shocked by the events unfolding before him.

Once they untangled Joe, the syringe was thrust into his backside. Within thirty seconds he was a mumbling non-threat. Two of the large men picked Joe up with ease and carried him out to the "Time-out-room", a padded cell reserved for the more unruly patients. The nurse got up from the ground and addressed Blake.

"Are you okay, dear?"

"I'm fine. Are you okay?"

She looked like a mess. Hair in disarray. Face beet red and scratches on her cheek and arms. There was a trickle of blood on her lip.

"Don't you worry about me, sir! I was raised with four brothers." At that, she turned on her heels and walked out of the room. Just outside the door she turned around and offered.

"If you need anything, let me know." Blake needed a drink, but he thought better of asking for that. The bed was comfortable enough, but this was not where he wanted to be. What was it they said about a seventy two hour hearing? He had to get out of there.

He went to the nurse's station and asked for a way to contact patient legal services. She directed him to a wall of three phones. Next to the phones was a bulletin board with patients' rights, notices and other information required by law.

Problem was that most patients were so doped up they couldn't think straight, much less make a phone call. Various patients were walking around in circles or just stood staring at other worldly realms. Some spoke a lost language, having conversations with themselves. Some laughing, some crying. What in the hell am I doing here?

As he reached for the phone the white bandages spoke to him. The red spots of blood seeping through. The words he heard were, "You tried to kill yourself." Did he though? He was, after all, in the middle of a blackout. He liked to think he wasn't that much of a loser, but he wasn't able to kill himself properly. He could have done a better job, couldn't he? Maybe it was a subconscious cry for help? He picked up the phone to dial. Called the available attorneys for patients' rights. Set up a lawyer who would set a hearing. What would he say? Was it an accident? How do you accidentally try to kill yourself? It was a blackout and the wounds, for the most part, were superficial. No arteries were cut. Now, swimming out to sea was harder to explain. He was hot? Scared? That's it.

He was coming out of a blackout, and he was scared by the big bad police! Isn't everyone terrified of cops nowadays? Of course they were! He was drunk, high and blacked out. Therefore, he wasn't aware of what he was doing and was not responsible! He didn't hurt anyone and barely cut himself.

He was an alcoholic and an addict. He needed minor counseling and maybe some bullshit A.A. meetings where people met for coffee and shared their feelings. He had been invited once and thought they were a bunch of phonies and most of them were there to pick up lonely girls. But he would go to a meeting if it meant getting out of here!

He devised his plan for manipulating the court. His day in court came and he shared his idea with the lawyer.

His legal rep was not used to clients so coherent and articulate. They were usually manic or drugged up. Their appearance and speech always told the court to continue the order of committal for psychiatric treatment. But this guy, the attorney thought, might have a chance to get out. Never mind, he needed help. The lawyer was tired of his dead-end job and never winning a case.

Blake had cleaned up nicely, shaved and combed his hair. Still too skinny but looked more presentable than before. His attorney acted as if he was on stage and performed superbly. As Blake spoke slowly, he calmly explained that he was depressed but not suicidal. He came to Galveston to unwind and partied a little too much. The blackout was something he had never experienced before.

Awakened by sirens, he ran for fear of the police chasing him. He admitted to having a problem with alcohol and drugs and asked for assistance in getting sober. The judge didn't even ask him about the water rescue two miles out to sea.

By some miracle and the work of his lawyer, the court was merciful and ordered him to intensive outpatient therapy. Holy shit! He hid his excitement. Blake was about to be free from this nightmare. So he thought. Down the street from the hospital, the white van waited patiently for the last man on the list. His time had come.

CHAPTER 50

Doctor Van Hook implemented the ventilation sedative once again. He wanted to check on Milo and draw some blood. Although the pipe chase entrances had been sealed, Milo's blood couldn't lie. Doc had to be sure Milo wasn't getting drugs some other way.

He would try to get Milo fully detoxed and attempt one last time to help Milo make that life-or-death choice. Phase two was about to start, and they were running out of time. He doubted Milo would accept this final chance, but the doctor didn't want any more deaths on his conscience.

The orderlies cleaned up the rooms and filled the refrigerators. Mike, Bam and Betty were seemingly cured from their addictions. They had chosen the right path. As for Pookie, he pushed him out of his mind. As he drew two vials of blood from Milo, he remembered Janine going to the black fridge and opening the door. She had stood there for several minutes while the others encouraged her not to open it.

It was so fascinating to him how people came together in situations like these to help one another. To help in carrying one another's burdens. People, once self-centered and destructive, were finally clean and thought of others' wellbeing. But Janine drank. She sat in front of the black box of misery and cried and drank, then she passed out. Woke up drunk and tossed back a few more and passed out again.

The blood from Milo showed a small amount of narcotics left in his system. Good, detox. He went back to the control room to observe along with Marie and Matthew. Matthew was about to leave to get some much-needed sleep. Matt addressed the doctor as he entered the room.

"Hey, Doc." Van Hook was still upset at Matthew for his slip up, so he was curt and only made eye contact with Marie.

"Good morning, everyone." The sedative was starting to wear off and their main focus today was on Janine. She had not touched the narcotics but was drinking from the time she woke up until the time she passed out. She had not eaten. Van Hook instructed the orderlies to empty her black fridge in anticipation of Phase two. Last chance for everyone. God, he wished his son was here. Truth be told, he would have probably ended up like Milo, but he would have at least tried.

"Some people are just lost." At this remark Marie turned from the monitor.

"You think she's lost, doctor?"

"Um, no, I don't. I was just thinking out loud, Marie. I do not think she is as far gone as Milo, but this will be her final chance before Phase two." Marie experienced fear, anxiety, and excitement at that statement. Phase two. Where tech interaction starts. Not physical though, just communication with each patient through the intercom system.

They anticipated a lot of cursing and many questions. Once they answered the who, the what and the why's, the last chance therapy would start. If the last remaining patients couldn't be swayed at this point, well, that was it. The black refrigerator will be filled, then leave them to it. Marie shuddered at the thought. Phase two is almost here. One more patient.

CHAPTER 51

Janine woke up. She wiped the drool from her chin. She was lying in front of the black fridge. She brushed the crusty sleep from her eyes, popped her neck and reached for the door.

"Hey!" She managed, as the door was opened to emptiness. She jumped up and almost passed out from the dizziness and ran a few feet to the white fridge.

"No!" She shouted to the refrigerator full of food.

"Why?" She screamed and slumped to the floor.

"Why? Why are y'all doing this to me?" She managed between sobs. Marie was typing furiously to help Janine during this time with more messages on the wall. But Janine saw nothing.

Her eyes were like windows in a rainstorm. Only alcohol could bring sunshine to wash away the rain and the flowers of salvation to bloom once again. She drank a coke when the crying paused and deliberated her situation. She needed a drink, badly. No more alcohol meant the shakes and withdrawals would arrive soon. Fear gripped her like an assassin at her throat.

"Please. Please. One more bottle. That's all I need. Then, I'll stop! Please!" She shouted to the walls and her unseen captors.

"One more, please." The age-old cry from the alcoholic and addict. One more. Always one more and then they could stop. This fallacy was told a million times a day by millions of people and every single time, ten bottles was not enough and one bottle was too many. It was never enough for the alcoholic and only a psychic change would help.

Marie knew that's what the program helped create. Why, God damn it, did some people not get it? This both saddened and infuriated her. Partly, because she honestly cared for these patients. Mostly, because it diminished the hope that her husband might one day change. But she couldn't and wouldn't give up hope for him.

CHAPTER 52

They released Blake. His clothes were filthy when he arrived, so the hospital provided him with scrubs. While inside he was able to shower and shave so he was ready for the world. As he walked down the street he thought about his car. His precious Corvette. It's probably in a tow yard or stolen by now. He had no money. Good job Blake, he told himself.

He saw a man panhandling with a cardboard sign that read "anything helps". When he came within a few feet of the beggar, he asked Blake for some money.

"I wish I could, buddy." The man noticed the hospital band on Blake's wrist.

"Just get out of the nut house, huh?"

"Um, yea, I guess so. I got picked up at the beach." Looking at the bandages on his arms it seemed like a light bulb went off in the poor man's head and his eyes opened wide.

"Oh shit! You're the guy that swam to Mexico running from the Popo's! Dude! You're famous!"

"Well, I didn't quite make it to Mexico but um, yea."

"Wow! I ain't never met anyone famous before! You got any dinero for me man?" Blake stood there feeling uncomfortable. This disheveled and awful smelling man had more than he did. Blake had absolutely nothing.

"I'm sorry. I, uh, lost my wallet in the ocean. Lost my car somewhere too. Lost my place to live. Lost my wife. Everything." His voice was just a whisper at that last statement.

"Everything."

"Well, shit! I'm doing better than you!" At this, the man laughed. It was a big, loud toothless laugh. As horrible as the situation was, Blake joined in. He laughed for a few minutes straight. When his sides hurt and tears began to fall, the pair locked eyes and stopped.

Standing on the sidewalk, these two different people from two different worlds looked like they belonged together. The reality hit Blake like a hurricane powered wave against the Seawall. He had more in common with this vagabond than he cared to admit.

The panhandler was homeless, strung out and reeked of alcohol. Blake thought this man was better off than him because at least he had a source of income. At some point this man must have given up and succumbed to his addiction and became content to live like this. On the street hustling for change and deciding on a drink or food from day to day. Sleeping whenever or whenever he could. Is that what I have to do now? Is this my destiny? Blake played out the final days in his mind. As Blake walked away the man was still talking.

"There's a soup kitchen off of 33rd and a church on 15th ..."

He saw himself sleeping on a sidewalk on cardboard and an old lice ridden blanket. Eating out of garbage cans and begging for change to buy a beer. Could he hustle enough for cocaine like his buddy Mike? Those days are probably over. He needed a drink and a fat line of coke to top it off.

"Man, my life sucks." He said to no one in particular. He came upon a church. One of those old nineteenth century churches they spent too much money to build. Why did they do that, he asked himself. Wouldn't it have been better to spend the money on feeding the poor? The church was grand with huge stone steps and tall stained-glass windows depicting various bible scenes.

He wasn't in a blackout but felt like he was on autopilot. Blake walked up the steps and opened the eight foot tall, solid wooden doors. He hated church. Never went. His wife had tried to get him to go, but he refused. Now, in this house of God, he looked up at the thirty foot ceilings adorned with beautiful paintings. Again, he thought what a waste of money better spent on the homeless. The church was empty with rows and rows of long wooden pews.

A priest appeared and held his gaze for a moment. The priest motioned for Blake to approach the altar. Blake turned around hoping he was communicating with someone else. Nope. He's calling for me. Shit. Blake walked slowly towards the priest. A memory of fifth grade flashed in his mind. He was called up to the chalkboard to answer a mathematical equation of some sort. He was so nervous that he dropped the chalk, and picking it up, he bumped his head to the pleasure of his classmates that gave their approval with laughter. He ran out of the classroom and hid in the girl's restroom by mistake.

Later, when he was found, he had a hard time explaining why he was curled up in a ball inside a girl's bathroom stall. He shook away the memory. This wasn't grade school, this was a church. And this was a priest about to, what, impart some Godly wisdom to him?

He stopped five feet from the priest. At least sixty years old, short and a head full of white hair. He had large coke bottle style glasses that reminded Blake of a cartoon character he loved as a child. Mr. Magoo.

Blake looked above the altar at an eight foot crucifix of Jesus. The pain was unmistakable on his face. The word excruciating was created to explain the agonizing pain Christ must have felt while metal spikes were driven through his hands and feet. Combined with hanging on a cross there was no way to describe the sheer magnitude of what he felt up there. How could people downplay the enormity of that event to explain a bad day or headache?

"I haven't seen you here before my son." The statement woke Blake from his daydream.

"Um, no, father, is that what I call you? I, uh, never go to church."

"Well, my name is John if you're more comfortable with that."

"Okay, John. Yea, I." He lifted the arm with the hospital band on it and both arms were still bandaged.

"Oh, I think I, I recognize you from the news." Blake lowered his head as if to pray but the shame he felt was overwhelming. He cried. It was a silent cry. The priest placed his hand on Blake's shoulder.

"Son, you've come a long way. I don't mean you're trek from the hospital. I mean your journey through life. I only know what I saw on TV and where you are now. I don't know all the details that led up to your decision to do what you did and jump in that water. But whatever it was, you were obviously in great despair. And whenever we reach the point in our lives where we are too overwhelmed and we don't rely on God, well, the enemy comes for us. He'll trick us into thinking our only choice is to give up hope.

"Drown our sorrows in alcohol, drugs or," he paused for effect, "a vast ocean. But there is always a better choice than that son." Blake lifted his head to look in the priest's eyes. He wiped away his tears and focused on his words.

"You were delivered from the hand of the enemy. You may or may not believe in God, I don't know your faith. But he believes in you. Some people like to blame all the chaos in the world on the devil and that may be true. But I think most of the destruction comes from within each and every one of us."

Blake had never cared for the preachers that espoused the bible to get people's money to buy fancy cars and build big churches. But something about this humble old man spoke to his soul. If that was possible.

"As long as you wake up each day you have a choice."

"What choice father, um John?"

"You can choose life." The priest could see the puzzled look on Blake's face.

"Up until now you have been surviving your bad choices. I assume drugs, alcohol or both?" Blake nodded his head to affirm.

"More of the enemies lie. Every day you chose that path to numb the pain of life until it was unbearable and chose to, well, you chose the final journey. The journey you cannot come back from." Blake took all he was saying and processed it. God, enemy? He didn't know what to believe. The priest must have had divine understanding because he could see the doubt in Blake.

"Whether or not you believe what I say, the fact remains, you've been through hell, and you were burned, but you made it through! You made it back. Believe in divine intervention or not. Now, you are looking for something. Anything different. On this day in this church, you have a choice. I hope you choose wisely." And with that, he walked away reciting the Lord's Prayer.

'Our Father, who art in Heaven

Hallowed be Thy name'

He disappeared behind a door. Blake stood there for a moment. Choose. More talk of choices. His wife's words. X-wife. God, he missed her. Could he ever get her back? No, life as he knew it was over.

He walked out of the church and blinked the sun out of his eyes so he could see. It took a few moments as he walked down the steps. He looked down the sidewalk one way then the other. Choices. Which way to go? Cars lined the street in both directions. He must be close to the beach because he could hear the waves crashing. He chose the direction of the beach.

As he walked down the sidewalk, he could not decide what to do. Homeless shelter? Rehab program? Anything he contemplated was overshadowed by his desire for a drink and a bump. He was oblivious to his surroundings. As many addicts before him didn't see what was coming even though they chose the path, the van pulled up and repeated the method of abduction. Blake didn't even put up a fight. He welcomed the darkness. He welcomed what he thought was the final journey the priest spoke about. But there was one more journey left for Blake whether he was ready or not.

CHAPTER 53

Marie received the news. Although she was ready for Phase two, she felt trepidation for her husband's arrival. Of course she wanted him saved, clean, and sober, but thoughts of Milo and Pookie raced through her mind like a runaway train. This was his last chance, the only way. She had tried everything else.

When she saw the news of the attempted suicide, she was devastated. She almost gave up hope, but the doctor reassured her they would retrieve him from the hospital upon his release. She was amazed that Blake talked his way out of there within seventy two hours. But then again, he was a bright man when he used that brain of his for something other than a trash can for all of his problems.

He just arrived and was still under the sedative and safely tucked away in his room. She watched him sleep on the monitor. Milo was stirring again and began destroying his room once more. The orderlies were tired of rearranging his room afterwards but that was their job. She wondered about the long term effects from the knockout gas they used occasionally to restore order. The patients figured out this subtle trick recently and Marie heard them discussing it. Although Milo was maniacal, obsessed and dangerous at times, he was extremely intelligent.

He was the one that discovered the pipe chase in order to obtain more narcotics. He had the others riled up for a moment looking for an escape route, luckily, they had given up. She was worried they would find the other access points. Now, she watched and listened as the others tried to reach Janine with words of encouragement. She mostly woke, cried and slept. Her body was trembling from withdrawals. Rarely speaking to her friends, she would walk around the room reading the walls.

Marie hoped Janine would begin to comprehend the enormity of this opportunity available to her. Blake looked so peaceful sleeping in his room. Beautiful even. She had not seen him shaven or showered in longer than she could remember. At home, when he was drunk and high, he would usually ignore his appearance and her as well. To him, she was an annoyance. A pest even. A nag.

He had told her to go and didn't seem to care as she walked out the door. She was knowledgeable enough to know it was the addiction that was clouding his judgement. The drugs telling him lies, and whispering to him that he didn't need or love her. The only need he seemed to care about was his next fix. This was a chance for his mind to reset and realize what was important to him. That she mattered, and this was a way for him to rejoin life.

Restore his sanity. But first, doesn't one need to acknowledge they have a problem and what they were doing was insane? How many dictators throughout history thought they were doing the world a favor by killing millions and waging war? She wasn't comparing her husband to the likes of these maniacs but just their delusions. They did not realize their actions were insane.

She must show him that giving up all hope and discarding those that love you and slowly killing yourself was insane. She must show him he had something to live for. That there were other choices. A better way to live and to cope.

But most of all, that he had the power to choose. He stirred and her heart skipped a beat. He sat up and looked around. He walked to the toilet and relieved himself. His reaction was the same as the others. He was talking to himself while looking at the messages flashing on the walls.

He watched the t.v. for a second. Disgusted with CNN, he switched to FOX news. She silently laughed at this. They often had heated debates about his conservative viewpoints. But she respected his perspective because he never tried to convert her to his way of thinking like an overzealous preacher. He was never mean in his explanations and always apologized for any arguments in the past. That is, until his addiction took over.

He switched off the tv and opened the white refrigerator. He studied the choices of food. Then attacked the fridge like only a person that was starving could. He didn't wait to find a spoon. He tore open a container of yogurt and squeezed the contents into his mouth, spilling some on his chest. He squeezed another. Grabbing huge stacks of lunch meat, he shoveled it in his mouth and choked. He washed down the mess with a Dr. Pepper. Still not satiated, he ate some chips and several handfuls of ice cream. Once he was full, he walked around the room addressing his invisible captors.

"What is this place? Who the hell are you people? Why have you kidnapped me? Fucking answer me!" Bam was the first to hear him and asked.

"Hey! Who is that?"

"Blake! Who are you?"

"This is Bam."

"Oh hey. I heard about you, but we've never met. You went missing a while back."

"Yea, bro this place is a trip." Betty heard Blake and thought she was dreaming.

"Blake? Oh my God! You're here! Holy shit! I'm so glad you're, I mean, not glad you're here but glad you're not. Well, I don't know what the hell I mean! But everyone else is here too!"

Mike heard his friend and was excited to hear his voice.

"Corvette Blake! What's up brother! Man, it's good to hear your voice!"

"Betty? Mike? Wow! Everyone is here! This is crazy!"

"Yea it's crazy!" Shouted Pookie."

"But so cool!" He sang through drunken lips.

"It's everything you'll ever need, homeboy!" Pookie continued to sing while the others had another reunion. Marie just listened and prepared Phase two.

"Have y'all met the people that run this place?" Blake was hoping someone could shed more light on his situation.

"No." Bam answered.

"But there are more important issues you should know."

"Don't touch the black refrigerator! Don't touch it!" Mike screamed.

"What the hell is the black refrigerator? Mine is white." Mike spoke with intensity.

"Imagine right now, placed in front of you, an unlimited amount of cocaine."

"What?" Blake was incredulous.

"What the hell are you babbling about?" Bam took over.

"This place is an experiment, a test. After a few days, whoever is in charge will provide you with all the alcohol and drugs you could ever consume."

"Why in the hell would someone do that? I mean, that sounds great and all but…"

"Don't give in, Blake!" Betty sounded frantic. The thought of a beer, multiple beers and a Scarface pile of cocaine. Damn! Imagining this gave him chills. He ran to the toilet and threw up. His retching was so loud that the others heard.

"It's okay, Blake. We all went through the withdrawals. You must fight it."

"Fuck that! Fuck y'all! Give me some of your shit- I'll kill you!" Milo barked like a rabid dog chained at hell's gates.

Pookie joined in the conversation.

"Blake ma man! You finally made it! So, sit back and chill! Have a drink on me!" His laugh echoed throughout the facility.

"Don't pay attention to him, Blake." Betty continued.

"All of us have experienced this black refrigerator and it's terrifying and exhilarating at the same time."

"But that's the point." Remarked Bam.

"But why?" Blake couldn't for the life of him, understand the why.

"We think it's an experiment to see what choice we'll make. Have you read the messages on the walls?"

"Yes, I have." Blake looked at the walls flashing before his eyes.

'Choose.'

'Choose Life.'

"But why? Why go through all of this? Kidnapping? Who are we for someone to care about or experiment on?" Blake was so confused, and Bam offered more insight.

"I think because it's not so much that someone cared or not cared but that we didn't care about ourselves. Whatever the case, I think the point is that we were killing ourselves with our bad choices. Now we have a chance to choose differently or keep doing what we were doing and speed up the whole death process." Betty chimed in.

"Watch us die or watch us live." The realization of her recent insight frightened her. She had not spoken about this perspective until now and it petrified her. In the beginning, she had thought of her captors as impartial observers offering door number one or door number two while recording their choices. Taking notes. Now, she saw them as possibly being evil doers taking bets on who would survive or not. No, that can't be, she thought. The messages are all so positive. So helpful. Bam broke her away from this path of thought.

"All we can do is guess and listen to the messages! We have a new outlook on life because of all this regardless of their intentions. We are cured from our addictions!"

"Speak for yourself!" Milo shouted.

"What's his deal and who the hell is that?"

"That's Milo. He's one of the first few that went missing. I guess he has given up. They took away his black fridge and withdrawals are making him nuts." Betty was sad for Milo.

"Fuck you! I ain't no quitter like y'all! I can handle my shit! Give me back my fridge God damn it!"

"Damn, he sounds bad." Stated Blake. Blake was horrified at the prospect of going through several days of withdrawals. He was only able to hold together recently because of the psyche meds he had received in the hospital after his swim. Mike spoke up.

"Look, Blake. You may not be able to resist but know that we are here for you. I gave in but I had some kind of, I don't know what to call it. Spiritual transformation or some shit. But whatever it was, I had my friends encouraging me. I guess I had some kind of awakening. I realized there is some kind of purpose to all of this, and it is not for me to die here. I am clean and have no desire to live like that again. So, keep that in mind. You don't have to live like you did before." Marie was so thankful for these patients encouraging Blake. She wanted to run down the hall and hug and kiss each and every one of them.

CHAPTER 54

Janine was dreaming of Blake. They were in his corvette with the top off, wind blowing through their hair. Laughing, smiling and singing.

'I like big butts and I cannot lie,

You other brothers can't deny....

Then she snapped her eyes open to Blake's voice. What? The dream faded away and she was back in this awful place.

"Blake? Blake? Is that you?"

"Janine? Janine! Hey!" Blake was glad Janine was here and that she was okay. If here was a better place to be that is. Better than the streets for sure.

"Are you okay, Janine?" She could tell he genuinely cared about her wellbeing.

"I'm okay, I guess. Withdrawals suck. I need a drink. My black fridge is empty." A pitiful laugh escaped her lips.

"I don't think I can make it through this, Blake. It's so hard!"

"Hold on, Janine!" Yelled Bam.

"You can do it, girl!" Betty shouted.

"Come on, Janine! We are here for you!" Mike showed his concern as well.

Marie witnessed them join forces to lift one of their own out of a lake of fear and despair to save her from drowning. She hoped Blake would take heed and learn from all of this. She envisioned the miracle of Blake sober. Doctor Van Hook had been observing. He wasn't as emotionally invested in the new arrival as Marie but understood her concern. He knew he could count on her commitment.

"Marie, Phase two is here."

"I know, doctor." The doctor looked directly into her eyes.

"I need you to remain objective and focused and no matter what, do not break protocol."

"Yes, doctor."

"Also, He must not know it is you, so make sure you utilize the voice changing software."

"Absolutely, doctor." Each patient's room, in addition to the surveillance system, had two-way communication set up. With Phase two, daily communication would be necessary to add more benefits to the healing process of each patient. Would Blake be able to resist the black refrigerator?

She shut out any negative thoughts. Marie understood that this was the last and only chance to save her husband from himself. Or maybe this was the last time she would see her husband alive. Again, she had to shake away the negativity.

"Recite the Serenity prayer, Marie." She whispered to herself.

CHAPTER 55

Milo had reached a point of evil, fever pitch. He snarled like a dog and screamed threats and obscenities constantly. The others shut him out as best as they could. Orderlies did not go to his room anymore because he had not eaten in days and his refrigerator was full. He was a madman in a room with blood-stained walls running around in circles until he heard the voice.

"Milo." He stopped. Marie was speaking through the voice filter. Milo's eyes darted around the room looking for the source.

"Milo, I'm here to help you." Milo began a frantic search for the voice.

"Milo, please calm down. I'm here to help." He was still running around the room searching.

"Then give me back my black fridge!"

"Okay, Milo." At that glorious statement, he stopped dead in his tracks.

"Wh-wha, What did you say?" He knew what was said but couldn't believe his sudden great fortune.

"I said, we will return your black refrigerator."

"Don't fuck with me, bitch!"

"I am not, Milo." She thought better of his matching his vocabulary.

"The black refrigerator will be returned by tomorrow, but we need something from you first."

"I need my shit now! Don't play with me bitch!"

"Milo, listen to me. One more day. If you calm down. Stop destroying your room. Next time you wake up, you will have the black refrigerator."

"Are you for real? No bullshit?" Milo was intently focusing on the words of this Wizard of Oz magician speaking from the walls as he sat down on his bed.

"I give you my word, Milo. Stay calm. Take a nap and it will return."

"Okay, whoever you are. One day! You better not be lyin'!" With that she switched off the mic. Doctor Van Hook nodded at Marie with approval and a hint of a smile.

"Good work, Marie." They had taken Pookie's black fridge as well, but he didn't react the same way. He just shrugged it off and went back to sleep. She switched the intercom back on.

"Pookie." Pookie stirred.

"Who is that? Where you at?" Pookie got out of bed and looked around the room. He started in one corner and worked his way around until he stood in the center of the room and stared up at the ceiling.

"What you want with me? Why y'all got me locked up in here?"

"Good question, Mr. Pookie. We are offering you a chance at a better life."

"Better life? I ain't never had a room this nice, ever! This bed makes me sleep like a baby. There are no roaches- and until yesterday, I had all the drinks I could ever want! Why y'all take my drink?"

"To give you one last chance. There is a better way, Pookie."

"Yea, you sure right. That black box is the better way!" He laughed, despite going through the shakes.

"Why you give a damn about 'ol Pookie anyways?"

"Because we care and want you to care."

"But why, fool? Tell me why?" Marie paused, looking for the words.

"To show you. To show the world that people in a hopeless situation with alcohol and drugs no longer have to suffer. That they can be free from substance abuse."

"Abuse? I ain't never abused nobody!" He broke out in laughter again.

"Mr. Pookie, please pay attention. The words all around you are there to help you in this program. Tomorrow you will have your black refrigerator back and one last chance to change your life for the better. Choose wisely." With that, she switched off.

"What the hell?" Pookie scratched his head and thought about what was said. Damn! He forgot to ask any important questions. All he really cared about was more drink. Maybe she was right though. Maybe he had serious issues. But as usual, he reasoned he wasn't as bad as other people on drugs. It was just alcohol and he ain't never hurt no one. One more day.

He began to read the messages once again. He read the Serenity prayer out loud this time. A vision of his grandmother Edith filled his memories. Her nickname was Gigi. She was a firm believer in whipping him for his various sins. He saw himself young and scared, having to go to the backyard and pick out a good switch to receive his punishment. He knew better than to come back with a little one! But as Pookie walked around this hospital room, his frame of mind began to change. He remembered the sweet moments of his Gigi. Always with a hug for him even when she was mad. She told him he could choose whatever path he wanted in life and that it was up to him. Her words had him often daydreaming of becoming an astronaut.

Growing up, he loved movies about space and alien invasions. He pictured a space warrior traveling the universe in Star Wars hunting Darth Vader. He chuckled at this rediscovered memory. A lone tear slowly made its way down the scar marked path to his mouth and he tasted salt. The tear was for his Gigi. The tear was for lost hope and dreams of something more.

Something more than that poor South Texas town and that dilapidated shotgun shack he had once called home. Something more than beans and cornbread every day. Though, Gigi had the best cornbread recipe in Texas. At least that's what everybody said. He had dreamed of something more than sweating and breaking his back like his Papa did his whole life. A hunched over old man. But that was his path. Nothing fancy, but an honest, hardworking man.

Old dogs can't learn new tricks. Gigi's words echoed through his mind. This place was trying to tell him something he already knew. Had already been taught. To choose a righteous path. That was his plan at fifteen years old. Then both Gigi and Papa died in the same year. He was placed in foster care with a house full of nine other children. The government paid an old bitter woman to take care of all of them. All she did was beat them and use most of the money to smoke crack. So, he ran away. His life of hustlin' and drinkin' destroyed all his good upbringing and he became content with the lifestyle.

As these revisits to the past and the messages on the walls swam through his vision, He started to see with more than his eyes. He felt the presence of Gigi with him, and his hands stopped shaking. He hadn't noticed at first. He recited each phrase he saw, and Gigi's voice spoke to him. He smiled brightly as her churchy, corny words all made sense now. So did the voice from the walls.

"I don't have to live like this anymore." He spoke out loud to the ceiling again.

"Damn, that black ass box!" He shouted.

"I choose life! It's my choice Gigi!" He felt Gigi's embrace and he let the warmth consume him. He knew his life had changed. He had won the battle with himself. He lay in bed and closed his eyes and dreamed of fighting alongside Princess Lea. Damn she was fine! Lightsaber in hand, he whooped Darth Vader's ass. He was a hero.

"Janine. Janine." Marie spoke to her hoping to help her through the withdrawals.

"Are you the one making me go crazy?"

"Is that what you think, Janine?" Janine's hands trembled and so did her voice.

"Why did you bring me here?"

"We brought you here because your life was over, you just didn't know it yet."

"What the hell are you talking about?"

"With a life of alcohol and drugs you have three promises. Jails, institutions and death."

"So, this is an institution? They don't usually kidnap you and keep you locked up by yourself."

"Don't they?" Marie asked rhetorically.

"Most hopeless addicts are sent away. Committed and against their will. In those places they pump you full of drugs. Again, against your will."

"But you give us drugs here! That's crazy!"

"Is it really, Janine?"

"Yes!"

"The alcohol and drugs placed in your room are freely chosen. Nobody forces you to use them. You're a smart girl, Janine. You have figured that out. Everything here is about choices. We've been telling you that every single day."

"But aren't the drugs in those other places supposed to help?"

"Do they really help? I'll answer for you. The meds those Psyche doctors provide cure nothing. Absolutely nothing. Some may alter the chemicals in your brain and help you function better, but for the most part, they numb you to the main source of the problem. You!"

"Me? All I have to do is stop drinking and I will be okay."

"No, Janine. Drinking is only a symptom of your problem. Your problem is you and your thinking. You choose to drink because you think it's okay to do so. You think drinking will help your problems go away, but things only get worse over time. The people that don't die early end up with so many health problems or legal troubles. It's inevitable."

"So, it's hopeless!" Janine felt even more defeated as she wept.

"No, it's not! You still have a choice! As long as you have a heartbeat, you can choose. Read the messages. Talk with your friends. Pray or meditate. But choose to not open the black refrigerator."

"What do you mean? Y'all took it away!"

"It will return tomorrow." Nausea hit her stomach and she hurried to the toilet to wretch. Needing a drink filled her with such longing, but she knew this unseen voice was right. Drinking and the occasional drug usage never helped her. Ever. Her life never amounted to anything worthwhile.

Living in a crack motel. A hooker. Her best friend was a hooker. It all seemed so hopeless. But the messages that flashed all around her said different.

'It's all up to you' flashed in front of her.

"Up to me? Can I really change?" She asked herself. But Marie heard and answered.

"Yes. Yes you can, Janine." Marie turned off the mic.

CHAPTER 56

Dr. Van Hook was impressed with Marie's ability to encourage each patient. Such passion he thought.

"Marie."

"Yes, doctor?"

"You know it will be different for Blake." Marie didn't respond and the doctor continued.

"For one, he just arrived. Two, the others had time to experience longer withdrawal symptoms and a few days of withdrawal medication. Three, they had more days of interaction with each other and more time to ponder their choices. Tomorrow, Blake will receive the black refrigerator along with the other patients."

"We usually gave them a few days before, doctor."

"That's right, Marie, but no longer." Her hope for Blake took a nosedive and her heart sank. Doctor Van Hook could see the disappointment on her face.

"Don't do that, Marie. Never lose hope. Even when the situation looks hopeless. You never know who is going to get it. Don't give up five minutes before the miracle." Marie was still feeling the enormity of what tomorrow would bring.

"You said it yourself, Marie. As long as they are alive there is hope. But it is up to them to choose their destiny."

Marie seemed to straighten up and grow taller. She lifted her chin and managed to smile.

"You're right, doctor." She prepared herself mentally for the next patient.

Bam was doing push-ups and a squat routine. She didn't want to interrupt him, so she moved on to Betty.

"Betty. Betty." The voice startled her.

"Oh! Who's that?"

"Betty. I am here to help you."

"Who the hell are you?"

"I am one of the technicians that work here to help guide you through the program."

"Why did y'all kidnap us?" Marie paused. How could she answer satisfactorily to anyone in this situation?

"Please allow me to ask you a question first. If you were not brought here, shown another way to live and given this opportunity, what would your future have looked like?" That question was easy for Betty to answer but she could not bring herself to say it out loud. Instead, Marie did it for her.

"I think you are intelligent enough to know the answer, Betty. If left unchecked, your choices could lead you to incarceration but definitely the misery of addiction, then death."

Betty knew this to be true.

"So, all of this is to save me? Save us?"

"No, Betty. Only you can save you. You have to choose that. All of this is to help you choose."

"But why? Why us? Why me?"

"Why not you, Betty? You ask that question because you feel you are not worthy of help. Those feelings of shame, guilt, pain and resentment are lying to you. You woke up today. That means you have another chance to change. You've already changed. It's been days since your last use. You've encouraged new arrivals to do the same. That black box will return tomorrow, and I believe that won't be a problem for you. Keep doing what you are doing. Keep that hope alive and keep working with others and you'll be fine." Betty processed the information. It was true, she had been clean for days. No cravings and she felt great. She hadn't been this happy and free in years. Well, free in her mind.

"When do we get out of here?"

"We are in what we call Phase two of the program, Betty. After everyone becomes more aware of the purpose, then comes Phase three."

"What is Phase three?"

"That is preparation for release. I think you will get out of here and create a wonderful life for yourself."

"You think so? I've done absolutely nothing with my life."

"Not true, Betty. Look at the past week. You've transformed your mind. You've made choices you never thought possible. Hold on to that newfound power tomorrow." Microphone off. Marie stood from the monitors, stretched and watched Blake. He would be the last one to talk to. She prayed the Serenity Prayer again. She asked her God to give her strength and went home to get much needed sleep. She felt deeply for these people. She hoped their sobriety held true through Phase two. All the messages would stop tonight, and they will be left with the black refrigerator and their thoughts.

Blake had less time with the constant behavior modification. Milo seemed calm for the moment, and she felt a little hope rise for him. Hope is really all she had. Most days that was all that kept her going. It was amazing she wasn't an addict. Or maybe she was. Hope in hopeless situations was like a drug, wasn't it? She hoped and prayed so many sleepless nights for Blake. She fed on that hope. Craved it even. She cried. She begged. Like an addict needing a fix. Hope was her drug, and she would never recover. At least she hoped not.

Betty yelled for Bam.

"Bam! Hey Bam!"

"What's up, Betty?"

"You talk to her yet?"

"Talk to who, Janine?"

"That woman!"

"What woman?"

"The woman that runs this place!"

"Wait. What? You talked to someone That is responsible for all this shit?"

"Yeah, and she s-"

"Bam." Marie was now addressing him.

"Bam."

"Talk to you later, Betty! Yes ma'am, I'm listening."

"First of all, I would like to say we are all very impressed with your progress here at the facility." Bam said nothing.

"Are you hearing me okay, Bam?"

"Yea, I heard you." The aggravation in Bam's voice was undeniable. He had been kidnapped, and in his mind tortured. Although he had been cured of addiction, he wanted answers.

"Bam, I detect anger in your voice."

"Damn right I'm angry! I mean, I pretty much figured out why we're here. It's some kind of experiment, right?" Marie didn't answer so Bam continued.

"Right, okay. So, I understand the kidnapping and secrecy and all but what's next?"

"What's next is that the black refrigerator returns tomorrow."

"What? Why? I ain't worried about that thing but there are a few of us that are still suffering because of it! Why in the hell would you do that?"

"I understand your frustration, Bam. But consider this. The entire world is a giant black box. Alcohol and drugs are everywhere. There are 100 times more drugs on the street than here. Some cities out West allow meth and heroin use recreationally. Like there is such a thing! So, this last test will strengthen your resolve."

"Or tear it down?" Bam's insight into the methods of this program impressed Marie.

"That is correct, Bam. You have learned a great deal since your stay with us."

"Okay, so, fine. I've changed. Made the right choice." On the word choice, he emphasized with extreme sarcasm.

"Then what happens when I don't give in to the big bad box?"

"Another great question, Bam. We have entered Phase two. Once this is over, Phase three is planning your release and reintegration back into society."

"What am I going to do out there?"

"We will help you, Bam. With housing. A job. Training if you need it. This is a great opportunity that has opened up for you because of your sobriety."

"You know, that sounds great and all. But why do so much for me? For all of us? We are nobodies."

"That's where you are wrong, Bam. Everyone needs help. Not everyone wants it. Most don't think they need it. You want it. You took it. You learned. Most of all, you passed it on to others. Don't you see the incredible impact one person can have on others when they choose the right path? You transformed people's lives. That is what we are trying." She stopped to correct herself.

"No, what we have accomplished here. We have set a great change in motion. We hope you will sustain this change when you are released into the community and bring the message of hope to others."

His laughter came through the speaker like steam, burning with cynicism.

"You want me to be your preacher?" He was still laughing.

"You're not preaching, Bam. You have been and will be sharing your experience, strength and hope with anyone that will listen."

"Why would I do that?" Bam indeed wondered why he would do that. He wouldn't use again. He knew he wanted something different out of life, but he wanted to get away from that crime infested area and start fresh.

"I'm pretty sure I ain't going back to my old stomping ground. I'll relocate. Somewhere. Anywhere but there."

"That's great, Bam. But you cannot escape the temptation by just changing your geography. You can't escape the addicts either. They are everywhere. With what you've learned here, your new way of living will be a testament to the power of choice. People will want what you have and if you are truly cured, you will want to freely give away the gift that you've been given. I wish you well, Bam. We'll talk soon."

Marie turned off the intercom. Man, Bam thought. I'll be out of here soon. He had been in jail a few times and when he knew he was about to get out, he anticipated getting high. But this time was different. He had hoped that his life would be extraordinary. He was a little nervous but confident. His thoughts traveled back to Janine. He was troubled by her predicament. He and Betty tried their best to help her, but she got caught in the spell of the black refrigerator. He wanted to do more for her but knew she must make the choice herself. Tomorrow will be here as quick as a crack rock goes up in smoke. He was rooting for Janine. Milo was a goner for sure. At least he had quieted down.

"Janine? Janine?" She was asleep Bam guessed

"Mike."

"Huh? What? Who is that?"

"Hello, Mike."

"Who is that?"

"Mike, I'm glad to see you've been doing well. You've chosen a new path. How do you feel?"

"Feel? Um, well, Like I want the hell out of here! Why is all this happening? Who are you people?"

"This is happening because we wanted to provide you with a path to success. The only way to do that was to guide you toward choosing life over death. You've done that. The 'we', are a team of experts that designed this program that made your chance at a new life possible."

"Yea, I guess, but why are we still kind of locked up?"

"Well, Mike. Unfortunately, this was a necessary part of the program. Could you have obtained sobriety in that motel? Developed hope for your future on the streets?" Mike lassoed her point and realized that he would have never got clean without this place. And this place wasn't really like jail except for the not being able to leave part. This place was safe from criminal predators and violence. The only battle here was with himself. Thank God he had come out of that war alive.

"I understand. But when do I get out of here?"

"Tomorrow, the black refrigerator will reappear."

"What in the fuck? I'm clean! Why? I've ignored it and then you took it away! Back? I don't want it!" Mike's pulse was racing. He was confused and frightened. Marie sensed as much.

"Please calm down, Mike. We know that if you were released today, even though you are clean with a newfound hope, temptation will await you on every street corner. This is just a way to reaffirm your resolve. Stay strong. You'll succeed." With that, she signed off.

So far so good. One more to go. She played out every scenario in her mind. The excitement gave her butterflies and made her nauseous, just like an alcoholic anticipating their next drink. She must calm down and prepare for his questions so she doesn't inadvertently reveal herself. Time was running out. She would take a break, eat and drink some coffee. You can do this Marie. She had no doubt. But could Blake resist the temptation? He was pacing his room and reading the messages. Every so often he would stop and read one of them more intently. The Serenity Prayer. Her favorite. Did he know that was her favorite prayer? She must have said that prayer a thousand times softly to herself at home. Would he make the connection? No. That prayer was so old and millions recited it every day. But Blake didn't know millions. He knew her. She would find out soon enough. She finished her coffee and one half of an egg salad sandwich. She sat back down at the bank of monitors. Before she turned on the microphone, she fixed her hair. Why was she doing that? He couldn't see her. Dr. Van Hook noticed this nervous gesture.

"You'll be fine, Marie. Stick to the plan. Focus on the goal." She checked to make sure the voice masking software was on and switched on the intercom.

CHAPTER 57

Blake was trying to eat but the withdrawals made it hard to keep anything down. The food was so good! He walked around the room between naps assessing his situation. White refrigerator. Black refrigerator. Choose life. Changes. Choice. Serenity Prayer. So familiar. A voice opened a window to his mind and his thoughts escaped.

"Blake."

"Hello?"

"How are you feeling?"

"Who are you?"

"I am one of the people in charge of this facility."

"Okay."

"Are you feeling better? You've been through a lot this past week. "

"Fine, I guess. I'm a little shaky but a drink would be nice." Marie wanted to tell him she was here. That she was the one trying to save him. Instead, she stuck to the plan.

"Blake, that's how you ended up here, isn't it?"

"What do you mean? I ended up here because you kidnapped me."

"You are correct."

"But why?"

"To offer you a way to escape the prison you have built for yourself."

"Prison? This is the only prison that I see, lady!" She switched off the mic. Oh Blake. She was frustrated and wanted to scream. Wake up Blake! She took a deep breath and turned the mic back on.

"Let me ask you a question, Blake. If you were released right now, what would you do?"

"Get a fucking drink!"

"You're going through withdrawals and so you think you need a drink, right?"

"Yea, like I said before I need a drink. So what?"

"So what? Thinking you need a drink to solve your situation is the reason we brought you here. That is why nothing you have done works to fix your problem. Drugs and alcohol are your answer for everything. Look at your situation when we picked you up. No money. No car. Homeless. Nothing. And I bet all you could think about was getting messed up!"

"So what!" Blake was deeply disturbed by this woman telling him things he already knew. Of course, he couldn't do anything right. Failed marriage. Failed career. Failed life!

"So what! You brought me here to tell me how much of a loser I am? I already know this, lady." He lowered his head as well as his voice.

"You're here to find hope."

"Hope?" At this word he laughed.

"Hope?" He stood. Walked around the room.

"All of this?" He turned around in circles with his arms spread wide.

"This is hope? A pretty jail? Cryptic messages flashing everywhere? Good food? Hope? The only hope I have is that Black refrigerator will come soon, and it has some cold beer and plenty of nice, white and flaky cocaine!" Dr. Van Hook shut off the microphone. He could see tears breaking down the floodgates of her eyes. He attempted to stop the flow.

"Marie, remember your purpose. Our purpose. Pull yourself together. I would take over, but I know how important this is to you so please, focus. Show him the way." She straightened up in her chair, pushed away from the table of monitors and stood. With new resolve, she grabbed the mic and turned it on.

"Blake, you are here because you gave up on your life. You gave up on your family. Gave up on yourself." Images of his wife shot through his brain like a sniper's bullet. She was still talking.

"Look around you, Blake. Focus on the words. They make sense if you just focus. Find hope once again. With hope you can do anything." He had given up on everything, this much was true. Long before his wife left him, he had buried himself in his addiction, wanting to dig a grave deep enough to never climb out. But he could never find the bottom of that hole until now. He couldn't dig any deeper. Or could he? Thoughts of the black fridge bombarded him like a mobile home in an East Texas hailstorm. The words on the walls made sense. Of course they did. But the storm in his mind clouded all but the desire to get wasted. She was 100% right. He was here because of his choices to drink and get high. Why couldn't he stop? Because he had no hope for his future. What future? He had nothing. He was nothing. All he cared about was the next drink and a pile of white snow. He had blocked the voice out. She was still rambling. He was reminded of his wife trying to reason with him while he was wasted. What a nag! At times, he missed her nagging. But that is not what he needed right now. He needed a drink.

"I need a fucking drink!" His scream startled Marie and she stopped her animated pacing and counseling to Blake.

"Blake, this is your last chance. I hope you see that. Choose life Blake. Choose life before your life is over." And with that, she turned off the intercom, set the microphone on her desk and practically fell into her chair. Her hope was waning. She was mentally fatigued. She watched her husband. He was visibly shaking. He walked around his room reciting the phrases with a mocking tone.

"Please. Please. Please," she said softly. "Please Blake, figure this

out." Dr. van Hook spoke to Marie.

"Marie. I know this is difficult for you. I empathize, but there are other people in this program. They all need your care and concern."

"I know, doctor. I'm focused. Don't worry. Everything is being prepared." And prepared it was. The orderlies were loading the little black refrigerators with various narcotics and plenty of alcohol to wash it down with. Plenty of syringes as well. Doubt continued to pollute her mind like a South Texas landfill. She mustn't lose hope. No matter what. That's all she had. She would do whatever it took to help these people. But would she watch another person kill themselves by overdose again? The two women that died in the beginning were shocking. Only thoughts of saving her husband kept her from quitting. She wouldn't stand by and do nothing while he ended his life with an endless supply of poison. Even if he gave into the black fridge, there were other counseling sessions she could try. Would that be enough? Her vision of them driving away into the sunset was fading and replaced by her chasing him into a valley in the middle of a tornado. The winds were destroying everything in its path. There was a face in the tornado, and it was Blake's. With each rotation his face changed from sadness to fear, then anger. All these emotions built up speed and threatened to engulf her. Now, she ran. Ran as fast as she could. The tornado nipped at her heels. The centrifugal force turned her around to face Blake. His face was replaced by a tombstone. She was jolted from her vision by the doctor's hand on her shoulder.

"Marie. Marie."

"Huh? Oh sorry, doctor."

"You look tired, Marie. Go home. But come back early. Tomorrow is a big day. I need you fresh."

"Yes, doctor." On her way home she prayed for renewed strength. Also, she asked for more hope. Her stash was getting low. She needed Her daily fix. For hope is all she had, right?

CHAPTER 58

Matthew sent the odorless gas through the vents one more time. Once all the patients were asleep, the orderlies entered their rooms and brought each patient a black refrigerator. Since they hadn't removed Milo's, they loaded it up. The other refrigerators were filled to capacity with everything that might tempt them.

"Dr. Van Hook. Everything is ready." Matthew had his doubts about the next part of Phase two. Marie had arrived early to oversee and told Matthew not to worry. Matthew had been a mental wreck since his snafu. The Doctor was going over his checklist while Matthew looked over his shoulder. All of them waited for the patients to awaken. Marie hardly slept a wink in anticipation of her husband's test. She looked at each monitor for just a few seconds then back to Blake's. She must focus. She was trying to be impartial but that was impossible. She would help everyone as much as she could. Come on Blake, she told herself. You can do this. Milo stirred. Of course Milo would be the first one to rise. His tolerance for narcotics was unbelievable. He could probably smell the drugs in his sleep. Marie felt bad for finding that amusing. Doctor Van Hook looked up from his clipboard and noticed Matthew was too close and gave him a look of disapproval.

"Oh, sorry, doctor." Matthew retreated as the doctor approached the bank of monitors. Matt spoke.

"Look at Milo. He must have a natural radar for this stuff." Again, the doctor frowned at him.

"More like Milo has built an extreme tolerance to most drugs and sedatives including our sleeping gas."

"Right." Matthew felt stupid for what he said, and the doctor always had a way of adding to it. Matthew left the room to walk the halls.

"Marie, we are almost to the end. The results are promising, although some may not make it. You must mentally prepare for that possibility. Remain objective. Do not let your feelings get in the way."

"Of course, doctor. I've been preparing for this moment for a while." How long had she waited for this? Months? Years? Blake's addiction has been in full swing for at least 2 years. It had been six months since the divorce. She counted the days until this moment. But now they focused on the most extreme case.

Milo woke and sat up in bed. He looked around the room. He Stood and went to the toilet. A knowing grin was on his face. He moved Slowly with purpose. To Marie and the doctor's surprise, he took a shower first. They could hear him reciting the various phrases from the Walls. Change. Choices. Choose life not death. I'm worth it. Once showered, he dried off with his towel and got dressed. He walked to the Serenity Prayer flashing above his bed. He began to recite.

"God grant me the serenity…."

"Doctor, do you think he is finally…" Milo stopped half way through, turned toward the black fridge, then looked up. His eerie, demon-like laugh flowed through the facility like lava from a volcano. Seeping through the walls and burning their ears. His laugh was louder and more maniacal by the second as he seemed to look directly into Marie's eyes. She watched him move slowly to the fridge. Never taking his eyes off the unseen camera. How did he know where to look? The hair on the back of her neck rose and she quivered like she was touched by the devil himself. He stopped a foot away from the treasure trove of narcotics and spoke.

"I bet y'all were standing there, watching and waiting, thinking I had chosen." He said the next part with air quotes.

"The right path. Right?" He laughed again.

"Fucking idiots! This is all that matters. He opened the black refrigerator. Milo pulled out several syringes and a bag of heroin. He seemed to be in deep thought. He manipulated the bag of tar between his fingers like a Las Vegas card trick. He flicked the bag away and tossed the syringes. No, not yet. Not time for that. He grabbed a baggy of methamphet amines.

"This is what Milo wants." Dr. Van Hook was visibly shaken at the prospect of Milo on large amounts of speed. Milo on heroin was calm, subdued. Milo on Meth was unpredictable, out of control and dangerous.

"And remember the promise I made to all of you?" They looked at each other for a second. No one could remember a promise that Milo had made. "I will kill every fucking one of you." The way he said this with such conviction alarmed Marie and the doctor.

CHAPTER 59

Bam woke up and had a childlike grin on his face as he said The Serenity Prayer. He saw the black fridge. It did not faze him in the least. He immediately went to the corner of the room and addressed everyone.

"Hey! Hey! Everybody wake up! Hey! Janine! Blake! Mike! Pookie! Wake up! Betty, get up!" As they slowly woke, they wiped the sleep from their eyes. Each one of them looked around their rooms and saw the ominous sight. The refrigerator looked much larger to Mike. Fear congealed his blood. He couldn't move. He had reviewed this scenario in his mind more than once and thought he was prepared. He wasn't. Janine was terrified. She had tears in her eyes as she walked to the fridge. Betty jumped out of bed and ran to the corner to speak to her friends.

"Hey, everyone! Don't give in! Please! Stay strong! We can do this!" Pookie rolled out of bed and landed with a thud. He Shook his head to wake up more and stared at the black refrigerator. Then, unceremoniously, he walked to the fridge and opened the door. He perused the buffet of wine before his eyes.

"Man! They got T.J. Swan up in here!" He grabbed the bottle, unscrewed the cap and turned it upside down. He held it a few inches from his mouth and let the liquid splash like a waterfall from a mountain. He swallowed most of it and a trickle ran down his chin. Within a few seconds, the bottle was empty and he grabbed another without cleaning himself. In another dimension, Gigi was crying. But Pookie never noticed. To some people, the power of alcohol was greater than God. The doctor and Marie didn't notice because they were fixated on Milo. Matthew returned and shook them from their trance. Captain Obvious pointed out the first failure of the day.

"Oh Pookie." Marie said to herself. Janine was still crying in front of the refrigerator. Marie took this opportunity to speak to her.

"Janine, It's okay. Just breathe. Turn to the nearest wall and focus." Marie typed a new message.

'Your Life. Your Choice. You Can Change. You Are Worth It!'

"Janine, you can do it as long as you don't pick up. Things will get better if you don't use" Janine turned back to the black fridge and plopped down to sit. Not crying any longer, she appeared to examine the black box. She rubbed her hands on the top then the sides. Slowly, methodically, as if she was communicating telepathically. Was she willing the box to speak? Everyone already knew the language of what was inside. Despair, shame and death. That is all alcohol and drugs had to offer and all they ever spoke. She opened the box. She opened it and she drank.

CHAPTER 60

Blake was sweating profusely. It's here! It's here! His head was swimming with thoughts of an endless supply of cocaine. His body was yearning for the chemicals to ease the pain. He went over some of what the mysterious woman had told him. But, at this moment, his addiction was superseding all rhyme or reason. The insanity told him he could use and everything would be okay. It wouldn't turn out like the last time, right? His mind always told him that and he never argued. Marie spoke.

"Blake, wait!" Blake was walking toward the answer to all his problems.

"Blake, stop!" Blake opened the door to paradise on Earth.

"Blake, please don't do this!" Blake reached for the nearest bag of treasure. A blank face with no emotion opened a bag of powder. The robot-like man stuck in his nose and inhaled.

CHAPTER 61

Milo was so high, he sensed he was floating and weightless like a cloud swimming in the sky. A wisp of evaporated water. But eventually, that cloud will dissipate or become more dense and turn into a storm cloud. It will rain on everything. Milo was walking around his room scanning for something. His mind told him there was another way out. Janine continued to drink. She could hear the others call her name, but she blocked out their appeals. She couldn't change. She wasn't worth it. She did not believe any of the messages on the wall applied to her. What if she could stop drinking? Then what? Get a job? Find a husband? Who could ever love her? She was broken. Just keep drinking, she told herself. Drink my problems away.

The freaks come out at night!
The freaks come out at night!
The freaks come out!

Pookie was singing one of his favorite songs by an 80's Rap group called Whodini. Life was great. He had free liquor, a nice warm bed and plenty of food. The only thing missing was. A woman.

"Man, I need a woman!"

CHAPTER 62

Mike couldn't get out of bed. He was shaking uncontrollably and frozen where he sat. Like a northern wind had blown in; his teeth chattered. His stomach hurt, but it wasn't hunger. The butterflies within demanded to be fed. But what do butterflies eat? The butterflies could only be satiated by two things. Drugs and alcohol. And only a few feet away was the motherload. Something deep inside Mike repeated the same thought. Everything will be fine if you get high. No more problems. No more pain. No more nothing. Don't worry. He grabbed his head and screamed.

"Noooooooooooo!" Like a butterfly sets on a flower to feed, Mike flew out of bed to feed on the contents of the Black refrigerator.

CHAPTER 63

"Bam."

"Yea, Betty?"

"I think we are losing them." They both had begged, yelled and pleaded with the others to not use but failed.

"We can't give up, Betty! I've learned that as long as I wake up each day, I have a choice. At any point in this place someone can change!"

"But they have to want to, Bam." He thought about that statement. Those words had never occurred to him prior to this facility. All he wanted, as far as he could remember, was to get high and drink until he passed out. Now, he could not imagine going back to living that way. That person looked like someone else. It was like watching a foreign film with no subtitles. Life was about choices. He surveyed his room and the flashing messages. These words saved his life. He thanked his nameless God. He thanked his mother.

"We can't give up, Betty."

CHAPTER 64

Marie had tears brimming but refused to cry. She repeated to herself, 'I must stay strong.' The doctor was irritated and had argued with Matthew over something. She wasn't really paying attention and sent him on an errand. It was the doctor that broached the subject first.

"Marie, there is still time." Marie looked up at the doctor from her seat at the bank of monitors. Her eyes emptied like the sky during a summer rain, but her voice belied her despair.

"I know, doctor. Bam and Betty are fine. The rest." She paused and wiped away the rain.

"The rest can still find hope." Dr. Van Hook shook his head to the affirmative but had no more hope for Milo. He was vehemently destroying his room screaming bloody murder. How could they ever allow him to leave this place? He pushed away the hope that he would overdose and meet his fate. End his miserable existence. Obviously, he had spent his life too chicken-shit to put a gun in his mouth. The doctor thought terrible of himself for thinking this. But what more could he do? Milo was clearly psychotic and meant them harm. He was shouting as much now.

"I'll kill you all!" Echoes of his promises echoed through the entire facility.

Marie focused her attention on the one that mattered more than them all. No matter how impartial she tried to be, this was her x-husband. He still lived in her heart. Once a beautiful castle, now a condemned building, his heart still resided there, nonetheless. He was crying, snorting cocaine while sitting on the floor. He had a beer in one hand and a bag of powder in the other. A white spot on the end of his nose. He depicted one of the lifeguards that had rescued him from the sharks. He lowered his face into the bag and inhaled once again. No rolled up dollar. No straw. Just his nose. She was curious to know if in the history of snorting cocaine use, had anyone ever done that? Images of Tony Montana came to mind. But he wasn't Scarface. This was a tragedy playing before her eyes. The hero in the story was dying, and by his own hands. She felt helpless. She wanted to run to him. Hold him. Wipe his tears. Take away his pain. Save him.

"It's his choice." She said out loud. Her inner dialogue gave her strength. Speak your heart, Marie without revealing yourself. Find the words.

"There must be a way out of here." Milo kept saying to himself in between threats of death to his captors. He hoped that would distract them from realizing his true purpose. He had upended the white refrigerator. The black fridge as well. He was careful not to damage the precious payload inside. He smashed the t.v. and threw the nightstand across the room. He picked it up again. Before he threw it, he noticed The Serenity Prayer above his bed. What bullshit, he screamed and threw it with all his might and it shattered into pieces onto his bed. With the crash there was a loud echo. He had heard that, hadn't he? A strange echoing sound. Is that a fucking door? He stood for a second and caught his breath. He concealed his excitement. After a minute or so, he casually walked to the bed as if he was in a park taking in the scenery. He grabbed the mattress and pulled it off the box spring. Then, yanked the box spring from the frame and tossed it aside. Next, the frame screeched as he slid it from the wall. He walked back to his stash and picked up a bag of meth. He dropped a shard on the floor, crushed it under his fingers, then pinched it and brought it to his nose. Once the burning chemical entered his sinuses, he walked back to the wall his bed once blocked. He placed both hands side by side and his face between them on the wall. There was a small opening behind the refrigerators. Was there one behind the bed? His recent genius was fueled by a substance once used to make super soldiers. In reality, it created psychopaths impervious to most pain and devoid of feelings. No limitations and indestructible. His hands slid up and down the wall and side to side until he found a spot. The door clicked and opened a half an inch. He stopped and turned around. Did they notice? They hadn't noticed when he found the pipe chase. Could he get that lucky again? If they did, they would just come storming in or put him to sleep like they did on occasion. He had figured that out several days ago. After a few minutes he walked back to the door and slowly pushed it open. He was teeming with expectation. Who would die first?

CHAPTER 66

Marie took a few minutes to gather her thoughts before she spoke. She watched with great sorrow as Blake drowned in a sea of despair overflowing with beer and cocaine. Her heart was breaking by the minute.

"Blake." He looked like a bobblehead toy as he looked for the voice.

"Blake."

"Yea, what do you want now?" His speech was slurred as he spoke.

"Leave me alone, lady!"

"Do you want to die, Blake?" That question almost killed his buzz and his head snapped up to answer.

"What the hell kind of question is that?"

"Do you want to die, Blake? It's a significant question. Your answer determines our next course of action."

"Course of action?" Blake did not know what to make of this line of questioning and was getting upset.

"Please answer the question, Blake." Blake contemplated the question. The last couple of years of his life flashed before his eyes. His addiction building momentum, then his wife left. Divorced and living in a crack motel. He Snorted up all his money. He saw Himself at the beach, blood, sand and ocean. He felt the sting of the salt water on his wounds. The despair and fear as he swam out to sea was bombarding his brain like Galveston waves on the Seawall. Where had he been swimming to? To an end? No, when faced with being ripped apart by sharks, he swam back to shore. So, he didn't want to die. So, what did he want? How had his life become so tragic? Drugs and alcohol. But millions of people drink

beer every weekend at various sporting events and don't rip open the cans and gouge their skin to pieces. Although his life was out of control, the thought of not using it did not compute. He couldn't imagine a life without alcohol or his powdery savior. His wife's image took over the beach scene. Her face was the sunny sky. The people on the Seawall were erased. The sirens were silenced and replaced by her words. "Choose me or the drugs." Marie was still waiting for an answer from Blake.

"I'm waiting, Blake."

"Um, uh, I don't know the answer."

"You don't know if you want to die or not? Think, Blake. Have you anyone in your life that you care about? Anyone that cares about you?" He didn't want to talk to this woman about anything this deep. He wanted to forget.

"None of that matters anymore."

"Why do you say that, Blake?"

"Because I have nothing. The one I did care about left me and now I am nothing. This." He held up his beer and a bag of coke.

"This is all I have. All I am." Marie choked back tears. Since the divorce, the occasional tinge of regret would creep up on her but she would shake it off. She did the right thing. Again, that remorse tried to affect her thought process. She remained determined to finish what she started. She would save her husband. X-husband.

"Blake, your hesitation to answer the life-or-death question means you don't want to die. Oh, you might have thought about it, but you don't want to. You may even think you have no reason to live but that's not the same. If you had one wish. One wish to change everything in your life for the better, what would it be?" Blake knew the answer. It came immediately but he was afraid to speak it. He didn't believe in magic. This wasn't a fairytale, it was a nightmare. But the answer was screaming to be released.

"To get my wife back." He spoke those words as the tears streamed down his face. Marie reacted as would anyone else in this situation. She was elated and tears of joy flowed. In contrast, the sadness Blake felt brought him to a new depth.

Every time he thought of his wife, the pain required more substances to wash it away. She wiped her face and took a deep breath.

"Blake, what if you could get her back?" Blake let go a pitiful laugh. No joy behind it.

"What in the hell are you talking about? How in the hell could that happen? Are you saying you could bring her back?" He choked on his laughter while drinking, and beer shot out of his nose.

"No, Blake, I can't make any promises about her. But what I can promise you is that if you stop using, your life will get better."

"Stop using?" There it is again. Stop. He couldn't fathom life without his Chemical God.

"You must stop, Blake. You must find hope again. This place is designed for two purposes. Look around you at the messages. Life. Change.

Choices."

"Yea, yea, I see all that bullshit. That's one, what's the other purpose?"

She didn't want to answer him. She looked at the doctor. His cold, hard stare told her to say it.

"Death, Blake. Death. You have been killing yourself for whatever real or imagined reasons for a long time. You cannot deal with life on life's terms."

"Death? Life's terms? What the hell does that even mean? This sounds like some Twilight Zone Alcoholics Anonymous bullshit! Are you a friend of Bill?" He tried to manage a laugh, but truth be told, he was terrified.

"Death is no bullshit, Blake. You keep using as your way of dealing with life. And in here, sooner rather than later, you will die."

"Okay, whatever. What's this riddle, 'life on life's terms mean?" What was this crazy woman talking about? He thought he was crazy but this lady was nuts!

"Life happens, Blake. A lot according to the choices we make. Good or bad choices determine the outcome. But life also comes at us sideways with situations that make absolutely no sense. Life throws circumstances at us that are completely unfair. And the normal people deal with it. They don't look for the answers in a bottle or snort a line looking for a reason. They don't destroy their life with depression and resentment because life didn't turn out the way they wanted. Frequently, life does what it wants, and we don't like it. Deal with it. Acceptance is the key. Accept the dilemma and move on. Look for a solution and do not focus on who is to blame. Stop thinking like a victim. The main solution to problems in life, especially if the problem is you, is do not use!" She sternly emphasized the last part, do not use. "Using only makes it worse. A horrible day sober is far better than a great day wasted." God, this lady is making no sense.

"Leave me alone. None of this matters. Only this." He held up his answers to life once again. He finished his beer and stood to retrieve another. Baggy. Nosedive. Inhale. These were all the answers he could understand. Marie switched off. The doctor could feel the tension within her. Marie wasn't crying but the look of sadness was apparent. Marie left the

room. As she walked down the halls, she thought of giving up. But her hope was too strong. She would not give up until the end, no matter what that was. Life or death. Whether or not Blake thought he was worth it. To her, Blake was definitely worth all of this. This whole program. All this planning was for him. What more could she do? An alcoholic or an addict could never recover until they made the choice to stop, after admitting they had a problem of course. The sad part was that some never made it to that point because they couldn't admit that there was a problem. Blake knew he had issues, but his real problem was he didn't care anymore. No hope. Marie was frantic. The thought of Blake dying in this place was horrifying. She returned to the monitor room.

"Dr. Van Hook, I have an idea."

"For what, Marie?"

"To save Blake." She sounded almost excited, thought the doctor.

"Run it by me."

"Okay, so you remember the breakthrough with Bam?"

"Yes, but I do not understand what you mean."

"I know what to do, doctor. Let me get the orderlies ready." The doctor looked puzzled, then finally understood what Marie wanted to do.

"No, Marie! You can't be serious!"

"It's the only way, doctor!"

"Absolutely not!"

"But doctor! It worked with Bam! And this is my husband."

"Ex-husband Marie."

"I know, doctor, but I have to try!"

"The thing with Bam was a real hallucination not a manufactured one. We got lucky!"

He thought about it for a moment. Bam thinking he was seeing his mother did help. Bam had been sober ever since the incident and he played a vital role in helping the others.

"It will work, doctor! It's the only way! It's his last chance! He's dying!" The doctor empathized with Marie and relented.

"Okay, Marie, but do you think entering his room is a good idea?"

"Doctor, even if he doesn't believe he is hallucinating, I am in no danger from him!"

"But you will risk exposing your involvement in the program. So, just be extra cautious."

"Got it!" As she was exiting the monitor room he was still speaking

"I will have people outside the room on stand-by just in case!" Marie readied herself mentally. She wasn't sure this would work but she was desperate. Blake was in a tailspin with the ground coming up fast! Could she catch him before he crashed? She obtained a small flashlight and made her way to the pipe chase. Once outside his room, she prayed a silent prayer.

CHAPTER 67

B lake was sitting in bed drinking whiskey. He was trying to slow his racing heart. He must have snorted a half an ounce in a couple of hours. He was on his fifth shot and decided to drink straight from the bottle. The messages on the walls were blurry. So were the images of his wife. Marie switched off the lights to Blake's room from the pipe chase. She opened the small door behind the white refrigerator. She pushed the fridge out of the way.

"What the hell?" Blake was sitting on the bed when all the lights went out. He couldn't see the glass in his hands and missed his lips as he took a drink. He wanted to stand but thought better of it for fear of falling. Marie stood a few feet from Blake. She clicked on the flashlight and shone it directly in Blake's face.

"Hey!" Blake was startled.

"Who's that?"

"Blake." Marie's voice was no longer filtered. Blake sat silent. He was wasted and partially blinded by the light. What he could see was an image that swam like a bioluminescent fish in the middle of the room. Although the vision was hazy, the voice was familiar.

"Blake."

"M-M-M-arie?"

"Yes, Blake, yes."

"Are you here?"

"In a way, Blake. Blake was mystified. Was this a ghost? Was his Marie dead?

"Marie, are you dead?" She didn't answer that question.

"Blake. You've been brought here by these people to save your life."

"Oh, Marie!" The longing in his voice almost compelled her to wrap her arms around him.

"Marie, I miss you! Where are you?"

"Blake, listen. I need you to focus on my words. This is your last chance to change your life."

"I tried, Marie. I tried." He was softly crying now. The pitiful manner in which he spoke sounded like a defeated man.

"You need to stop trying and start doing. This is your life at stake. You are out of money. Out of options. You are out of time. There are enough drugs in that black refrigerator to end your misery once and for all. You must find enough hope to lift you from the pit of gloom you have dug for yourself. If you can't find enough, then take all the hope I have."

"But, Marie, I have lost everything! Most of all, I lost you!"

"As long as your heart beats, the battle is not over. Right now. Right here, you have a chance to choose the right path. That's what the place has been trying to tell you! The same thing I tried to tell you. Find that hope before it is too late!" He sat on his bed and felt he was teetering on the edge of a cliff and debating whether or not to jump. But Marie's words and her otherworldly presence filled him with something. He didn't know what. But he did. Love. His love for her warmed him and he knew it wasn't the whiskey. The light seemed to disappear and the apparition before his eyes was beautiful. Marie's aura occupied the majority of his thoughts and the pain of losing her could only be comforted by numbing his feelings. Of course, it never really worked. She was right. He would die. Die in this place. Alone, with no one. 'Please choose Blake. Me or the drugs.' Her ancient words rattled his memories. Choose life, not death. Then come find me. He didn't notice her slowly backing up, switch off the light, drop to her knees and crawl out. His vision was still whitewashed by the light. She pulled the fridge back into place and shut the door. Did her plan work? Dr. Van Hook watched and listened. He had no hope for her husband but dared not tell Marie. But hadn't he once thought the same for Bam? Betty? You never know who is going to get this thing. Psychic change. Spiritual Awakening. Or when faced with a life-or-death situation. Those three things seemed to be the "why" some got it. His son broke into his thoughts. Just starting out his life. Sons should never die before their parents. How many college kids die from overdose? He knew the numbers were staggering. How many could he help with this program? This must work. The need to legitimize this program and show the world this method of recovery could change lives, was everything to him. He would prove the method to his madness. Blake just sat there. Marie's spirit or ghost or whatever it was, had him in a stalemate.

"What the hell was that?" A shiver went up his spine. The total darkness around him lit up again, but this time it was a bright, sunny day on the Seawall. He and Marie were passing each other on scooters. They each looked back to catch another glimpse. She crashed. He helped tend to her wounds. They fell in love. These pure, perfect memories filled his soul and erased his pain for a moment. As the pain tried to darken the day and threaten to wash it away, he grabbed a hold of the thought and held on. He walked the Seawall with Marie. He lived the first few years of his marriage in that brief time sitting on that bed. When a storm appeared to rain on his walk with her, he saw the word hope spelled out in the clouds and he floated up to the sky and grabbed hold and his whole being seemed lighter. Now, he stood in the dark. He was taller. Stronger. The buzz floated away but not his hope. His fear and despair dissipated like fog after dawn. This was hope at its highest form. He chose to focus on all the good he ever had in his life. The unconditional love of a father that never gave up hope on him. The love of a woman that was the best thing that ever happened to him. This place that somehow found him when he was lost and brought him back from insanity. He wondered if he could get his wife back. The answer eluded him. But what he did know was that he was choosing to be sober and anything was possible. The urge to drink left. No, he banished it away with love and hope. He chose. He threw the bottle of whiskey and it shattered against the wall. He upended the black fridge and stomped on its contents. Then, he saw the newest message to light up the wall.

'The choices we make determine our fate.' He knew everything would be better.

"Today, I choose. I choose."

As Marie made her way back to the monitor room, she did not notice Milo opening the door to the pipe chase. Pookie was enjoying some Mad Dog 20/20 and singing as usual.

"This is the life!" He was happy. Never mind he was confined to this room. He didn't notice Milo opening the secret entrance from the pipe chase.

"You can't keep running in and out of my life, keep running. Got to love me some Gap Band!" Pookie didn't see Milo pushing the white refrigerator out of the way.

"Keep running!" Milo was standing in Pookie's room watching Pookie singing on his bed. Mid song, Pookie opened his eyes and saw Milo. At first, he didn't know what was happening.

"Am I dreaming this shit?" He said out loud.

"Nah," Milo replied. "This is a nightmare." Pookie launched himself out of bed.

"What the hell is going on, man?" Pookie was a few feet away from Milo, knees bent, and hands up and in a boxer's stance. Many years in the street had prepared Pookie for the occasional scrap. Pookie was usually a laid-back guy but he wasn't one to back down from anything.

"Get out ma room or Ima fuck you up!" Pookie started to circle Milo.

"Hey, bro chill! Chill, bro! I found a way out! I'm going to get us out!" Pookie stopped and dropped his hands. The realization that this man was able to sneak into his room, turned on the sober switch in his mind. His buzz gone, for the moment, he spoke.

"Where are we gonna go?" Milo motioned for the small hole in the wall by the white fridge.

"There? Through that hole? Then what? Back to the streets? Hustlin' and beggin'? Duckin' them po-po's? You know, some days I make just enough to eat a little and drink, but not enough to get a room. I didn't mind though. I would just sleep on the bench at the bus stop. At least until the laws would run me off."

"Stop reminiscing, Pookie! Let's go!" Milo went to grab Pookie's arm.

"Get off me, fool!" Pookie pulled away and went to the black fridge. He opened it and grabbed a bottle of Ol' E., twisted the cap and took a healthy swig before he spoke again.

"Look out, fool." This." He looked around the room with arms raised, beer in hand.

"Is all I need. What's out there that I ain't got right here?" Milo couldn't argue with that.

"You're crazy! Suit yourself, but I'm getting the fuck out of here! But first." He walked to Pookie's black fridge.

"You don't use drugs if I remember correctly, right?"

"That's right, fool. Just the drink."

"Then you won't mind if I take yours."

"Help yourself." Milo opened the refrigerator and pocketed everything he could, even the syringes. Pookie watched as Milo crawled through the small door and disappeared into the pipe chase.

"I ain't that crazy! That fool is crazy! Who would want to leave here?"

CHAPTER 68

Marie was talking to Janine, trying to reach her on a different level. Janine was so drunk that she couldn't stand, so she sat in front of the black fridge. No longer crying, but she had a look of anguish on her face. She crawled to the toilet and did the dance that nauseous alcoholics performed on occasion. Wrapping her arms around her partner, hugging tightly, she released her last meal while depressing the lever. She watched the water spin, then passed out with her head in the bowl. Arms still clinging, she looked ready to dance again when she came to.

With a little light coming from through Pookie's room, the pipe chase was easier to navigate. Milo opened the door and investigated the Hallway. He deduced that they hadn't yet noticed his escape and re-entered the hallway. The cameras weren't hidden in this area and he looked up at one. He had an idea. He ran back to his room and grabbed a piece of wood from something he had broken during his fit of rage. Once back in the hallway, he proceeded to smash all the cameras. He only counted four. This is too easy, he thought. He went back to the pipe chase entrance. There were at least 4 different entrances from what he could tell. He walked in then crawled to

Betty's entrance. He entered stealthily. All his experience breaking into homes in the middle of the night came back to him. Like riding a bike. She was asleep. Damn, she was gorgeous. She never liked him though. Once, he tried to pay her for her time but she refused! He remembered being so pissed off at that rejection. How dare she! Getting denied by a prostitute!

"Not today, bitch." He whispered in the dark. She heard a sound, or was she dreaming? Being sober has its advantages. You're no longer passed out drunk. You sleep soundly but wake up much easier. The first time Milo snuck into her room he was on a mission for drugs. This new mission was special. As he walked toward the bed he might as well had trumpeted his arrival because his shoes squeaked and startled Betty to wake up. She opened her eyes and bolted upright.

"What the hell?" She didn't have time to react. He set upon her faster than a Tesla going from 0-60. He pushed her down and ripped at her clothes. He was insane with lust and didn't care about whether or not she was a willing participant. Since her recent clean time, she regained a healthy strength and was able to fight back. Even though she was a prostitute, she prided herself in being in control of her body. She would sleep with who she wanted to when she wanted to. She clawed his eyes. He screamed and this momentary distraction gave her the opportunity she needed. As she screamed, she bent her knees up and with her feet knocked him off the bed. Her screams alerted the others and Bam was the first to speak.

"What's the matter, Betty?"

"Milo broke into my room!"

"What the fuck, Milo! I swear, if you hurt her, I'll…" Milo heard nothing but the bloodlust flowing through his body fueling his desire. He would have her and nothing would stop him. Pookie heard the scream and heard her say Milo's name. He was smart enough to know what was up. Pookie poured out his forty and crawled through the pipe chase. He heard the furniture crashing and the grunts of two people engaged in a fight. He entered her room and held up the forty ounce bottle menacingly as he yelled.

"Milo!" Milo had her pinned beneath him as he was ripping away at her pants. His pants were down around his ankles and his intentions were clear to Pookie as his manhood announced as much.

"That ain't much of a weapon for this fight, fool." Pookie cracked the bottle over Milo's head. Milo was down for the count and Pookie ran to aid Betty. She was a mess. Clothes torn. Her shirt was ripped open exposing her breast. He fished a shirt out of the dresser and handed it to her.

"Thank you. Thank you." She managed between sobs.

"You cool, Betty?"

"Yes, Pookie. Yes. Look out!" Betty's warning came too late. Milo had retrieved a piece of broken furniture and slammed it against Pookie's skull. Blood oozed out of a large gash and he hit the ground face down. Blood trickled from his ear.

"He's a goner!" Milo proudly announced.

"Now, where were we?" Fear, combined with rage, filled Betty with the courage to catapult herself into the air and land on top of him. She punched and kicked then bit his nose. She looked like a wild dog fighting for a scrap of meat. And she got her scrap. A piece of his nose tore off as blood ran down her chin. Like a pit-bull tasting blood for the first time she was out of control. She spit the flesh on the floor and the scream that escaped Milo's lips was better than those in horror movies. The sound reverberated through the halls. She was upon him again. Blinded by wrath, she would fight until the threat was gone. After the shock of having a part of his nose ripped off by human teeth faded, he grabbed Betty by her waist. Never mind her fingers were now in his eye sockets. He picked her up in the air and slammed on her head. WWE Smackdown could not have done any better. When she hit the floor there was a loud crack. She didn't move. Nor would she fight again. Her eyes were opened and didn't blink. Betty was gone.

"Shit! Shit! Shit!" Milo didn't want her dead. But the deed was done. He turned around and tripped over Pookie's body.

"Dammit!" Was he dead too? The answer came with Pookie suddenly punching Milo square in the mouth from a sitting position. Although not much power behind the punch, blood shot out along with a decayed tooth. Recovering quickly, Milo pushed Pookie down and straddled him. He punched Pookie over and over until he was unconscious. Milo reached into his pocket and took out a preloaded syringe and plunged into Pookie's arms. Not being a dope fiend, Pookie's veins were healthy and made easy targets.

"No, No." Pookie said before the venom hit his blood stream. His eyes rolled back in his head and he was gone.

CHAPTER 69

Marie had looked up from the monitor of Janine's room for a moment. She was feeling discouraged at her inability to reach her. She saw the carnage before her eyes. The doctor had just walked back in from working in his private office. She turned toward the doctor and saw his confusion turn to fear then shock. Both, unable to move. Both unable to speak. What would they do now? There were no contingency plans for murder.

"Betty!"

"Betty!" Mike and Bam were hysterically calling her name , but she would answer no more. Janine was still passed out on the floor.

"What the fuck is happening, Bam?" Mike had been taking a nap and woke up in the middle of the assault.

"Milo attacked Betty!" Bam was so furious, he felt helpless and was shaking.

"What?" Mike didn't understand.

"How in the hell did he get in her room? I remember he had said he found a way out, but I thought he was full of shit!"

"I don't know, Mike! I just heard her scream and Pookie yelling too! I think he got out somehow and tried to help her. I heard Pookie yell, then I heard more crashing!"

"Hey, Pookie!"

"Pookie!" They both yelled for their friend Pookie but he couldn't answer.

"Doctor! What are we going to do?" Marie was terrified. Milo had disappeared from Betty's room and the hallway cameras were not working. Two lifeless bodies. The scenes on the monitor were surreal and ghastly. Furniture was smashed. The refrigerators were open and tipped over. Its contents all over the place. Blood splattered on the walls like a psychotic graffiti artist run amok. Marie switched off the flashing messages. It seemed moot at this point.

"Marie, stay calm. We must deal with this in the appropriate manner."

"Appropriate? What in the world is appropriate, doctor?" She trembled at the prospect of Milo attacking Blake.

"We have to call the police, doctor!"

"No! We can't, Marie!"

"But doctor!"

"No, Marie! Everything we have worked for. Everything we've tried to accomplish will be lost. We'll go to jail! Everything will amount to nothing!"

"Doctor!" Marie couldn't believe what she was hearing. People were just murdered!

"Their bodies are right there, doctor! And you're worried about the sanctity of your program? That ship has sailed, doc!" The way she said "doc" was definitely facetious. She never spoke that way to Doctor Van Hook.

"What would you have me do, Marie? Call the police? Call them and tell them that we are running a medical facility without a license? A facility full of kidnapped, homeless addicts that we are experimenting on? And, during our illegal experimentations, one of our psychotic patients broke out of his room, high on meth I might add, and is on a murderous rampage? Oh yea, and we supplied him with all the drugs he wanted?" The doctor let out a chuckle that was more of disdain for her idea than humor.

"And by the way officers, this junkie psychotic killer is lost somewhere in our facility! Please help us! Well, Marie, I don't think that will play out in our favor!"

"I don't know, doctor! But we have to do something!" He picked up the phone but didn't call the police. He called Matthew because he was late, as usual. So unreliable. Where were the orderlies? What the doctor didn't know was at the sound of the carnage in Betty's room, the two orderlies on duty high tailed it out of the facility. They wanted no part in whatever came next. They didn't sign up for murder. Who cared if these nutjobs killed themselves with an overdose, but murdering each other? They were just there for a paycheck and felt no loyalty to the doctor. He couldn't reach Matthew.

"Dammit!" he slammed down the phone.

"Where are the orderlies?

"I don't know, doctor."

"I'll be back." The doctor left the control room. Marie was left with her thoughts and the scenes before her. Bam and Mike were still pleading for an answer from Pookie or Betty. Janine was okay. She was just drunk. Blake had miraculously sobered up. The nightmare she was in prevented her from celebrating. It was bittersweet. The room was dark and she could feel a storm on the horizon. She must do something. Anything. Think, Marie. Think. She switched on the mic and turned on all the comms.

"Everyone please listen. Stay calm. We are resolving the issue with Milo. We are attending to Betty and Pookie." The need to lie to these people was necessary. She feared their reaction to the truth.

"Please just stay calm." She watched as Blake, Mike and Bam walked to their beds and sat down.

The doctor ran to his office. A large room with a large desk in the center. Medical journals lined the walls. In the far right corner was a locked medicine cabinet. It was always stocked full of narcotics. Some legal, mostly not. He shut the door and stood there for a minute staring into space.

"Think! Think! Think!" He couldn't. The usual brilliant, quick-witted doctor was dumbfounded. He walked to the medicine cabinet.

"The source of so many woes." He fished the key out of his pocket and opened it. He pulled out a bag of cocaine and tossed it on his desk. He pulled out another key and unlocked his desk. A white, dusty mirror lay in the back of his top drawer. Further back was a glass straw. His heart was racing. His palms were sweating as he sat down to line up his options. This was helping him think of an answer was his reasoning. The doctor snorted several lines and leaned back in his chair.

"Think. Think. Think."

CHAPTER 70

Milo was walking the hallway. His bloodlust still not satiated; he came upon a door. He turned the knob and slowly opened it. He saw a woman sitting at a bank of computers. She was crying. Head buried in her folded arms on the desk.

"So, we finally meet, Mrs. Wizard." This shocked Marie and she jumped to her feet to face this drug-infused maniac. Blood covered his clothes. His face was black and blue and he had several deep scratches trickling more blood. One eye was swollen shut but he still had a wide, almost joyous grin. One tooth was missing in the center. Throw on some white makeup and he would look like a psychotic clown from a B-rated movie. Marie was glued to her spot with terror. She chose her words carefully.

"I'm Blake's wife. I helped bring him here as well as all of you to try to help you. Milo just stood there smiling. Bleeding.

"The doctor went to go get help so please stay calm. Milo approached her slowly.

"Help? Help? Oh, you've helped us alright." At that he laughed. The laugh was so sinister, fear traveled to her very soul.

"Milo, please. The doctor is calling the police." Another lie.

"They'll be here any minute." This statement stopped Milo's stalking. His smile left his face and he looked in deep thought.

"Hmmm. I see. Where is this doctor, Marie is it?"

"Yes, Marie. I believe he went to his office down the hall to the right." She was hit with a momentary twinge of guilt for giving up the doctor to this madman. But she was in survival mode.

"In his office? Well, alright then. Carry on." It was almost comical the way he spoke. It was as if he was a fellow colleague sharing the day's activities or the company gossip. Milo turned on his heel and left.

"Oh, my God!" She spoke these words in relief to an unseen God and because of her narrow escape. She was still trembling but a new purpose rose within her. She sat down to look at the remaining patients. The storm was here and threatened to release its torrential downpour. Marie knew what must be done to weather the storm. She darted from the room and cautiously entered the hallway. This was the only way to save these patients from further bloodshed. To save her Blake. She might end up in prison but no one else would die.

CHAPTER 71

"Hey, Mike, you good?"

"Yea, Bam, but what are we going to do?"

"I don't know, bro. I haven't heard anything from Janine for a while and I'm worried."

"Me too. And we still don't know what the hell is going on with Betty and Pookie exactly."

"Fucking Milo!"

"Yea, Mike. Fucking Milo!"

"Try Janine again!"

"Janine!"

"Janine!" They tried to contact Janine but to no avail. Mike tried Blake.

"Blake! Hey, Blake! You alright?"

"Yea, Mike, I'm good. But I don't think Janine is. During the whole Milo thing, she didn't make a peep. Do you think she

is…"

"Don't even say it, Blake!" Bam pushed away the thought of Janine lying in her room dead from alcohol poisoning or worse. At the hands of Milo.

"She's just probably passed out drunk."

"I hope so, Bam. I hope so.

CHAPTER 72

arie walked carefully through the hallway towards the patients' rooms. She stood in front of Janine's main door behind the bed. Once opened, she peered in and noticed she was still passed out on the floor. She navigated around the bed and knelt by her body. Delicately, she checked for a pulse. She breathed a sigh of relief.

"Thank God." She whispered. "She's still alive." Janine stirred and managed to open her eyes.

"Who? Who? Who are you?" A drunken owl came to mind. Marie suppressed a laugh. She must be in shock, she thought, to find anything humorous about this situation.

"Who are you?" Janine sat up.

"I'm Marie. I work here at the facility. I need you to come with me."

"Huh? Where are we going?"

"Out of here. You need to go. It's not safe any longer."

"Wait. What? Not safe? What happened?"

"There is no time to explain." She helped Janine to her feet and guided her from the room. They entered the hallway and made it to an exit door. It led to the loading dock where every patient first arrived. At the door she stopped to face Janine. This poor girl was a mess. Obviously, still under the influence of alcohol, scared and confused. She looked her directly in the eyes and firmly held her shoulders.

"Listen to me. You must go. We tried to help you. We did our best but sometimes the pain of the past is too hard to let go. Your time here is done." Marie reached into her pocket and pulled out an envelope that contained money.

"Take this. It will help you get started. Find a women's shelter. Get off the streets. Try again. Please try again. Get your life straight. This should have been a wakeup call, but." She was out of words for this young lady. Marie opened the door

to let her out.

"Wait. What about my friends? Bam, Mike, Betty.." Marie cut her off.

"They'll be right behind you. Just go and good luck to you." She pushed her out the door. Marie went back to the rooms. This time she went to Mike's room. As she walked in and around the bed, Mike was standing in the middle of the room staring directly at her.

"Hey! There was a door there the entire time? Damn! Where's Betty?"

"No time to explain. Come on!" Mike followed her to the exit. Mike was still asking about Betty.

"Look, Mike. You need to go. You made it. You succeeded. You' re going to be fine. Your friends will be right behind you. If you hurry, you can catch up to Janine!"

"Oh! Janine? Okay!" He practically ran out the door but not before she handed him an envelope.

"What's this?'

"A little to help. Stay out of trouble. Good luck."

"Thank you!" and Mike was gone. Bam's turn. She walked into his room to find him nervously pacing, mumbling some prayer, while eating a sandwich. He looked like he might have been exercising as his shirt was removed and his muscles were glistening in the light. He stopped cold when he noticed Marie.

"Who the hell are you? Where is Betty? Is she okay?"

"She's fine. Everyone is fine. But now you have to leave! Your friends have been released. Come this way!" He followed her to the exit and she gave him an envelope.

"This is not much but I don't think you will have any issues starting a new life for yourself. Good luck." Bam ran down the street at full speed. One more. She was scared stiff. How would she explain this to Blake? Would the shock knowing she was behind all of this cause him to relapse? Would he hate her? Before she crossed that bridge, she needed to do one more thing. She ran back to the control room. Once inside, she placed her hand on the phone, gathered her thoughts and dialed 911.

"911. Do you need Police, Fire or EMS?"

"Police! Send the police!"

"What's your emergency?"

"There has been, um. There has been an attack!" She hung up. She knew the operator would trace the frantic call back to the facility and the police would arrive shortly. She looked at the monitor of Blake's room and he was pacing like Bam had been. He was cured. Her joy was overshadowed by the deaths and her spontaneous exit strategy. She turned on the intercom.

"Blake."

"Yes! Yes! How is Betty? And what about Pookie!"

"There is no time to explain. I need you to walk over to your bed and pull it away from the wall." She waited for him to obey.

"Why am I doing this? What is going on?"

"Please just do what I say, and all will be revealed." Why so mysterious, he wondered, but still he complied.

"Then, feel on the right side of the wall, halfway from the floor." Although Blake was confused, he continued to follow her directions. He found a latch flush with the wall and instinctively pressed it until it clicked. The door popped open ever so slightly.

"Now, enter the hallway, go right then right again until you come to a large metal exit door."

"But what then? Where do I go? Where are my friends?" Marie didn't answer him, but sprinted from the control room and exited the facility the same way everyone else did. She made sure the others had left the area and walked around the side of the building. There, under a dark cloak used to camouflage a car, was Blake's Corvette. After the Seawall incident, she retrieved it from the impound yard. The bar that Blake left it at thought it was abandoned and had it towed. She drove it around to the exit door. She held her breath. Blake walked out slowly. She got out of the car and stood there waiting for Blake to realize what was happening. She realized she was still holding her breath and he was just standing there, staring at her and his Corvette. She was about to scream his name when he yelled.

"Marie!" He bolted from the loading dock and around the car to stand in front of Marie. He was blinking back tears. He grabbed her in his arms and seemed to envelop her entire body. Her head was buried in his chest. She was crying as well but remembered the urgency to leave immediately.

"We have to go, Blake!"

"What about.."

"Now Blake!" The tone of her voice commanded action.

"I'll drive." He got in the passenger side for the first time since he owned that car and did so happily.

CHAPTER 73

Milo stood at the door in the hallway that had a large glass window in the middle. He saw movement. A man in a white Coat. Perfect. He tried the doorknob. Locked. The doctor heard the jiggle of the door and stood up.

"Aaaaa, what'up Doc?" He sounded like Bugs Bunny. The look of horror turned the doctor's face white as his coat. He steadied himself on his desk for fear of passing out.

"Open the door, Doc, let's talk." The doctor was immobile and didn't say a word. He tried to make himself invisible and even closed his eyes like he did when bullies used to beat him up as a child. Of course it didn't work. And like the bullies of old, Milo would get what he came there for.

"Have it your way, Doc!" Milo threw his body against the door.

"Ow! Shit! That door is pretty tough, Doc!" Milo stepped back and kicked the door below the doorknob. The door made a cracking sound on the second kick flung open with a crash.

"Stay back!" The doctor shrieked.

"What's up, Doc." His mocking tone shot adrenaline through the doctor's blood stream so swiftly, that he went blind for a few seconds. When the doctor's vision returned, Milo was only a few feet from him. The doctor held his hands up in supplication.

"Wait! Wait! Wait! Listen!" Milo stopped approaching the doctor, but was still close enough to reach out and touch him if he felt inclined to do so.

"Okay, Doc, shoot."

"Look, Milo. This was an opportunity…" But he was cut off.

"An opportunity?" Milo's maniacal laugh pierced the doctor's heart, he was frozen and felt mute.

"Well, Doc?" Van Hook shook off the momentary frostbite of his brain and continued.

"Yes, an opportunity. A way for hopeless addicts and alcoholics to find sobriety and live a normal life. And…" Milo interrupted again.

"And what, Doc? A way for you to get your rocks off, watching people get high as a kite on the drugs that you provide? Come on, doc!"

"No, Milo! All of you had a choice! We gave you choices! Some of the others were cured!"

"Oh, really?" Milo took another step toward him.

"Yes! Your friend Bam! Betty! Even Blake! They all chose! They chose life!"

"And I choose death!" With that, Milo grabbed the doctor by his lapel with both hands and lifted him off the ground. Now, face to face, the doctor could smell the meth on his breath, and the murder in his sweat.

"No! No! Milo! Look, I can help you! There is a cabinet full of drugs behind you! And, in that safe I have over \$100,000! You could start a new life!"

"A new life?" His blood curdling laugh was too much. The doctor started whimpering like a scolded puppy.

"Doc, my life was over before you kidnapped me! You have just sped up the inevitable. Wait a minute. You said drugs?" Milo had been holding the doctor off his feet the entire time. He turned to look behind him and seeing the cabinet, threw the doctor against the wall. He was knocked unconscious and Milo walked to the cabinet. What a glorious sight!

"Jackpot!" He screamed. He searched for the right substances.

"It's time to finish this party!" He found a bag of heroin and two syringes. Mixed with a little meth, he heated up the sweet mixture of ecstasy. He drew up both the syringes until each one read 100 units.

"Doc! Hey, Doc!" He slapped the doctor's face several times until his eyes snapped open.

"What? Huh?"

"Come on, Doc. Let's party!"

"Nooo!" Milo picked the doctor up and brought him to his feet. His legs were a little weak and he was barely able to stand. But before the doctor had a firm footing, Milo punched him in the nose sending Van Hook across the room while his blood flew in all directions. The doctor let out a groan and collapsed on the floor, barely conscious.

"Oh, no, no, no, no! We're not done yet Doc! Get up!" He couldn't of course. The doctor's fight or flight instinct had evolved into freeze. He couldn't move. His body rebelled at any command his mind came up with. His body had admitted defeat and awaited its sentence. After all, Milo made a promise. Milo picked him up again and punched him in the mouth, this time, shattering a few teeth in the process. The doctor lay in a pile of broken flesh choking on blood. He was trying to plead with his assailant.

"No! Wait! Please!"

"No, Doc! You had your chance to do and say all you want. Now, it's my turn! Besides, I made you a promise!" He walked back to the cabinet where he had set down the syringes.

"I'm gonna take you on a journey, Doctor. A journey of which there is no hope. A journey where there is no return.

CHAPTER 74

Marie was driving explaining everything to Blake. Every so often, through tears, Blake would ask a question.

"I'm sorry, Blake! I didn't know what else to do! I felt there was no other way! I love you and told you over and over, but that wasn't enough! You had every opportunity to choose me over the drugs."

"But, Marie, kidnapping? Free drugs? I, I, I could have died!"

"You would have died anyway!" Marie screamed through her sobs.

"But, I had hope! Even if you had none! You gave up but I didn't! I prayed and made this crazy decision to save you and it worked!" He knew what she said was the truth, but he was still in shock that she was behind all of this nightmare.

"Do you want to get drunk, Blake?" The question was easy to answer.

"No! Of course not, Marie!"

"Do you want to snort cocaine?" Another easy answer.

"Hell no! Never again!"

"Then, you have beaten this disease. So, hate me if you want, that's fine. All I care about is your life!" Her last statement erased any resentment and any doubt. She saved him. Loved him. She was there for him the entire time. Patiently waiting for him to come to his senses and make that Psychic change. He was free. Free to love her once again.

"You have hope again, sweetheart! You have chosen life. Now, choose us!" He had already chosen. When he jumped in that corvette and let her drive him away, he had chosen. His life was renewed and so was his love. They sat in silence as Marie navigated the nighttime streets of Houston. They passed several Police cars heading to the facility,

sirens blaring.

"Where to now, Marie?"

"Home, Blake. Home."

"Where's that?" Blake turned to Marie and saw her tear-stained cheeks glistening in the street lights. She stopped at a red light and returned his gaze.

"Wherever we are together Blake, that is home."

CHAPTER 75

The police arrived at the facility. Guns drawn, they entered through the loading dock because the door was still ajar. There were three police cars with two cops per car. A Sgt. gave orders to the EMS just as they pulled up.

"Wait here until we clear the place."

"You got it, Sgt." The EMS stood by and prepared the necessary equipment for anyone that might be injured. The Sgt. brought up the rear and noticed the eerie silence. The other officers looked to each other as if they were about to speak, but the Sgt. made a "shh" sign with his finger against his lips and motioned them to proceed. He pointed at two officers one way and two in the opposite direction. The remaining one stayed with him. With an officer in tow, the Sgt. made his way toward the Doctor's office.

Two officers took the stairs to the basement and found a steel door. A loud creaking sound from years of rust annoyed their ears as it was opened. The entire room was stainless steel. On the back wall were several small square doors. Four rows across and three high. One open door revealed a body. A second door. A body. Cold and obviously dead.

"Damn." An officer whispered. After further inspection, they radioed for the EMS.

Two other officers looked in the open doors to the vacated patients' rooms. Careful not to make any noise, they whispered.

"Was this a fucking hospital or something?"

"I guess so. What the fuck? Is that cocaine?"

"Yes. And heroin."

"Holy shit!" Then, they saw her. Betty. The death stare made up their mind as to whether or not she was gone. They radioed EMS. They walked further into her room and saw another victim. Pookie. An officer knelt down to check his pulse and Pookie sat straight up, knocking the policeman over.

"What the fuck? Po-pos? I ain't done shit officers!" His speech was slurred from alcohol, heroin and a mild concussion.

"What happened here, sir?" The officer was getting off the floor with his gun pointing at Pookie.

"Man, I don't know fool. These people kidnapped me and. Hey, don't point that shit at me! I told you, I ain't done shit!"

They radioed EMS again.

The Sgt. and his backup came upon a busted door. The scene was disturbing to say the least. Desk was overturned and papers were everywhere. Drugs spilling out of a cabinet and two bodies. They rushed over to the bodies after holstering their weapons.

"What the hell?" The Sgt. exclaimed.

"Are those syringes in their arms?"

"Yea, Sarge." The officer felt for the doctor's pulse, while the Sgt. felt for Milo's.

"Looks like they both overdosed, Sgt."

The Sgt looked around at the rest of the carnage. Blood masked the doctor's face. Blood was all over Milo and they could tell it wasn't his and his knuckles were the evidence.

"What the hell happened here tonight fellas?" The Sgt. continued to examine the scene and saw his officer standing in front of a wall.

"Um, Sarge, you're going to want to see this." The Sgt. walked over to look. There, written in blood by someone's hands, were three words.

FUCK YOUR CHOICES

EPILOGUE

CNN BREAKING NEWS

This is CNN breaking news. We are here at the horrific scene in Houston, Texas with a shocking discovery. Police were called to this facility and found several bodies. Initial reports are that a deranged doctor kidnapped innocent, homeless people and performed experiments and tortured them to death. The doctor was found dead with one of his patients as well. The police are calling his death an escape attempt by one of the patient's.

In other news, President Trump has been caught breaking the law once again…

FOX BREAKING NEWS

Fox news comes to you live from Houston, Texas. A tragedy has occurred. Police have found a hospital with several dead bodies. One of those bodies is a doctor who devoted his life to helping drug addicts and alcoholics get off the street and find hope once again. Preliminary reports say the patients attempted to break out and killed the doctor in the process. We will keep you up to date as this tragedy unfolds. In other news, Democrats are on another witch hunt, accusing President Trump of…

AUTHOR'S NOTE

This story was a work of fiction but inspired by actual events. Some of the graphic scenes are true. I told this story because of the seriousness of addiction. The two final fictional news pieces were to show that life is about perspective. People see things differently. Part of this world sees addiction as being weak or having a sinful spirit. The other part sees addiction as a disease. Either way, there is no denying that addiction is an ever present, destructive force in this world. It tears families apart and ruins lives. I make no excuses for addicts or alcoholics behaviors. I only implore that if anyone finds themselves in the position of dealing with someone that has this deadly issue, to be mindful of the pain or trauma that precipitated this problem. And if possible, find them help. There are thousands of programs all over the world designed to bring hope to the hopeless. At one time I was hopeless. Now, I find joy every day when I wake up to another chance to do something special with my life and my family. If, by some miracle I can help one person with this book to realize there is HOPE, then this journey will be worth it!

Thank you for taking the time to read this book.

Choose this day to Forgive, Hope and to Love.

It's your CHOICE.

ABOUT THE AUTHOR

Christopher Clark is a resilient and powerful voice in the world of recovery and transformation. His life is not just a story, it's a testament to how far someone can fall and still rise again. After experiencing poverty for a time in his youth, Christopher's early years were marked by instability and hardship. As a young man, he struggled with drug and alcohol addiction, which led him down a dark path filled with chaos, pain, and survival at all costs. That path included homelessness, prison, and surviving both a shooting and a stabbing. At his lowest point, he was living on the streets, battling addiction and carrying the weight of a life he no longer recognized.

But Christopher's story didn't end there. Through a spiritual awakening and a deep connection to a higher power, he began the hard work of recovery, mentally, emotionally, and spiritually. What followed was a complete transformation. Sober and focused, he found healing and strength not just in recovery but in writing. Words became a way to process the past, make sense of the pain, and reach others who were still in it.

Today, Christopher writes with raw honesty and unwavering compassion. His work is deeply personal and rooted in lived experience. He writes not as someone who studied these struggles from the outside, but as someone who has survived them and came out stronger on the other side. His mission is simple but powerful: to offer hope. Through his books, he connects with people who feel broken, lost, or forgotten, reminding them that redemption is real and that a better life is always possible.

Christopher now resides in Houston, Texas, with his wife, Marie, and two huskies. Whether he's writing about addiction, trauma, recovery, or the power of faith, Christopher brings heart, grit, and truth to every page. His story is one of pain, but more importantly, of triumph.